Unmarried Women

》》》》》》》》》》》 《《《《《《《《《《《

Matilde Serao

Unmarried Women

Stories

TRANSLATED FROM THE ITALIAN
BY PAULA SPURLIN PAIGE
FOREWORD BY
MARY ANN MCDONALD CAROLAN

NORTHWESTERN UNIVERSITY PRESS
EVANSTON, ILLINOIS

》》》》》》》》》》》 《《《《《《《《《《《

Northwestern University Press
www.nupress.northwestern.edu

Printed in the United States of America

10 9 8 7 6 5 4 3 2 1

ISBN-13: 978-0-8101-2404-2
ISBN-10: 0-8101-2404-1

Library of Congress Cataloging-in-Publication Data

Serao, Matilde, 1856–1927.
    [Short stories. English. Selections]
    Unmarried women : stories / Matilde Serao ; translated from the Italian by
Paula Paige ; foreword by Mary Ann McDonald Carolan.
        p. cm. — (European classics)
    ISBN-13: 978-0-8101-2404-2 (pbk. : alk. paper)
    ISBN-10: 0-8101-2404-1 (pbk. : alk. paper)
    1. Women—Italy—Naples—Social conditions—Fiction. I. Paige, Paula
Spurlin. II. Title. III. Series: European classics (Evanston, Ill.)
PQ4841.E7A2 2007
853'.8—dc22

                                                                    2007012853

♾ The paper used in this publication meets the minimum requirements
    of the American National Standard for Information Sciences—
Permanence of Paper for Printed Library Materials, ANSI Z39.48–1992.

»»» CONTENTS «««

Mary Ann McDonald Carolan

When Matilde Serao died suddenly of a heart attack on July 26, 1927, at the age of seventy-one, Italy and her adoptive city of Naples, in particular, mourned the passing of a national treasure. The masthead of *Il Mattino*, one of several newspapers she had founded, was draped in black for two days. News of her death and funeral covered the newspaper's entire front pages on the July 27 to 28 and 28 to 29 editions, which included first a drawing of her and then a photograph of her corpse. The list of telegrams expressing sadness over the loss of Serao filled the interior pages of the paper; condolences came from Queen Elena d'Aosta, Mussolini, the poet Gabriele d'Annunzio, newspaper guilds, and regular people. Hundreds of Neapolitans viewed Serao's body before the funeral Mass celebrated the following day in the Chiesa della Vittoria, which could not accommodate all who wanted to attend. As the funeral cortege proceeded from the church to the cemetery where Serao would be laid to final rest, silence reigned in the usually chaotic streets of Naples: apartment gates were closed, shop blinds were lowered, hats were doffed, and heads were bowed as the caisson passed through aristocratic and impoverished neighborhoods alike.

To what can we ascribe this deep sense of affection and loss expressed by all walks of life in Naples upon the death of Matilde Serao? Was it her gift for literary expression revealed in the many novels, essays, and short stories she wrote in a prolific fifty-year career? Or was it her contributions as a journalist who founded and directed several important daily newspapers in Naples and Rome and penned thousands of pages of prose, ranging from investigative probes to society columns? Or was it her political activism in defense of Naples, evidenced in the invective she hurled at Minister of Interior Agostino Depretis when, in 1884, he called for the city's evisceration to combat the cholera epidemic? Or was it her ability to overcome a disadvantaged childhood and lack of early formal education to find success in the male world of letters and give voice to the marginalized female readership? Most likely this outpouring of grief resulted from a combination of all of the attributes that the author embodied, but most of all, Neapolitans showed their love and respect for Matilde Serao because she displayed immense compassion in her truthful descriptions of their virtues and failings.

Matilde Serao's early life reflected the political, social, and economic realities of the second half of the nineteenth century. The author, who was born in Patras, Greece, in 1856, came from a literary family. Her father, Francesco, an exiled Neapolitan, was a journalist, and her mother, Paolina Bonelly, a descendant of Greek nobility, was passionate about poetry. In 1860, after the Bourbons were expelled from Italy, the family returned to Francesco's hometown of Ventaroli, in the province of Caserta. Five years later they moved to Naples. After teaching herself to read, by borrowing books from friends and neighbors and by spending endless hours in the library, Serao enrolled in school (the Scuola Normale [Normal School] in Piazza del Gesù) for the first time in 1870 at the age of fourteen. Upon receipt of her teaching certificate, Serao entered and won a government competition in 1874 for a position in the state telegraph office, where she worked for four years. While there, Serao began writing articles for literary magazines, and in 1878, using the pseudonym Tuffolina, she published her first collection of short stories in a volume entitled *Opale* (*Opal*). In 1881, already a well-known journalist, Serao moved to Rome, where she worked as an editor for the literary journal *Capitan Fracassa,* and, in 1884, she published an essay entitled "Il ventre di Napoli" ("Naples's Belly"), a vitriolic response to the interior minister's assessment of the cholera epidemic that claimed tens of thousands of Neapolitans. Serao vilified the government's superficial solution to the problem—to raze Naples's overcrowded, yet vibrant, neighborhoods in order to halt the disease—and suggested instead that the government rebuild Naples through moral, social, and economic reforms. In this famous essay, later published as a book, Serao displayed her characteristic understanding of, and love for, her fellow Neapolitans, and especially for the women whose work and habits she chronicled so attentively. Her description of the daily habits of Neapolitan citizens, told in affectionate detail, reminds the American reader of Jacob Riis's 1890 illustrated examination of life in New York tenements entitled *How the Other Half Lives.* In 1888, Serao returned to Naples as the wife of Edoardo Scarfoglio and mother of four sons. After Serao and Scarfoglio separated in 1902, she founded a literary review, *La Settimana,* and a daily newspaper, *Il Giorno,* which she ran until the day she died.

Serao's life spanned a politically dynamic time in Italy that witnessed the expulsion of foreign rulers, the unification of the country, and the rise of fascism. The unification process began as *Il Risorgimento,* or the Resurgence, a series of struggles over contested lands and attempts to remove foreign rulers in the first half of the nineteenth century. Most of the peninsula was united by 1861, but it was not until 1870, when Venice and the Papal States were annexed, that Italy was completely unified. In the years immediately following the formation of the Italian state, an increasing divide emerged between the south of Italy, primarily an agricultural land, and the north, a center of industrial revolution. In fact, unification provided little relief for the economically disadvantaged south, which had exchanged the oppression of the Bourbons for continued poverty under an indifferent national government based in Rome. Unschooled in the ways of self-governance after generations of oppression and disappointed with the lack of economic progress, thousands of southern Italians decided to leave their country for America from port cities such as Naples.

In the south of Italy, a new literary movement known as *verismo,* or realism, was born to articulate the transformation of an ancient society by these new political realities. The *verismo* movement, which was founded by the Sicilian writers Giovanni Verga and Luigi Capuana, elevated the quotidian details of working-class and peasant life to the subject of art. Scholars have drawn parallels between *verismo* and the French naturalist school, in particular, the works of Zola, Flaubert, and Balzac. The regional character of *verismo* reflected the reality of postunification Italy as it attempted to transform the culturally diverse peninsula into a unified political entity. *Verismo* also aimed to educate northern Italians about the reality of the southern situation and inform them of the dignity of the inhabitants of the *Mezzogiorno* (a term that literally means "midday" that is used to refer to the south of Italy), who faced monumental and seemingly intransigent obstacles in the path to modernization.

Serao's journalistic style was perfectly suited for *verismo.* Her realist prose diverged from that of her male contemporaries in two important ways: first, she wrote about female, not male, protagonists and situations, and, second, as narrator, she did not distance herself from the hopeless conditions her female protagonists faced but rather offered her sympathy as she chronicled their sad lives. *Unmarried Women (Il Romanzo della fanciulla* [1885]) is an example of Serao's *verista* prose. The five stories about young women were first published in literary reviews such as *Nuova antologia, Fanfulla della Domenica,* and *Il Piccolo* before being collected in this volume. In her introductory remarks to the original text, Serao notes that these historically accurate stories are based upon memories and therefore infused with authorial subjectivity. She tells her readers in the preface that she rejected invention in favor of the memory of real young women with whom she had studied and worked: "Instead of fabricating a young girl, I evoked all the companions of my childhood; instead of constructing a heroine, I lived again with my friends from long ago." Serao knew her protagonists—of diverse social classes, ethnicities, and personalities—intimately. Two of her stories in this collection, "Girls' Normal School" and "The State Telegraph Office (Women's Section)," are profoundly autobiographical. This self-reflexive dimension gives her chronicles of everyday life psychological depth and texture. In all of the stories, except for "The Novice," Serao appears in the person of Caterina Borrelli, a spunky young woman who challenges the authority of teachers, bosses, and elders. The reader readily identifies this figure's signature behavior, which includes constantly adjusting her eyeglasses, writing in her notebook, and reading. As further proof that Borrelli is Serao's alter ego, scholars have pointed to the fact that Serao often signed personal letters with a version of her middle name, Caterina. In addition, her mother's maiden name (Bonelly, Bonelli, or Borrely, according to different biographers) approximates Caterina's last name, Borrelli.

For a woman in a prefeminist world, Serao was extraordinarily modern. The newly unified Italian state to which she and her family returned from exile in Greece adopted the Napoleonic law code that prohibited financial independence for married women. As "The State Telegraph Office" illustrates, this was in an age in which marriage often necessitated a woman's departure from the workforce. Yet, despite the restrictions imposed upon her sex, Serao became an enormously successful and well-known writer.

We must remember, however, that for part of her life, Serao's journalistic success was linked to that of her influential husband, Edoardo Scarfoglio, with whom she founded newspapers in Rome and Naples. That marriage, however, was fraught with conflict regarding Scarfoglio's extramarital affairs and the spouses' different perspectives on art and journalism. It ended in separation in 1902, after which Serao lived with Giuseppe Natale until his death in 1926. Serao voices her own skepticism toward the institution of marriage through the mothers in "In the Lava" who agree that they would not have married if they had known beforehand what marriage entailed. The protagonist of Serao's "Nevermore!" echoes the author's belief that marriage was justified as a means to motherhood. In that short story, Rosina tells her unmarried friend Emma that any marriage, even a bad one, is better than no marriage at all, because marriage allows you to have children. Serao knew the joys and pains of motherhood firsthand for she had four sons with her husband.

The overt sexism of the age influenced critical reception of Serao's works. While many of the important literary figures of the time, such as Giosuè Carducci, Gabriele d'Annunzio, Benedetto Croce, and Attilio Momigliano, appreciated her talent, others derided Serao for her seemingly masculine nature. The critic Ugo Ojetti voiced the opinion held by many of his peers that women writers were really men trapped in female bodies, and Verga supposedly called Serao a hermaphrodite. Politics as well caused problems for Serao. Famous for her opposition to fascism, the author incurred Mussolini's wrath on account of her antimilitaristic stance, which was especially evident in her last novel, *Mors tua,* published in 1926. In fact, some scholars have attributed Serao's loss of the Nobel Prize that same year to another Italian woman writer, Grazia Deledda, to Il Duce's disdain for her politics.

Matilde Serao occupies a particular position in the Italian literary tradition on account of her acute observations of working-class life in Naples as well as her gripping portrayal of female aristocrats as seen in short stories such as "The Novice." On the surface, Serao's stories provide a social history of Neapolitan customs at the end of the nineteenth century, from interactions at bathing establishments and on garden promenades, to exchanges between teachers and students at school, to relations between managers and their subordinates in the office. Her powers of observation go beyond the minutiae of everyday life to examine the ways, both subtle and overt, in which societal institutions such as marriage, school, and work repress women. Some young women in Serao's short stories, determined to circumvent their insufficient dowries or family objections, inevitably fail to marry the men they love. Others, such as Elvira Brown Castelforte in "In the Lava," succeed in marrying for practical reasons only to find such marriages of convenience profoundly disappointing. Some, like Eva Muscettola in "The Novice" or Emma Demartino in "Nevermore!" enter the cloistered world of the convent or remain behind the blinds of their lonely apartments when they cannot marry the men they love. Serao's female workers face long hours, unpaid overtime, and pitiful wages, and wonder, like Maria Vitale in "The State Telegraph Office," why they never have a day of rest. At school, students crumble under the pressure of overbearing school teachers and cruel examiners, only to graduate and find oppressive teaching jobs like that of Lidia Santaniello, whose position as a rural nursery school teacher in "Girls' Normal School" proves fatal to her frail constitution. Given the challenges these women face, we are not surprised, therefore, that many of Serao's characters do not survive their own stories.

Lest the reader lose hope completely for these pitiful creatures trapped in untenable situations, Serao offers female solidarity as an antidote of sorts. Young women seek the solace of other young women in places such as the girls' school, the women's section of the telegraph office, the sewing room of the Abandoned Children's Home, the bathhouse, the convent, or a new mother's bedroom. In these gendered spaces they freely express their thoughts to one another, and the plurality of this expression creates a choral effect. The remarkable number of protagonists—we follow the lives of twenty-four young women in "Girls' Normal School," for example—compounds this sense of chorality. Yet the author succeeds in distinguishing individual characters through the literary device of synecdoche, by focusing on a part of the body, such as an infected eye, a constant bloody nose, or an ugly red wig, to represent the entire person. Serao's insistence on emotional individuality also saves these marginal female characters from anonymity. In her precisely organized stories, clearly divided in terms of time and place, the author contrasts objective, straightforward arithmetic identification of the young women (the worth of their dowries, the number of telegrams they transmit, or their place in line for entrance to the bathhouse) with more nuanced, subjective descriptions of the individual's own fears and aspirations for the future. Serao weaves a compelling narrative out of the characters' relatively uneventful (and eminently forgettable) lives by giving voice to their inner thoughts about love and marriage. This narrative technique allows the reader to imagine how these young women would live their lives if the choice were theirs, not that of their father, or boss, or teacher, or husband.

Paula Paige's poetic translation masterfully renders in English the pace and tone of the author's Italian prose. This translation, which is both technically accurate and culturally nuanced, delivers the same sense of immediacy that we find in the Italian original. Paige's careful attention to detail mirrors that of Serao and makes a setting that is both chronologically and geographically distant accessible in English.

Finally, Serao's careful consideration of modest lives in *Unmarried Women* reveals the transformative power of literature. In "Nevermore!" the unmarried Emma is an Everywoman of sorts, for in Serao's words: "Life for her and for the others seemed a long, joyless path, a hard one without rewards or anyone to help them along the way." As characters such as Emma face the immutability of the future, we sense, and share in, Serao's profound compassion for their vanquished lives. The love and tenderness with which the author describes the *fanciulle* allows them to live again in the reader's imagination. In this way, Serao delivers Maria Vitale, Lidia Santaniello, Eva Muscettola, Emma Demartino, and many others from despair to immortality.

Unmarried Women

Girls' Normal School

I

While the eight o'clock bell was ringing, the students began to enter the very long, very dark, narrow corridor. Through the door that opened onto the stairway, framed by an iron halo in order to shed a little light on that humid alley of a corridor, came the day students; through the opposite door, which was small and half-closed and opened onto the boarding school, the boarders appeared, two by two. And immediately, two enormous long lines formed: along the left wall, closed, unbroken by any doors, were the day students; along the right wall, which was broken up with four doors, three classrooms, and the principal's office, stood the boarders.

"Now, ladies!" the student de Donato had already exclaimed three times. She was a large young woman of twenty-eight from Avellino who had been going to make her debut as a singer and then had lost her voice.

But the boarders didn't hear the signal; the day students went on chatting among themselves, with their hats still on their heads, their overcoats buttoned, their skirts hiked up so that they wouldn't get dirty, muddy shoes, books under their arms, holding a box of compasses, a roll of paper, or a paper bag containing their lunch, exuding all the humidity of that rainy morning. The boarders were quieter, in their dry gray dresses, their white collars, with black velvet ribbons in their hair, their books tied together with string or with a rubber shoelace, but Carmela Fiorillo, the kind one with black eyes and a purple mouth, had a nosebleed, as usual; Alessandrina Fraccacreta, the ugly, sentimental one, had a discharge from her right eye that made her look terrible, in spite of the powder that she secretly used and her hairdo, for which she was always being punished; Ginevra Barracco blew her nose constantly, crying without meaning to; Giovanna Abbamonte had a hangnail on her left hand, after having had one on her right hand; and all the boarders had the unhealthy pale look of girls living in a damp place who eat poorly and sleep with the gas on. Sing? Neither the day students nor the boarders felt like singing that morning: the day students were already tired out from their walk and from getting wet in the rain and from the mud underfoot; the boarders were depressed by that great Jesuit convent that oozed water through every wall and that seemed on the verge of collapse.

"Now, ladies," shouted Signorina de Donato, clapping her hands and intoning the first note.

Distractedly, about fifty students listlessly sang the first verse of the morning song:

> I have a divine father in heaven
> Who gives me light and life
> And who invites me to the banquet
> Of eternal truth.

It was slow music, with notes that were prolonged simply, as elementary as the first syllables of the alphabet; the singers sang without passion or warmth, understanding nothing, as though they were singing in a dream, and they pronounced the words as though they were in Hebrew. But the other hundred students weren't singing; a great mute pantomime of smiles, glances, signs, and smirks were exchanged between the lines, among the day students and boarders. A very severe rule from the principal forbade any relationship between day students and boarders, but because of this very fact, day students and boarders were united in couples and groups, so firmly that no punishment could undo them; because of this very fact, ardent friendships had sprung up that bordered on the passionate, invincible attractions that defied every punishment, and a continuous exchange of services—letters mailed, letters taken to the post office, cheap novels lent in secret, coins and oat soap passed from hand to hand; because of this very fact, there was nothing in these young heads but constant plotting to elude the surveillance of their superiors. Sing? In this hour that they were all gathered together, the strange network of love and hate, attraction and dislike, impatience and nervousness, tranquil affections and jealousies was evidently thick and sound. While the singers, so indifferent and bored and sleepy, sang the words

> I have an earthly mother
> Who scolds and consoles me,
> With angelic words
> Of comfort and kindness

one could see the passionate look that Amelia Bozzo, a boarder in the upper class, turned on Caterina Borrelli, a day student in the third class with a pug nose and nearsighted glasses that gave her a look that was part ironic, part disdainful, and Caterina Borrelli twirled in her fingers a wilted rose that Amelia Bozzo had given her three days before. Gabriella Defeo, a little blond boarder in the third class, affectedly turned her back on Carolina Mazza, a day student in the third class, with whom she had argued the day before, and Carolina Mazza pretended to be reading out of a notebook so that she didn't have to raise her eyes. Artemisia Jaquinangelo, with her hair cut short like a man's, her masculine face, and her skinny body like an adolescent boy's, wasn't singing, because

Giuditta Pezza, a day student in the first class, no longer loved her; Giuditta Pezza was smiling at Maria Donnarumma, but to no avail; Maria Donnarumma was vainly trying to find out whether Annina Casale had found any mail for her at the post office; Maria Valente was showing a card from a distance to her friend Gaetanina Bellezza, who was called "the Little Bottle" because she was small and round; a little bottle of scent that Clothilde Marasca had bought for Alessandrina Fraccacreta, the sentimental, flirtatious ugly girl, was being passed from hand to hand. The voices of those fifty lazy, bored girls, who were thinking of nothing, grew stronger, and they sang more and more mechanically, saying:

> I have a country to which is sacred
> My heart and my mind
> Which in the hour of danger
> Will keep me ever faithful.

The others were silent. The day students were getting tired of singing that stupid music and those silly words, in that dark corridor, without piano accompaniment, still wearing their rain-soaked clothes, with their cold feet and their arms tired from holding their books and notebooks, their stomachs barely warmed from a bad half cup of coffee that had been reheated from the night before; they were tired of singing, with the prospect of seven hours of classes before them. Especially those in the third class, who would be teachers in the upper grades and were overwhelmed with work, since they had to study the most disparate things and were subject to constant torment, didn't have the energy to sing. Giuseppina Nobilone was the unhappiest of all; she didn't understand anything, either about physics, or geometry, or arithmetic, or geography; she was always failing Italian language, and every six months she would pass, by dint of pushing, screaming, tears, exhortations, and prayers. Giulia de Sanctis learned all her lessons by heart, with immense fatigue, but if she happened to lose her thread, the whole class made fun of her. Cleofe Santaniello was intelligent and studious, but when she was called on to recite the lesson, she was seized with such trembling that the professors thought that she was a lazy, stupid student. Emilia Scoppa had never been able to learn not to write *receive* with an *ie* and *accommodate* with one *c;* Maria Caresse was excellent in history and hopeless in geography, while Checchina Vetromile was so good in everything that the professors did nothing but call on her, which worried her and made her feel under greater stress every day. What a strange idea, to make girls sing who have to take exams in thirteen subjects: arithmetic, Italian grammar and language, physical and natural sciences, history, geography, plane and solid geometry, morals, religion, line drawing, pedagogy, French language, calligraphy, and women's work! Those fifty who didn't care at all, who made fun of the exams or didn't think about them—stupefied more than ever by the monotony of that rhythm beat out by the clapping hands of de Donato, who was taking seriously her role as choirmaster—went on singing themselves hoarse:

> There are three rays in a flame
> That warm my heart and mind,
> I, a Christian and a devoted daughter,
> Will always live as a citizen.

Here the morning singing would have ended, but this last verse had to be repeated twice in a row, for emphasis, by the whole school, sopranos, mezzo-sopranos, and contraltos. The repetition on a higher note drew in another twenty voices so that there seemed to be a breath of gaiety in that long, narrow, dark room, but the saddest ones kept the closed mouths and blank faces of people who live inwardly, suffering in their hearts, lacking the courage to tell anyone else about their sorrows. Giulia Pessenda was thinking about her mother, a poor Piedmontese widow who went out to care for the sick and women in childbirth for two francs a day and who still blushed at having to present a certificate of poverty so that at least the school would buy her books; Clemenza Scapolatiello was dying of undeclared love for her sister's fiancé; Giuseppina Mercanti was forced to live in a house with her father's mistress, next to a sister-in-law who was cheating on her brother, in an atmosphere of corruption that robbed her of a sixteen-year-old's ingenuousness; Lidia Santaniello, at eighteen, knew that she had tuberculosis and prayed to God that he would at least let her live for another five or six years so that she could work and help out at home until her brother grew up. All of them were incapable of singing. But the one who never sang was Giustina Marangio, with that pale face of an old lady of eighteen, that viper's head who always knew all her lessons, who would never explain them to any classmate, who never lent her notebooks or books to anyone, who laughed when her classmates were scolded, whom her professors adored, who had no friends, and who was the embodiment of the worst evil, the great malice of youth, without a vein of kindness or light of gaiety.

After the singing, a great stir took place, as happens when military ranks are formed: eighty-five girls, all of the upper class, had disappeared from the library, a vast room that was all oak bookcases, with shelves that were empty of books, black and dusty with wormholes; the forty-two in the second class had gone into their lesson in a big, cold, whitewashed room that was elegantly adorned with two maps; and the thirty-one in the third class had gone reluctantly into the damp, low little room where their class took place. Through the doors, a loud chatter was heard, since the professors had not yet arrived, but the long corridor remained empty; here and there on the floor were muddy footprints left by the girls' boots. And a girl who was leaning against the jamb of the door that opened onto the stairway seemed to be contemplating those footprints. Since she was standing against the light, one couldn't make out the features of her face: one could only see that she was of medium height, thin, and dressed in black. She had been there since the girls had started singing, and she had listened, without taking a step, without daring to move forward; she had seen the classes form and disappear from the door of the classrooms, and nothing had been able to make her move. Now a rustle could be heard: it was Rosa, the caretaker, a big, tall woman with enormous feet and knotty wrists, who looked like a policeman dressed as a woman, wrapped in a wool skirt with big red and black checks and a red wool shawl. She was using a big noisy broom to sweep the mud out of the corridor, and she was muttering, in her usual good woman's grumbling way. When she got to the door, she raised her eyes and saw that little black figure.

"What do you want?" she asked her sharply.

"The principal," murmured the other, in a faint voice.

"He's not here."

"Isn't he going to come? Couldn't I wait for him?" And she asked it with such sweetness that Rosa was moved.

"He'll be here soon; go ahead and wait."

And she continued her noisy sweeping. Encouraged, the little black figure had the courage to walk down the corridor and to glance through the open door into the third class. The girls were all away from their desks, both boarders and day students, chattering and yelling: in vain was the student supervisor trying to impose order from the teacher's desk. She was a big fat girl, white, very good, not very intelligent, very precise and quiet, who had gotten to be supervisor only because of the gold stars that she had earned in conduct, and she was ill suited for that job: she didn't know how to lose her temper; she didn't have the courage to get angry with her classmates; her nice fat girl's inertia made it impossible.

"Oh, ladies, I beg you, quiet down!"

"Oh, Supervisor, my friend!" quipped Borrelli, pushing her glasses up on her nose, "What's this? You're affecting a Tuscan manner?"

"She's doing it to flirt with Radente, the Italian professor," added Artemisia Jaquinangelo, passing her hands through her hair like a man.

"Radente's not coming, Radente's not coming," exclaimed Defeo, the little blond, clapping her hands.

"It's barely eight; the bell rang fifteen minutes early," said Costanza Scalera in a low voice.

And she got out her watch. Costanza Scalera, a boarder, was considered a great lady because of this watch, the only one in the class: and she really looked like a lady, with her big, dark, curly head, wide green eyes, a very gentle smile, and a very elegant way of moving, but her great advantage was in fact that little gold watch, which she took out every minute. Someone had dared whisper in class that Costanza Scalera's sister mended silk sweaters, but that very aristocratic little gold watch had made that seem like slander.

Now the little black figure had arrived at the end of the corridor, walking slowly; in a corner there was a little zinc sink that was painted blue; a loose faucet dripped water into it, like an occasional tear; a small lead pail was attached to the faucet by a metal chain. Seeing that she was alone, the little figure dared to turn on the faucet, let a little water run first to rinse out the pail, then drank. But the water was warm, as water from a pump always is, and it had the bad metallic taste of stored water. She bent her head and dropped the pail; she went back toward the entrance, glancing timidly again at the third class, which she would never enter if the director didn't come. Some of the girls were sitting: Giuseppina Nobilone was going crazy, imagining that four professors were going to call on her to recite the lesson, and she was looking blankly at her stack of books; de Sanctis was sitting with her hands in an old muff knitted of black wool, staring fixedly at the wall and repeating to herself a passage by Passavanti; Emilia Scoppa was rereading her Italian language homework for the tenth time, worrying because she couldn't find the spelling mistakes that the professor would find in quantities; Checchina Vetromile was writing a quotation in a notebook.

In a group, Carolina Mazza, with her provocative eyes, was describing something interesting in a low voice to Giuseppina Mercanti, Donnarumma, Luisetta d'Este, and Concetta Stefanozzo, and they were listening to the story, one pale, one red, one smiling, one with lowered eyes; in another group, made up entirely of day students, Lidia Santaniello, whose cheeks were too red from tuberculosis, was telling another story to Caterina Borrelli, Annina Casale, Maria Valente, her sister Cleofe Santaniello, Scapolatiello, and Pessenda, which they were listening to attentively. Alessandrina Fraccacreta was holding a cloth handkerchief to her inflamed eye, and with the other was reading *Jacopo Ortis*, which she had open inside *The Little Furnace Man;* Teresa Ponzio was answering a letter that she had received from a day student—and the others were sitting up straight, talking, complaining about the bad weather, sighing, groaning, starting to fight among themselves to warm up, while Judicone, the supervisor, called the roll from a big class register. But in a moment the groups broke up, the girls went back to their desks; the ones who were reading or writing got up. The principal had come in.

He was a small, thin man with lively eyes and a blond goatee, taciturn, nervous, always in motion, who quickly explained his natural history lesson, was often sick, and was a rather good man, in spite of his coldness. As soon as he came in, he opened the window: he was an advocate of hygiene.

"Air, air," he said to the supervisor, Judicone. "Better to have a bit of cold than to breathe bad air."

And to the class that remained standing in silence, he added:

"Ladies, I present to you a new student, Signorina Isabella Diaz. Supervisor, assign her a place."

He went out, already worried and nervous because Professor Radente was ten minutes late; he paced in the corridor so that he could say something to him when he arrived. All the girls sat down: on her feet in the middle of the class remained the little black figure, bearing up under the curious stares of thirty-one girls. Now her features were quite visible. It was a flat face, without precise lines, with a yellowish coloring without even a trace of red; her eyes were very light, her lips purple and spotted from fever, her teeth bad. But what was striking was the total absence of eyebrows and eyelashes, of which there was not even a hair or a shadow; she wore an ugly, ill-made reddish wig that revealed black thread stitches around the part and came down too far on her forehead. Some terrible disease must have devastated her skull and face. She wore a black wool dress that had been dyed and had faded and a shapeless hat made of black cotton lace with some purple ribbons; she had no gloves and clutched an old, peeling small black leather purse in her hands. She was horrendous.

"Could you tell me your name?" asked Judicone kindly.

"Isabella Diaz," the poor girl answered, still rooted in the middle of the room.

Giustina Marangio snickered nastily at that name; Signorina Diaz gave her a melancholy look through her lashless eyelids.

"You'll sit on the last bench," the supervisor went on. "Make room for her, Mazza."

Diaz crossed the classroom and sat down on the edge of the bench, keeping her shapeless hat on and clutching her little purse to her waist; Mazza moved over toward the wall, with a gesture of disgust. After a minute, the nickname invented by Giustina Marangio, "the Bald Monkey," made the rounds, and as it was murmured, repeated, and whispered into one ear after another, Diaz heard it and neither blushed nor went pale.

"Let's say the prayer," Judicone intervened, to be kind.

"Yes, let's, since the Lord has caused Radente to be late today," exclaimed Caterina Borrelli.

"Radente's probably dead," went on Annina Casale, a pious, good creature whom the professor could not stand.

"Let's say the prayer, ladies," repeated the frightened supervisor.

The professor was there, at the door. They all arose, made the sign of the cross, and recited the Our Father in a loud voice. Lidia Santaniello had crossed her hands over her diseased chest, and Borrelli had lowered her glasses in respect. The prayer was over and Diaz was still standing, with her hands folded and her mouth open, as though she were still praying. The priest mounted the lectern; he was small and fat, with the round, smooth face of a pleasure-loving old Roman and a pair of ferocious white eyes that did not single anyone out and were terrifying. His hands were white and plump, with pink nails like a woman's; he was carefully dressed in layman's clothes. He paused for a minute to leaf through his papers and to read in the class register, feeling and savoring the fright that he induced in those poor little mice, whom he was playing with like a cat. Then he raised his head and called out:

"Mazza, recite the lesson."

"I don't know it."

"Why not?"

"I was sick yesterday."

Without commenting, he wrote "o" in the register.

"Casale, recite the lesson."

The poor thing did recite it; it was on the origins of the Vulgate, and she knew it well: but she was transfixed by those white eyes; she felt the professor's dislike and stumbled. Without pity, he let her stumble, looking off into space, so much so that she trembled and blushed, and finally fell back on the bench and burst into tears. Radente, the priest, bent over the register and wrote down "o."

"Borrelli, recite the lesson."

"I didn't learn it, Professor," she answered as she got up tranquilly, smiling.

"And why not?"

"Because *I'm* not a parrot, to memorize a whole passage by Passavanti."

"That's what the program calls for."

"Then the person who made up the program was a parrot. And then, excuse me, Professor, I don't know who this Signor Passavanti is, or in what period he lived, or what he wrote. If you could explain these matters to me, I'll learn the passage."

This time Radente knotted his blond eyebrows slightly, which was the angriest he ever became: Signorina Borrelli, with her unexpected sallies, almost always managed to hit his weak spots. This intelligent, insolent girl always argued for a quarter of an hour before she would say the lesson; he said nothing, put a zero in the register, and promised himself that he would talk to the principal about her. The student sat down in satisfaction, because at least she had earned her zero. The professor stared at the class for a moment and noticed Diaz:

"You, over there, are you the new one?"

"Yes, Signor Professor," she answered, in her small voice.

"You come from home?"

"Yes, sir."

"And what do you know? Nothing, naturally."

She didn't dare answer.

"And what do you plan to do? Here you don't relax, as you do at home; you come here to study, not to stare at the wall. Catch up for the day after tomorrow."

The poor thing looked at him, painfully widening those terrible lashless eyelids. And in spite of their terror of Radente, with that stone face, those wicked eyes, and that sharp voice, a note was circulating through the class on which a little verse was written, a variation of a song that was in vogue:

> I have told you so often
> Don't make love with Radente,
> Who is an impertinent priest;
> He writes zero and leaves.

II

De Sanctis sat up straight at her desk, her arms folded, her mouth still slightly open, her eyes glazed like a human parrot reciting the lesson: the professor of education had just interrupted her in the middle while she was spouting the four fundamental laws of education. Annoyed by that monotonous and idiotic murmuring, he had suddenly asked her if she really understood the law of harmony; the poor thing was bewildered and silent, unable to find her thread again; the talking machine had stopped. Estrada had made a little gesture of disgust and then had launched into a long, very literary, very poetic explanation of harmony in education. This is what Estrada always did. He had a superior mind, more versatile than profound, and was a brilliant speaker; and forced by necessity to teach pedagogy to the girls in the third class, he openly despised this task, and himself for doing it. He had already astonished his students during the first class of the year by explaining to them that pedagogy was useless; and this friendly skepticism characterized all of his explanations of any subject—of the reading method, of Froebelian systems, of Pestalozza and Ferrante Aporti; he would improvise an energetic, sentimental lecture that began with pedagogy and ended who knew where—with Goethe, Pulcinella, and Beaumarchais. Estrada was still young: he was a handsome man with blond side-whiskers that were just beginning to go gray, an ironic smile, and a sonorous voice. Estrada was beloved by a whole group of students—Carmela Fiorillo, Ginevra Barracco, Alessandrina Fraccacreta, Carolina Mazza—because they were also sentimental, because his warm words, that were partly disorganized, partly paradoxical, broke up the stifling monotony of the other classes. And it was said that Teresa Ponzio, the little one, was madly in love with the professor; it was said that Teresa Ponzio wrote him certain passionate letters that she would fold up in her pedagogy homework. But the studious ones, Giuseppina Nobilone, de Sanctis, Cleofe Santaniello, Emilia Scoppa, and Checchina Vetromile—since they were unable to follow him in those flowery wanderings and felt that they didn't know pedagogy and were frightened at the prospect of the exam program—hated this poetic, crazy professor, as they called him: they shrugged their shoulders at his lectures and studied by themselves out of the text, pretending not to listen to him. Only Isabella Diaz, with her face ruined by illness and her reddish brown wig falling onto her forehead, fought with Estrada in the name of pedagogy; she recited her lesson with such a deep sense of reason, with such tranquil logic; she repeated his arguments with the emphasis of a calm, humble person; she took up his words with such good sense that he finally let her have her say, while he listened patiently, with a mocking smile, because that ugly, horrendous girl seemed to him to be the very incarnation of pedagogy.

But that morning even Isabella Diaz was still as she listened to Estrada: the latter had gone from educational pedagogy to the music of Wagner, from Wagner to the legend of Lohengrin and Elsa, from Elsa to the myth of Psyche. The sentimental ones were listening openmouthed, some pale, some flushed, exhilarated by his voice, his words, and the overt and hidden meaning of what he was saying; the studious ones pretended to be reading the text or the arithmetic manual, but little by little that flood of eloquence overcame them, too: they raised their heads, attracted, almost seduced. Caterina Borrelli, who had literary leanings and whose letters of friendship to Amelia Bozzo were filled with rhetoric, was shaking her head like a fascinated bird; Teresa Ponzio, the "beloved of the sun," was drinking in Estrada's words. When he went from Psyche to talking about love, the last holdouts, who wanted a pedagogy class at any cost, raised their heads, enchanted by the direction that the lecture was taking. Among those who were moved was Cristina de Donato, who had had to break up with a tenor with whom she used to sing romantic airs at the conservatory, since she had lost her voice and he had enrolled at the Malta Theater, the amateurs' theater! Carolina Mazza, who had been in love with a student who had betrayed her, went pale in the face; Clementina Scapolatiello, who was hopelessly in love with her sister's fiancé, had tears in her eyes; Luisetta d'Este, the cunning little coquette, was smiling nastily; Maria Valente, who loved her cousin without her love being returned, bowed her head on her hands. And over them all—those who were happily in love, or wanted to be in love, or poor creatures who would never be loved—there came a great nervous trembling: even Pessenda, the very poor girl from Piedmont who was destined to teach in a country school in some village lost in the Alps, was very shaken up; even Isabella Diaz, with her eyes without lashes or eyebrows, with her purple lips spotted by fever, looked as though she were dreaming. And while the whole class was deeply disturbed, while Professor Estrada was leaving, while Teresa Ponzio threw her head back as though she were fainting, the viperous Giustina Marangio jumped up on the teacher's platform and wrote in large letters on the blackboard:

"Love is a terrible mistake."

"Mercanti, recite the parable of the wise and foolish virgins," said the professor of religion.

Mercanti arose somewhat tiredly, half-laughing and half-coughing, showing her teeth where an incisor was missing, and answered:

"Professor, you know, this morning I heard you say Mass."

The priestling Pagliuca, who was very dark in the face and bespectacled, smiled as though he were flattered.

"Recite the parable," he insisted.

"Professor, why do you say Mass in such a loud voice?" asked the other, a bit insolently, with her pale face and eyes that were already too malicious.

He explained why and talked about the Mass; the girls listened, giggling among themselves. He was a very deformed, dark little priest who made a lot of faces with his mouth and eyes when he explained the lesson and a number of ridiculous gestures when he talked about Moses or Christ. The girls could not take him seriously.

"Donnarumma, recite the parable . . ."

"Excuse me, Professor, first I have to discuss a difficulty. Is it true what nonbelievers say, that Jesus was too lenient when he pardoned Mary Magdalene?"

He made a scandalized face, squirmed in his chair, raised his eyebrows, and tried to justify Jesus's pardoning of Mary Magdalene. But these girls, especially some, didn't seem to be convinced; they looked at him with their crafty, incredulous eyes; he felt the irony in their expressions, and he got angry and cried out that it wasn't proper to question the facts of religion. Donnarumma, the big young woman from Castellammare, with her cow's eyes, somewhat embarrassed, recited the parable; Carolina Mazza could be seen prompting her over her shoulder, as she read out of the book. But there was worse: that account of the virgins who await the bridegroom with lighted lamps to enter the house with him as escorts excited their curiosity, excited comments from those girls who were already grown, some of whom had come up from the streets, who saw and heard everything, both good and bad.

Luisetta d'Este, Artemisia Jaquinangelo, Concetta Stefanozzo, Signorina Donnarumma, Mercanti, and Mazza, the so-called Unbiased group, had a rather good time in religion class: they were the insolent ones who would prepare a number of tricky questions to confuse the professor so that they wouldn't have to recite the lesson. He would let himself be taken in, a bit nonplussed by these ticklish subjects, and would get lost in a welter of words; the entire class was seized with a fit of laughter. Accordingly, after Estrada's class, there was a secular charge remaining in the classroom, a fantasy of amorous visions; the girls' nerves were on edge: when they heard the strange parable of the virgins, which needs a lofty mystical explanation, the girls looked at one another with smiles full of ulterior meaning, and they had to bite their lips in order not to laugh; they raised their books up to their mouths to hide behind, or they bent over their desks as though they were looking for something. The professor was staring, completely unsuspecting, with that obnoxious face of his, trying to understand something from that laughing murmur that was growing louder. Only the group of "Saints," the mystical group, the two Santaniello sisters, Annina Casale, Signorina Pessenda, Signorina Scapolatiello, Signorina Borrelli, and Maria Valente, looked severe or scandalized;

these girls, who were either very unhappy or very intelligent or very poor, were the victims of a mild religious folly that they were unable to repress. Every morning they met in the Church of Santa Chiara before they came to class and prayed for an hour; they wrote the initials "J. M.," the names of Jesus and Mary, on all their homework; they exchanged rosaries, amulets, little crowns, color pictures of saints; every Sunday they arranged to meet for Mass and vespers, first in one church, then in another; they observed all the triduums, novenas, and octaves in their free time; they wrote religious phrases in the margins of their geography texts and prayers in their geometry notebooks; they referred to each other as "sisters" among themselves. They formed the group that was opposed to the Unbiased one and they despised each other; the Saints were quieter and more lenient, the Unbiased girls were more talkative and more insolent.

"Isabella Diaz, recite the catechism lesson."

The ugly girl got up and talked about the sacraments, very softly, in her small voice, and her lips were trembling slightly; she moved her yellowish hands, which were always a bit damp, around on the desk. Nevertheless, that thin little figure, flat-chested in her old dress, spoke of the sacraments with such true piety, such Christian humility of interpretation, that the mystics turned around to listen to her, completely absorbed. The little priest nodded his head from right to left, as though he were expressing ape-like satisfaction; and Isabella Diaz went on describing the veil of mystery that shrouded the sacraments and what they represented. But on the seventh, marriage, the Unbiased girls started murmuring again, and giggling, and elbowing each other, making faces so that they wouldn't laugh, and Luisetta d'Este's shrill voice asked:

"Excuse me, Professor, what does the sacrament of marriage represent mystically?"

» «

The principal and professor of physical and natural sciences put his hand, which was as thin as a woman's, in the cardboard urn box and drew out a little roll of paper.

"Judicone," he said, as he opened the roll.

The supervisor went slightly pale, but she tried to smile and stood up to recite the lesson.

"Come up on the platform: then you can explain the machine from a practical point of view."

In fact, the Atwood machine, long, thin, and complicated, all brass and steel, stood on the teacher's platform like a small gallows. Judicone stood next to it; big and fat, with her good-humored full-moon face, the wide hips of a future mother, and her full white matron's throat: and slowly, she tried to explain to her classmates that difficult, delicate mechanism with which the fall of masses is measured. Pointing with the index finger on her plump hand, she touched the little levers, the small wheels, the little paper flyers, the clothespins; her eyes, which were a soft oil color, full of kindness, were fixed intently on that metallic mechanism, as though she wanted to extract from it every bit of truth. But after three or four minutes of explanation, she began to speak more slowly, her sentences became labored, she mixed up her words, and Judicone remained silent, her arms hanging down at her sides, looking at the machine, her eyes full of desire and of pain. She had not even managed to describe a third of it. The professor was stroking his blond goatee, with a nervous gesture that was habitual with him; and a bit of impatience and anger was building up in that good, patient soul of a man who has lived. The class had been stuck for a week on this important but difficult lesson on gravity, on these laws concerning the fall of masses, on this dreadful Atwood machine, unable to go on, bewildered, stupefied, unable to comprehend anything more. He had already repeated the same lesson three times at great length, applying theory to practice, dismantling the mechanism piece by piece; he had left the machine in class so that the students could practice on it, analyze it at their leisure. But it all seemed useless. Without saying anything to Judicone, he stuck his hand in the urn and drew out another name: the whole class kept their eyes fixed on that fatal little roll of paper; everyone feared for themselves; the Atwood machine was too diabolical.

"Cleofe Santaniello."

The intelligent, studious little thing left her seat, after taking a last look at her own notebook, where there was a drawing of the machine; Judicone returned to her place, with her face bent over the class register to hide her blush. Cleofe Santaniello studied the machine for a minute, touched it two or three times with the bony hand of one who suffered from rickets, and began rapidly, looking at nothing in particular, so that she wouldn't get mixed up. She went along well for a while, but unfortunately on the word "front anvil," she heard a soft voice, her sister Lidia's, quickly whisper "rear, rear." Cleofe stopped, trembled, lost her thread, and was unable to begin again: her nervous problem, which kept her from making a good impression in class even though she understood and knew everything, took over once again. The professor looked at her for a moment, so little and wretched, and perhaps out of pity he didn't rebuke her, but told her to go with his eyes.

When she was called on, Costanza Scalera got up, with her composed air of a great lady, and declared frankly that she could tell him the whole theory regarding the law, but that she could not describe the Atwood machine; the principal-professor shrugged his shoulders. The silent storm grew worse: a tremendous embarrassment came over the girls; they felt tremendous shame over their stupidity, their ineptitude. In the final analysis, they were too fond of this principal, who was not at all outgoing, but fair, who was short on praise, but incapable of treating them badly; and they lived in awe of him and wanted to satisfy him in every way, and his lessons were the ones that they studied most. What a humiliation for the third class that they still didn't know anything about the law of falling masses by the fourth lesson! And as time passed, their shame and confusion spread and grew worse: when they went up on the teacher's platform and stood beneath that little metal gallows, two or three others lost their heads because of an unknown terror, like people who get sick because they are afraid of illness. The Atwood machine seemed to grow; it towered over their heads; its mechanism of little wheels seemed to multiply: it seemed to acquire a soul, a metallic, mocking soul, that laughed at those girls' torments; they looked at it in fear, as though it were a monster. At a certain point, the principal stopped; there was a very long and deep minute of silence. Then he, who never scolded them, who never pronounced a word of blame, said slowly:

"I'm rather pained by what is happening."

The effect was startling: many of them went pale; tears ran down the cheeks of Judicone, who was so good; Cleofe Santaniello broke into sobs. The honor of the third class was besmirched. As the principal rose and was on the point of leaving, Checchina Vetromile, one of the best students, stood up, a bit red, and said in a voice that trembled slightly:

"Listen, Signor Principal, the fault isn't ours, or anyone else's. The lesson is difficult, and complicated: we've been studying it for a week without being able to master it. We've neglected everything else for this dreadful machine; perhaps we've done worse because we've gotten dull from having to repeat the same thing twenty times over. If you agree, let's leave the machine for a little while and go on: we'll take it up again in a week. We promise you that we will learn it perfectly; I can speak for the whole class."

But the positive and calming effect of these words spoken by this dear, beautiful creature was dissipated by a strident little voice exclaiming:

"Speak for yourself, Vetromile. I know the lesson; if the professor wishes, I can recite it."

It was Giustina Marangio, the pale girl with the thin lips and white eyes. The girls were overcome by a painful astonishment at this defection, or betrayal; the principal himself knitted his eyebrows, as though he was annoyed. And Giustina Marangio quickly mounted the platform, gave the Atwood machine a mocking look; in her voice that resembled a shrill file, without ever stopping or making a mistake, she described that system of brass and steel minutely and precisely, omitting nothing, applying theory to practice, considering the smallest pieces of that mechanism. At the end, when Giustina Marangio tilted the machine so that the class could see it better and placed her small closed fist on it, with her index finger extended, she seemed stronger and more evil than it was.

The class had emptied for recess. The boarders had gone to walk in the school; the day students, in that corridor that was like the bowels of the earth. There were only thirty minutes of recess in all, from noon until twelve thirty, to go up and down, in the half darkness, in lines of four or five or in couples of two. Here attractions and friendships were evident. Amelia Bozzo had fled the first class and, passing in front of Caterina Borrelli, had passed her a note; it said: "If you don't love me, I'll either go crazy or die." The Saints, in a line, who were still very sorry about the scandal that had happened during natural science class, tried to distract themselves by talking about the next Holy Week and about moving religious rites. Scapolatiello praised the parish of the Seven Sorrows; Valente preferred Santa Maria della Rotonda; Annina Casale was partial to her own parish, the Madonna of Succor; Isabella Diaz, that horrendous creature, was reading, as she walked all alone, barely able to see in that darkness, a religious tract entitled "Where Will We Be in a Hundred Years?"

The Zealots—Vetromile, Cleofe Santaniello, Giuseppina Nobilone, de Sanctis—were reviewing the arithmetic lesson, the last theorems of the square root, while they walked; Professor de Vincentis was supposed to come from one thirty to three for the last class. Since they were hungry, the Unbiased, of whom there were six or seven, had pooled their financial assets and collected fifteen cents; by dint of a great deal of begging, they had convinced Rosa, the caretaker, to buy them eight cents' worth of bread, six of mozzarella, keeping one cent for her trouble; then, while they were waiting, Carolina Mazza, who was melancholic and cynical, told them an off-color story that made them split their sides laughing. And all of them, both boarders and day students, the Sentimentalists, the Zealots, the Saints, and the Unbiased ones, breathed a little easier; after the recess period they had an hour of women's work: the teacher was softhearted, feeling sorry for the ones in the third class, knowing how burdensome their courses were; she was lenient and let them read and write or draw, provided that they turned in a successful piece of sewing, or mending, or patching at the exam.

They all made plans for that hour, which was almost free: Caterina Borrelli wanted to write a long letter to her friend Amelia Bozzo; the Zealots planned to review the physical-sciences lesson among themselves; the Saints planned to continue their conversation about miracles and conversions; and the Unbiased planned to have a long lunch. So that, although they had come back into the classroom at twelve thirty, while the teacher observed the work of two or three who had enough energy for this, too, the others didn't even turn back the lid of their desks, in which there was a green wool pincushion, so that they could sew. Caterina Borrelli was writing; Carolina was cutting the smoked mozzarella in thin slices and distributing it equally; Checchina Vetromile had turned the Atwood machine upside down, almost as though she were going to take it apart; Clemenza Scapolatiello had rolled up the sleeve of her dress to show her friends a little rosary of the souls in purgatory that she always wore on her arm below her elbow. In this general uproar, a rustle was heard: the two inspectors, a hunchbacked countess who was an old maid and a heavy marquise with glasses on her nose, entered with their glacial, disdainful air. They did their job for free, as though they deigned to help poor girls as a form of charity; they filled up their long, empty days by going through schools, introducing the proud airs of their silk dresses and jeweled earrings; they used their worthlessness to annoy students, professors, and teachers with their know-it-all observations and byzantine disputes. They were detested because they were neither good nor compassionate nor at all useful. But everyone had to pretend to respect them, or they went to the principal or wrote to the minister, upsetting everything like a couple of magpies. Consequently, their arrival was like that of a double Medusa's head. Even the teacher became confused.

"They're not working much, I gather?" observed the hunchback in the bitter tone of an envious old maid.

"These young ladies haven't been thinking about sewing for quite a while," the pedantic marquise went on. "They want to become too learned . . ."

"The program is rather demanding," the teacher dared to say.

"If it goes on like this, we'll report it," said the hunchback.

"We'll report it," affirmed the know-it-all marquise.

And they began to inspect the class: many of the desktops had been opened to give the illusion that they were sewing.

"You, Borrelli, why aren't you sewing?" asked the hunchback with the chin full of gray hairs.

"I'm excused from sewing because I have bad eyes."

"Where is your certificate?"

"At home, naturally, and the principal has the other one."

"If they all get themselves certificates, we'll have to report it."

And they went on.

"Signorina Mazza, are you sewing without a thimble?"

"I lost it, Signora Inspector."

"You'll prick your finger, and you could be more careful with your equipment."

Luisetta d'Este was coughing as though she were choking: when she had seen the inspectors come in, she had swallowed a big piece of bread and a little piece of mozzarella the wrong way; and she turned red, with tears in her eyes, and was coughing her lungs out.

"Do you always have this cough? Is it a chronic condition?" asked the old hunchback.

"No, thank God," the latter shot back between wrenching coughs, "*I'm* certainly not fifty."

"Signorina Vetromile, why are you using Italian thread? Don't you know that you should be using English thread? What sort of carelessness is this? Ah, you really, really do not want to give importance to women's work, do you? You'll see, you'll see, when the exams come, what a lot of failures you'll get!"

And the two harpies, with the trivial minds and cold hearts of childless women, the two useless, tormenting women, slowly, student by student, found a way to make some bitter observation, some offensive remark: they upset them all, student by student, by their words, intonation, the luxuriousness of their dresses (which was ever more evident), by certain head-to-foot looks they gave, by certain nauseated faces they made, certain haughty movements with their heads, or certain elegant gestures with their hands. That visit was a complete disaster: the ones who had planned to study could not; the hungry ones had to give up their lunches, which they had hidden under their desks and were unable to eat; those who were sewing were embittered because of their needles, whip-stitch or running stitch. Even Isabella Diaz, who was mending a piece of beaver, a very delicate task, was criticized for the way she did her stitches; and the hunchbacked lady with the hairy chin looked at her wig with deep scorn. At the door, the marquise with the pedantic voice gave a pep talk, reminding the girls that their sad condition made it necessary for them to be teachers, that they shouldn't have the audacity to think that they were independent and free, and that they should strive to win the indulgence of important and respectable people who would sacrifice themselves for them—for them who were basically so ungrateful.

That day de Vincentis's face was set in a frown. With the arrival of spring, he had been bothered by rheumy eyes, which forced him to always wear blue glasses, and arthritic pain had penetrated his bones. He was limping, leaning on a cane, completely wrapped in a heavy wool coat, with a wool scarf around his neck and flannel-lined beaver gloves on his hands; his long salt-and-pepper goatee moved as his face contracted nervously. But the girls were not much afraid of him that day: everyone, or almost everyone, knew the long and difficult lesson on the square root, since he had explained it clearly, with his mathematical precision. And, because of the importance of the lesson that they had to recite, and seeing him so out of breath and sickly, a kind of certainty mixed with pity sprang up inside them: certainty that he would have little time left to explain the new lesson and that perhaps, since he wasn't feeling good, he wouldn't even try to do so. They found this encouraging, because if he assigned much new material for a couple of days later, they would never be able to learn it in such a short time; it would be a disaster. Gently, Judicone asked him how he felt and offered him a wool beret for his head, which was already balding: he was in quite a bit of pain, one could see, but he was in control of himself; even the nervous movement of his goatee had stopped. When he called on de Sanctis to recite the lesson, she got up in a lively manner, went to the blackboard, intending to demonstrate the theorem: the professor interrupted her at the beginning, saying, "That's all" to her dryly, and then called on someone else. And so it went for the second, third, and fourth students: as soon as he saw that they knew the lesson, he interrupted them and sent them back to their places.

The others began to look at one another in dismay: their innocent plan had failed; their expectations had not been realized. They almost hoped that the girl who was called on wouldn't know the lesson, that she would stumble, that the professor would make her say the whole thing so that he could correct her, but in vain! The class was passing through a moment of arithmetical bliss; the professor listened, almost smiling; his algebraic brain and his teacher's heart were comforted. At two, when there was still an hour to go before the end of the class and of school, everything became clear: the astonished students saw that little old man, bent over from arthritis, enveloped in his woolens, take one knotty red hand out of his glove, write a long arithmetical formula on the blackboard, and they heard a strong Chilean pronunciation (which changed *d*'s to *r*'s and put *gh* before every *e*) enunciate the fundamental theorem of the third power:

"The cube of a number, divided in two, is equal to the cube of the first part, double product of the first for the second, double product of the second for the first, cube of the second part."

And, from that bag of broken-down bones, from that head whose eyes could barely see any longer, from that weakened, deformed hand, from that lucid, unconquerable brain issued for an hour a precise, persistent, continuous demonstration that explicated and rendered more and more complex the formulas and subformulas of the theorem. The board was chock-full of figures, of arithmetical signs, of roots, and of letters: at the end he had to write smaller, since there was no more space. No word of complaint escaped him because of his illness, nor did he stop: he kept on and on, like an old mechanism whose basic wheel is still solid. He stopped when the clock struck three and the bell announced the closing of school; he stopped and left. They . . . did not. They stared at the blackboard, stupefied and exhausted.

III

They pretended, some to be tranquil, some nonchalant, some absolutely indifferent: they all pretended, to the best of their abilities and knowledge, in order to hide their fear, worry, sadness, or nervousness. Divided into groups of two or three, sitting here and there on the disorderly desks in the third-class room, they pretended to admire each other, one because of a new dress that had been cut out and sewed at home, another because of a new hat that cost nine and a half lire in all, a third for a scarf that had been embroidered in their very brief intervals of leisure; they talked of ocean swimming, at Santa Lucia, Chiatamone, on the Chiaia Riviera, at Posillipo; they formed groups so as to spend less and have more fun: a bathhouse costs one franc, divided by four makes five cents a day for each person, and they would get there on foot, what did it matter? They talked of the big summer evening cheap treat, the Villa, the mecca of middle-class Neapolitan girls—the Villa, with its gaslight, music, crowd of girls and young men, with the iron chairs that cost a penny, and the moon and sea that cost nothing. Yes, they tried to look relaxed, but underneath all those smiles, the torment still leaked out; beneath that talk of clothes, beaches, and evenings out, the anguished thought persisted, "the other," the reason that none of them had slept at night, that they had exhausted themselves for eight months, and that in the last two summer months, June and July, they had slaved from morning until night over their books, notebooks, summaries, and formulae; the underlying, dominant thought for which they had been called to school that day at nine, for which they had gotten up at six, left the house at seven, and, after a good deal of walking around, all arrived here at eight, an hour early. This was the day of the oral exam, for the *diploma superiore*. And the exam—the exam was the fearful, agonizing, underlying, dominant thought.

So that, since these young souls weren't capable of pretending for long, they all involuntarily abandoned themselves to their own thoughts, no longer ashamed since everyone else was worried. Pale and dismayed, Annina Casale was leaning against the window-panes, looking out into the courtyard without seeing anything, and Caterina Borrelli, her aggressive friend, was lecturing her in order to give her courage.

"You're silly to be afraid. Haven't you studied all year? What are you worried about?"

"Everything."

"Do this: think that the examiners in there all know less than you do. Are you thinking that? Try to convince yourself and you won't be afraid anymore. Understand?"

"Yes, but I don't think so."

"Think about something else: they're going to fail me, too. We'll take the makeup exam together; we'll study together."

"What? You think they'll fail *you*, you who are so good and so daring?"

"I swear that they'll fail me, Nannì. I have a bad premonition."

Elsewhere, speaking in low voices, each one was describing her own special terror:

"Pedagogy, pedagogy. I'll certainly fail pedagogy," said de Sanctis, as though she were talking to herself. "I've never understood it; I've wasted hours and hours on it; even last night I didn't sleep because I reviewed the whole book. And if he asks me reading methods, what do I answer? I don't know anything either about kindergarten or about the simultaneous system . . ."

"For me, the difficult thing is physical sciences," added Carolina Mazza. "It's too complicated a subject: if you learn optics well, you forget acoustics; then electricity mixes you up, and you're lost . . ."

"I've always had bad luck in history!" exclaimed Mercanti. "I'll bet they'll ask me about the Crusades, those damned Crusades; how many were there, nine, or fifteen, or thirty-four?"

"And arithmetic. Does arithmetic seem to you like a joking matter?" asked Luisetta d'Este, smiling bitterly.

"Oh, God, arithmetic!" four or five repeated in chorus; they were getting more and more frightened.

Others had gathered around Checchina Vetromile, and haunted by the nightmare of the exam, their heads empty because they had studied too much, they asked and gave each other some last explanations in Italian literature, geometry, and chemistry, which left them even more confused. Checchina Vetromile described the thermometer to Cleofe Santaniello, in minute detail; Pessenda twice recounted Charles VIII's invasion of Italy to Emilia Scoppa. At the blackboard, Scapolatiello had shown Carmela Fiorillo how to find the lesser radius of the trunk of a cone, and those who were listening absorbed as if in a dream, repeated the explanation, stammering. Giustina Marangio, who already had one foot out the door, hummed as she rocked in a chair; alone in a corner, Isabella Diaz, who had sewn some dyed green ribbons on her old hat, clutched her purse in her hands. Then, as the clock struck nine, silence descended: Rosa, the caretaker, appeared at the door with a card in her hand and read the first four names:

"Abbamonte, Barracco, Bellezza, Borrelli: come to the exam!"

Abbamonte turned pale, Barracco made the sign of the cross, Bellezza picked up her fan very nervously, Borrelli gave Casale a kiss and resolutely straightened her glasses on her nose: all four filed out without exchanging a word. In a low voice, Isabella Diaz told them as they passed:

"May God help you!"

The others said nothing; already trembling and breathless, they didn't start to talk again for ten minutes. Since Casale no longer had Borrelli to cheer her up, she sat on the window ledge and recited Hail Marys to herself. Carolina Mazza was telling the sad story of Nobilone, poor Nobilone, who had failed the written exam and hadn't been able to take the oral one: a year lost, so many hopes gone up in smoke.

"And what will poor Nobilone do?" asked Donnarumma.

"What can she do? She failed four subjects. How can she be ready for the makeup in three months? She would have to pay tutors: the poor thing, she has so little money!"

"She could take the telegraphists exam," suggested Defeo.

"Sure! Three months of school at a cost of twenty francs a month, books, tutors, four positions, and thirty-five applicants."

"True, true," murmured two or three.

"Or she could teach nursery school," proposed Mercanti.

"Of course: fifty lire a month, and deductions, and you risk ruining your health!"

"True, true," repeated the others softly.

And each one of them felt deeply discouraged; each one was thinking of what she would have to do if she failed. And the moral issue of humiliation, which made them blush, gave way to the more urgent material one of pressing need; each thought of that long sacrifice of three years, going to bed late in order to study, getting up early when she wanted to sleep, going out in the rain, cold, or damp without an umbrella or coat, in flimsy shoes, coughing, eating little, scrimping in order to buy books, and going without a hat in order to buy a box of compasses. What agony failure was! What could they do then? Where could they find the money, the patience, the will, the strength to continue that life for another year? How could they begin again with that anxiety over exams, for the telegraph office, for nursery school?

Forty minutes had passed; the caretaker Rosa appeared at the door and read four more names:

"Casale, de Donato, Defeo, de Sanctis: come to the exam!"

But the exodus of these four others was barely noticed; no one paid any attention to Annina Casale's melancholy hesitation, to Defeo's mute resignation, to the false air of confidence of de Donato, who was really terribly afraid, or to de Sanctis, who looked like a poor beast on the way to the slaughter: those who had already been examined were coming back, the spotlight was on them; they were immediately surrounded. Abbamonte had met her old father, a retired official, in the corridor and had flung herself into his arms; now they were walking back and forth with his hand lovingly on her shoulder, and she looked blissful, very red in the face, with her eyes popping. The others were in the classroom: Barracco very pale with a red spot on her right cheek, like the imprint of a slap; Borrelli looking triumphant, with her braid half-undone and her tie over her shoulder; Bellezza very red, looking uncertain. And questions swirled around them: everyone wanted to know if the professors were grumpy, if the problems were easy, if they asked what was on the program, if the principal was nervous, if the ten-minute exam with each examiner went quickly, if geography was tested using a map.

"Not at all, not at all," Barracco answered nervously. "Geography is nothing: imagine, they asked me the rivers in Spain; who doesn't know that? De Vincentis is usually a bit of a grouch, but it's obvious that he doesn't want the school to make a bad impression . . ."

"The problem is pedagogy," continued Borrelli. "Estrada certainly did us a fine service with his poetry: instead, the examiner is very demanding; I swear, if I hadn't improvised a bit, at random, I would have failed. Excuse me, did he ever explain to us what ontological reflection was?"

"No, never, never," three or four answered, looking at one another. "That Estrada has ruined things for us!"

"I'll give you some advice," continued the neurotic Barracco, "never answer in a hurry; that's bad, the examiner gives you a mean look and asks you too much, and the time drags. I answered too quickly, and I had to recite Linnaeus's entire system; I thought it would never end . . ."

"Italian literature is difficult, too: I thought so; didn't I always tell you that Radente was a fool?" exclaimed Caterina Borrelli. "Imagine, they want to know the whole history of Italian literature, which we've never studied. Oh, that Radente! Why don't they fire him?"

"Don't worry about history of religion and morality: the questions are easy," murmured Barracco.

"Don't worry anymore about anything; the exam is not as hard as it seems," Borrelli exclaimed gaily. "I should leave, but I want to wait until Casale and two or three others get out. Now I'll write a note to Mama to tell her that everything went well. Oh, poor Mama, this will make her feel better!"

And her voice grew soft until she was crying; Barracco, who was near her, grew pale, trembled, clenched her teeth, and said in a heartrending voice: "Oh, Mama, Mama," then collapsed onto a desk and fainted. The fit of nerves, which she had kept at bay for three hours, had come at that name, "Mama," and Barracco had seen again, as though in a bad dream, the suicide of her mother, an unfortunate woman who, having been left a poor widow at her husband's death, with five sons and daughters whom she was unable to support, had thrown herself onto the pavement from the balcony of a disreputable hotel in an alley in the Guantai. In her paroxysm, great tears ran down Barracco's cheeks from under her closed eyelids, and the classmates around her didn't know what else to do, after they had loosened her dress, but have her smell a rose that Mercanti wore on her chest. Barracco had passed, but it wasn't possible for her to ever be happy, ever, with that dark vision of her mother's broken body down in the street: they were all talking in low voices about the tragedy, while Borrelli bathed Barracco's temples with a handkerchief soaked in water. And Bellezza wasn't smiling or crying; she wore her usual expression of doubt: inwardly she was convinced that she had done the whole arithmetic demonstration incorrectly. She didn't dare ask Checchina Vetromile if the false-supposition method was the right one to use to solve that "rule of society" problem: she didn't dare since she was afraid of finding out that she had been wrong.

"D'Este, Diaz, Donnarumma, and Fiorillo!" called the caretaker.

They all turned to watch Isabella Diaz go by. She was really so ugly, with her face without eyelashes or eyebrows, of a yellowish and rather greasy pallor, with that old reddish wig and that cotton lace cap with pea green ribbons, that she was sickening: and beside her Luisetta d'Este was so pretty with her petite beauty, Carmela Fiorillo so appealing with her Andalusian eyes and her lips as bright as pomegranate flowers, Maria Donnarumma so strong and pleasing with her robustness, that Isabella Diaz seemed uglier, shabbier, and more repulsive in contrast. Now Casale had come back from the exam, as well as de Sanctis, Defeo, and de Donato; their reports grew more and more contradictory. Defeo had done poorly in religious history, of all things, which is such an easy subject; Casale had tried valiantly, but precisely in history she hadn't been able to remember the name of the battle that Dante Alighieri had taken part in.

"Campaldino, stupid, Campaldino!" cried Borrelli.

De Donato remained silent; she knew that her performance had been mediocre, but she also knew that she had had a low pass in every subject. What difference do points make? They're a silly question of vanity; it's enough to have a diploma. As for de Sanctis, the phenomenon of transformation was complete: with flushed cheeks and shining eyes, she said that she had answered everything correctly: and her classmates, knowing how weak she was, exchanged skeptical looks without her noticing.

"Imagine," she said excitedly, "that the professor of physical sciences asks me, what is the instrument that is used to measure the degrees of heat of the temperature? The barometer, I answer. Who invented it? Several people did: Signor Celsius, Torricelli, and Réaumur. And I also described it to him. Fine. The same thing in pedagogy. What is the fundamental law of teaching? There are various laws; the psychological law sums them all up, and Signor Froebel was the one who applied it to reading methods. Fine. History, what about history? The Battle of Gavinana and Pier Capponi who exclaims to Malatesta Baglioni, "You are killing a dead man!" In geography: the Apennines, yes indeed; they begin at the Colle di Tenda and end in Calabria. And to think I was so frightened! The exam is simple; you can take it with an easy mind."

And the others didn't dare tell her, so as not to disillusion her, about her strange mix-up of the thermometer and the barometer; and what a muddle she had made of pedagogy, history, and geography; and they listened to her with a pitying smile as she distorted everything, prattling away like a silly, noisy goose. The excitement of those who still had to take the exam continued to grow, at so many events and reports, so many contradictions; and, while the fervor of those who had already finished overflowed into nervous gaiety, those who still had to be examined grew paler and quieter. By now they no longer thought about reviewing that still obscure bit of history; they no longer cared to have Checchina Vetromile tell them how light acts on plants: everything was useless now, everything was decided; they wouldn't ever learn anything more. They knew what they knew; what would be would be; a sort of mistrust of everything took over in those souls shaken by anxiety. And, as time passed, the fateful day became more and more complicated by events: there was the case of Luisetta d'Este, the pretty young thing who had never studied anything, except for some little things here and there, little by little, completely absorbed in coquettishness and flirting, and who had had the luck to be asked precisely the few things that she knew and to be passed, as though she were the most zealous and studious of students—and when she came back, the cheeky girl was laughing and making fun of exams and of the examiners and of the diploma and of everything that was scholastic, boring, and hateful, which made the good girls who had ruined their health studying very sad. There was the case of Scapolatiello, who the very evening before had heard them announce at home her sister's marriage to that young man whom she silently adored: they were getting married in September— there was no longer any way out—and that news had upset her so much that she had gone to the exam as though she were in a dream, understanding nothing of what they asked her, shivering as though in pain from time to time; she was given a grade of bad failure: now the unfortunate girl sat in a corner of the third class, without crying or sighing; she kept on repeating that the only thing left for her was death. There was the case of the two Santaniello sisters: one of them already had tuberculosis; she had been harmed by that year's work and the examiners had given her the diploma almost out of pity, looking at her with compassion and speaking in low voices among themselves while she stood there, very embarrassed and ashamed of her illness; and the other was anemic, timid, and very intelligent, but she lacked courage, and the examiners had to tear the words out of her one by one, with tremendous effort, because the poor thing was so timid and confused. And there was the case of Giustina Marangio, who, when she went up to the blackboard where Fraccacreta before her had found the surface of the pyramid, had pointed out to the professor an error in the demonstration, which he hadn't noticed; she had redone the demonstration triumphantly, and because of her Fraccacreta had gotten a five* in geometry.

Then they all—whether happy or unhappy, thoughtful or merry, looking daggers at each other, holding grudges, envying, or loving each other—had waited until three in order to read the verdict, the official results of the exam that were posted in the courtyard. All of them more or less knew the results, but a last bit of curiosity spurred them on. And de Sanctis remained stupefied at having received fives, fours, even zeroes, in every subject. And the greatest miracle of all was Isabella Diaz, who since she had had the highest number of points, had come in first.

IV

Three years later, from a notepad, mementos, memories:

Judicone took the competitive exam, got one of the highest grades, and taught first grade for a year in the elementary school in the Porto neighborhood. Then she immediately married a clerk in the Bank of Naples and had two children in two years. She has gotten very fat.

*D

Emilia Scoppa took the competitive exam for elementary school teachers and didn't pass; she took the telegraph office exam and didn't pass that either. She found employment as a salesgirl in the Miccio stores, in the clothing department, and when she sees her former classmates, she is ashamed and hides.

Since she couldn't wait for the competitive exam, Pessenda immediately accepted a position as a country school teacher in the town of Olevano in Cilento, with a salary of five hundred francs a year. During the extreme cold two years ago, she was unable to get an allowance for heating her house; after she had written in vain several times to the school inspector and to the superintendent of schools for a subsidy, her old mother fell ill with bronchitis and died. The following year, due to greater budgetary expenses, the town of Olevano reduced the salaries of elementary school teachers by a hundred lire; Pessenda stayed on and put up with it, having no better prospects, since there were no other positions for country school teachers and the competitive exams in the cities were growing more difficult. Last summer, Pessenda did not go away on vacation, perhaps because she could not afford to go to Piedmont; in August she came down with typhoid fever, which was not properly treated by the town doctor. Because a rumor spread through town that her illness was contagious, she was abandoned by everyone, including the peasant woman who came to do the heavy chores; thus it is hard to tell when she died, since she was almost black when she was found in bed, in an unfurnished room, with the windows open and a burned-out lamp on the floor in a corner.

Caterina Borrelli and Annina Casale didn't take the competitive exam for elementary school teachers; they took the telegraph office exam, which they passed; they have been there for three years.

Borrelli is a terrible employee; Casale, instead, is excellent, both in the work and in her behavior.

Cleofe Santaniello took the exam and barely passed it; she teaches first grade in the elementary school in Montecalvario. She lacks moral strength and energy; her pupils drive her crazy and don't do well on exams; moreover, she is always sickly and is often absent in the winter. One day she fainted in class. The principal of the school and her superiors are not happy with her: they had to give her an assistant for a month, at her own expense. They put up with her because of her sweetness and her poverty.

Lidia Santaniello didn't take the exam, since she was ill with bronchitis. When she got well, she was given a position as a nursery school teacher in the Mercato area, with an annual salary of six hundred lire. She had 134 pupils. Unable to cope with such tremendous fatigue, she asked unsuccessfully for an assistant in her section. The constant din, having to teach songs to 134 little ones by singing herself, having to teach them gymnastics by gesticulating, stamping her feet on the floor and clapping her hands, having to take them out for recess in a big, damp courtyard, circling for an hour around a well, finally destroyed her health, which had already been undermined. She continued teaching in spite of her illness, because she lacked the courage to abandon the little children whom she loved so much, content to teach them their short children's songs in a very weak voice, without getting up from her chair; often the little boys and girls were quiet for a whole day, only because their teacher had begged them to be good because she felt very bad, since those little children loved her very much. When she could no longer function and had to stay in bed, there was a constant procession of little boys and girls through her bare house, coming very quietly to visit the teacher; since she could no longer talk to them because it tired her so, she had them sit around her bed and she would smile at them: they were quiet so as not to disturb her. When she died six months ago, the town paid her funeral expenses; the children each paid a penny so that they could take her flowers, and they all followed the coffin two by two, holding hands, as when she used to take them out for recess around the well, and they sang the little songs that she had taught them in her wasted voice.

De Donato, who didn't dare take the competitive exam, went to direct the elementary school in Avellino; she gives singing lessons to the wealthiest girls in town, and she herself sings the romances of Tito Mattei—"He Didn't Return" and "It's Not True"—at the musical society of Avellino.

Carmela Fiorillo did not take the exam; she was a country school teacher in Gragnano for a year, but when the son of a rich pasta manufacturer fell in love with her, she had to leave town and go teach in a village in Upper Savoy, for a salary of four hundred lire a year. Since there was no housing in the village where the school was located, she lived in a neighboring village and had to walk four miles every morning and evening, coming and going. One day last winter about three, when she was returning home, she was surprised by a snowstorm: and whether because of the cold, fatigue, or lack of food, since she hadn't eaten since the day before, she fell down on the road and let herself die, of weakness and frostbite; the Alpinists found her two days later. The town awarded her a small marble tombstone, in recognition of her zeal and love of her humble tasks.

Giustina Marangio took the exam, passed with flying colors, teaches third grade in an elementary school in the Chiaia neighborhood, and even managed to get the principal of the school transferred to Portici, so that she could take over as principal, with an allowance. It is she who invented a new method of punishing girls: putting the rag that is used to clean the desks and blackboards on their heads, filthy with ink and chalk powder. And it is she who invented a new way to discourage pupils from coming to school late: the teacher stands at the door with her watch in hand, and anyone who arrives after eight inexorably has her lunch taken away. Many little girls stopped coming after this.

Bellezza, Fraccacreta, and Jaquinangelo repeated the third year of the course: Fraccacreta is shut up in the nuns' convent at Sant' Agostino alla Zecca, where she is a teacher. No news of Bellezza or Jaquinangelo.

De Sanctis is repeating the third year of the course for the third time.

Teresina Ponzio, the "sun lover," took the exam, passed, and taught ninth grade in a school in the Vicaria neighborhood with mediocre results, because of inattention to her work. At the same time she published some love poetry in a literary journal called *The Sea Gull* and a sentimental story entitled *Love Scorned* in a pamphlet put out by the editor Carluccio of Naples, with the dedication: "To you, who must not love me." Twice she was called before the superintendent and scolded for these fanatical publications, but nothing happened. One day, while the inspector of schools was visiting her class, testing the pupils and finding them extremely behind in their studies, as well as badly behaved, he saw her quickly hide a white piece of paper beneath her roll book: when she was asked to hand it over, she became upset, cried, and gave him the paper. It was a love letter to a well-known Neapolitan man with a wife and children: and even though her love was not reciprocated, it still showed that Ponzio was guilty of a corruption that was incompatible with her delicate mission as an educator. She was fired. There is no trace of her.

Luisetta d'Este. She became a governess in a rich family: she will soon marry one of its old relatives who has disinherited four nephews for her. Still pretty.

Mazza. She is acting in a third-rate company in provincial theaters. She was recently in Albenga.

Mercanti. She is teaching in the convent of Sister Benincasa after her stepmother and sister-in-law did everything in their power to get her to leave the house. During vacations she makes artificial flowers: she was awarded a prize at the last Milan Exposition.

Barracco. She couldn't wait for the results of the exam; she went to teach in a town in Calabria, Citra. It seems that the rather severe winter climate had a bad effect on her nerves: she made two or three requests to be transferred, but to no avail. She wrote long letters to the inspector, the superintendent, the minister, imploring them all to take her out of that misery, but in all her correspondence the beginnings of nervous hysteria were evident. When the inspector came to her village, she threw herself at his feet, crying and agitated, begging him to somehow help her to get out of that hell: the inspector was touched and promised to do something to help her. Afterward, it seems that he forgot. Last year in March, she bought from the pharmacist, on three separate occasions, three Spanish fly capsules for gas, on the pretext that she was ill, and she took all three. For two days she suffered from atrocious spasms; she repented her suicide and called her sisters, brothers, and friends, but it was not possible to save her. After her death, they found her journal: since she had no one to whom she could write about her problems, she turned to an imaginary being. The journal was sent to her oldest sister; it was horrifying.

Maria Valente. After passing the exam, she teaches in the elementary school in the Avvocata neighborhood, in first grade, with good results, but she has never been promoted because she has no one to recommend her.

Abbamonte. After passing the exam, she is an elementary teacher in the Royal Convent Boarding School of the Miracoli: nothing to say.

Checchina Vetromile. After she passed the exam, she taught successfully for a year, then married a shoe merchant who has a national factory of shoes, which he also exports. Checchina keeps the accounts, deals with correspondence, and oversees sales: when her schoolmates come to buy shoes at her shop, she gives them a discount and ties their packages herself with blue ribbon.

Scapolatiello. She did not take the exam, did not repeat the third class, or take the makeup exam; she didn't even take a position in a nursery. In September, her sister got married and remained at home: since they were poor people, they didn't travel; the newlyweds spent their honeymoon at home.

Scapolatiello professed an intention to become a Sister of Charity, but she didn't have the money for the dowry. One day, after three or four futile attempts to succeed in something, she was on the balcony, on the fourth floor, with her sister and brother-in-law: she told them that she was going up on the roof terrace for a moment. She went up to the terrace on the fifth floor, wrote on a little piece of paper, "I love you so much, don't forget me," rolled up the sheet of paper, called down to her sister, blew her a kiss, first threw the paper onto the balcony, then threw herself down onto the street. Her sister and brother-in-law saw her falling past them, like a bundle of rags. She probably died of a stroke before she reached the ground.

Isabella Diaz. She had the highest grade on the competitive exam. She immediately began to teach in fourth grade, at the Gesù School, with exceptional results. She simplified the method of syllabication and changed the way geography is taught for the better. She founded a kindergarten in Portici and a nursery school in Pozzuoli and reorganized the schools in Sarno. She still looks horrendous. She was awarded the first medal of honor at the last pedagogical conference. She is the principal of the largest school in Naples: it is she who initiated the abolition of the old methods of punishment.

»»» «««

In the Lava

I

A hoarse sailor's voice that came from inside, distant and rough, cried out, over the noise of the waves against wood:

"Call!"

Immediately, a fat, blond young man, his face shiny with sweat, in a colored shirt with a very open neck, with no undershirt, a shiny black light jacket, and a flashy red silk belt that held up white summer trousers stopped rocking in his straw chair at the entrance to the hall labeled WOMEN and, turning toward the waiting room, shouted in a stentorian voice:

"Thirty-seven!"

There was a movement in the room, which was crowded with people. Eugenia Malagrida and her mother, followed by their servant, tried to make their way through to the hall, which led to the women's bathhouses, since they had number thirty-seven. But Eugenia and her mother were short, fat, and stocky; they had the swaying, ridiculous gait of geese; the mother, fortunately, since she no longer had any pretences, wore a dark wool dress that was not too tight, and her face was serene; but Eugenia was squeezed into a raw silk blouse that dominated her and made her appear fatter because of its light color, and her shoes were too small for her fat, round feet. In addition, the servant who was following them was loaded down with bags, umbrellas, fans, and cakes strung on her fingers; and under her arm she also had a bottle of marsala to revive her mistresses' spirits after their swim. When the three women had crossed the room, the movement of fans resumed, women's chatter started up again, louder than the noise of the sea, while the breeze blew the big raw canvas curtains trimmed in blue, and Signor Canavacciuolo, the owner of the establishment, the blond country squire who was calling the numbers, wiped his sweaty forehead with a yellow silk handkerchief.

Elvira Brown, a very beautiful Neapolitan girl who was married to an old man of English origin, was talking quietly with Margherita Falco, her future sister-in-law, her brother's fiancée. They had number sixty-two; it was ten o'clock; they would never get through before one: and Elvira Brown was worrying that that suspicious, angry, nasty husband of hers would make a jealous scene when she got home. Margherita Falco, a nice, slender creature with a pair of thoughtful eyes and a sweet smile, was listening to her, trying to comfort her, saying that Brown was not unreasonable, in spite of the natural pigheadedness of old men, that they would work it out . . .

"You just don't know, you don't know," murmured Elvira Brown, shaking her beautiful head and making her big jeweled earrings sparkle.

Yes, for as much as Margherita could see and understand, she couldn't appreciate the extent of the evil jealousy of that old man with the reddish wig, false teeth, and big hands warty with chilblains who had wanted a young, beautiful wife, whom he covered with clothes and jewels and tortured with his vile whims of a nasty, stubborn old man. Oh, Elvira was well aware of what awaited her when she went home, and she looked down in a melancholy way at the card with the number sixty-two, while Signor Canavacciuolo, obeying the sailor's voice from inside that shouted, "Call!" turned toward the waiting room and shouted, "Thirty-eight!"

Instead, Annina Manetta, so quiet, with her tranquil air, was very satisfied to have number sixty-four. Her lover, Vicenzo Spanò, had not yet arrived; her mother, who was opposed to this love, fretted and fumed with impatience; her little sister Adelina, who was devilishly crafty, giggled and ate biscuits with pepper; Annina, sure that she would see Vicenzino, kept her stubborn girl's invincible calm.

Twice her mother, nervous and bored, had sent Adelina, the younger one, around to try to trade their number, because she wanted a lower one in order to enter sooner, but Adelina had wandered around the room, had drunk a glass of iron water with lemon at the water vendor's, and had come back empty-handed: in reality, she was in league with her sister, who wanted to wait.

The room was filling up more and more: it was ten thirty. The two de Pasquale sisters had arrived with their mother, two blond, powdered actresses who received applause and amateur awards in private theaters and also in the solitary, abandoned, distant one of San Ferdinando, where the actors have taken up residence: they made the public go wild in *Giorgio Gandi*, in *Marcellina*, in *Our Good Peasants*, in *The Myrtle Pavilion*, using up their time, health, and money; they were always surrounded by admirers, but they couldn't find husbands, and they had carried over from the stage into life a good deal of powder in their hair and on their faces, a bit of lipstick on their lips, and certain oblique glances of young principal actresses.

The three Galanti sisters, all nice brunettes, with big black eyes, lavish curves, too robust, but with mustaches like their mother—a big woman who herself looked like the revolutionary general whose widow she was—had a circle of officers and of elegant young men; they were chatting and laughing, showing white teeth, a bit wild in their attractiveness, especially Riccarda, who had a little mustache and thick, scowling lips like an African. The Galantis had dowries;

they had been educated in the noble boarding school of the Miracles, and they had a certain disdain for the de Pasquales, the wretched blonds who did their best to express passion in the *Basket of Papa Martin* and hadn't come up with a single fiancé in five years, since they were twenty. The two groups pretended not to look at each other, but the Galantis were irritated that that elegant young man, the Marquis Geraci, was always attached to the skirts of Elena de Pasquale, the prettier of the two sisters: the de Pasquales were jealous of Riccarda Galanti's big coral earrings and of Emilia Galanti's gold bracelet.

"Call! Call!" yelled the sailor from inside.

"Thirty-nine, forty," shouted Signor Canavacciuolo, fanning himself with a five-cent Chinese paper fan.

The August sun beat down very hard on the wooden roof of the waiting room. It was a rather big covered gallery, sitting on large beams that the waves couldn't hit, linked to the beach by a wooden pier that creaked under peoples' steps. It was a gallery without windows, with curtains blowing in the warm western wind showing the great, blue, glittering sea, the great, poetic, young, fragrant sea: indeed, when a half curtain on the left was raised, one could see Vesuvius, in a delicate gray, softly crowned in white. Enrichetta Caputo entered, followed by her mother, and the girl's beautiful eyes blinked as she looked for someone. She was dressed simply in linen, with a very open sailor's collar that showed off her white neck, with patent leather shoes and blue stockings, but the dress cost twelve lire, the shoes ten, and her stockings were cotton: a poor person's outfit, in which she managed to be pretty and attractive.

Behind her came the mother, a small, puffy, untidy woman, dressed like a servant, with a hat that was falling apart and yellow leather shoes. Enrichetta remained on the threshold, a bit uncertain, clutching in her hands a very torn leather purse; the Galantis, who were kind, called out to her. There was a noisy exchange of kisses.

"I was looking for Eugenia Malagrida," Enrichetta Caputo said then.

"She's already gone in," answered Riccarda Galanti.

"But she said that she would wait for me," murmured Enrichetta.

She and her mother looked at each other for a minute, disconcerted. Poor as they were, one the widow, the other the orphan of a captain who had died heroically at Capua in 1860, trying to live on a small pension, they attached themselves instinctively to rich girls or to those who were less poor than the ones that Enrichetta had known at boarding school, where the generosity of the government had found her a place. Enrichetta spent half her life in the house of Eugenia Malagrida, the fat, ugly rich girl, acting as her companion, entertaining her, flattering her, combing her hair, dressing her, provided that she, from time to time, would take her to the theater, invite her to dinner, or take her for a ride in her carriage.

Poverty, and the desire to be seen, in order to find a husband, led her to live a humiliating existence that often made her shed tears when she was by herself. Enrichetta certainly couldn't go swimming, since she didn't have any money, and she clung desperately to Eugenia Malagrida, so that she would take her with her. But she and her mother had to come on foot, from the Pavilion of Divine Love in old Naples, a convent without nuns that the government gave as living quarters to soldiers' families: they came on foot in the sun to the Villa, and sometimes they happened to get there too late. Eugenia Malagrida had already gone into the bathhouse, forgetting with the indifference of the happy that her friend couldn't go in swimming without her.

So that morning, mother and daughter had been left in the lurch, since they had nothing but a ten-cent piece in their pockets, and already they were looking at Signora Brown and Margherita Falco, exchanging smiles and greetings, thinking that they would hang on to them in order to get into a bathhouse; these two women were alone and so polite! But at that moment Elvira Brown, who was still afraid of being late, had managed to exchange her number with that of a young man who had taken it for the family of his beloved, who hadn't yet come; and, as they were calling number forty-three, Elvira Brown and Margherita Falco got ready to go in. Now Enrichetta Caputo and her mother looked at each other in despair: how could they go swimming? And they still had to chat with the Galantis, mother and daughters, with the forced smiles of the suffering, and they didn't move, didn't go buy a ticket, as though they had forgotten what they were doing, so that Riccarda Galanti, the dark one, noticed and, in her kindness, said to Enrichetta Caputo:

"Why don't you come in our bathhouse?"

"There are already a lot of you; I would inconvenience you," said the latter, biting her lip so that she wouldn't cry.

Immediately, Enrichetta's kind face brightened: her mother, the fat servant with a face sprinkled with freckles, felt reassured and got up, dragging her big yellow shoes, and went to buy two pennies' worth of cakes. It was eleven thirty; there were no more empty seats left in the room; the young men remained standing in light, elegant summer suits, their straw hats thrown back on their foreheads, dangling their yellow wallets on cords, flanking or surrounding the girls. The heat became unbearable; elaborate curls came undone on sweaty foreheads; mothers and older relatives fanned themselves noisily. Caterina Borrelli, with two fat braids thrown over her shoulders, in a percale dress too short in front, her glasses perched bizarrely on her nose, with her ironic smile, fanned herself with an edition of *Il Piccolo* folded like a fan, rocking in a masculine way on her chair as she laughed in a low voice with her friend Annina Casale.

They were both graduates of the Normal School who had passed their exams with flying colors and were having a good time on vacation, spending half the day at the beach, going back home at three as hungry as wolves, sleeping after lunch, as all middle-class Neapolitan girls do in the summer.

Of the two, Caterina Borrelli was always the one who had a few lire in her pocket, and she spent them for pastries, cakes, and cookies; they would eat before, after, and while they went swimming; they were famous for their appetite in the establishment. Signor Canavacciuolo, a witty Neapolitan, would say to them:

"May Santa Lucia save your eyesight, my dears, because there's nothing wrong with your appetite."

Now a skinny, pale, balding young man in a faded coat had sat down at the piano and was playing a polka. The piano was out of tune and the polka was shrill, but all the girls were caught up in the thrill of the dance. Enrichetta Caputo nodded her head in time to the music, forgetting her poverty. Riccarda Galanti hummed the tune of the polka; the de Pasquales, the powdered blonds, lay back in their chairs, overcome by a lively enthusiasm. Caterina Borrelli twirled her glasses around her index finger.

All those girls there gave in to the youthful passion for dancing, to that physical and spiritual tingling sensation that not one of them could resist, even the ugliest, the most deformed. Even Maria Jovine—the pale, dark, crippled girl, so elegant, so perfumed, decked in lace, with gloves that went up to her elbows, a parasol with a carved ivory handle, and a big fan that had been painted by an artist, the poor cripple who had a dowry of a hundred thousand lire and who couldn't find a husband—even Maria Jovine, sitting beside her mother, a beautiful woman who was still young, kept time tapping with her fan on her fingers: she, the unfortunate cripple who would never be able to dance. Suddenly, the music stopped: all of those heads, those trembling hands, those tapping feet were still. The pianist, hired by Signor Canavacciuolo to cheer up the swimmers, had gotten up and looked shabbier and stiffer as he stood; he went to drink a glass of sulfur water, in which he wouldn't even let them put lemon so that he would only have to pay two cents for it. But nobody was paying any attention to him anymore: a rumor had spread:

"The Altifredas! The Altifredas!"

Everyone turned to look toward the beach, toward that big area of dark sand that divided the sea from that shady green of the Villa. People were overcome by the liveliest curiosity. The Altifredas were two beautiful, haughty young women: they arrived in their own carriage with two horses, with a maid and a swimming instructor, and a servant who carried their bags, the life jackets, and a basket with their lunch. Dressed with exceptional taste, shading their beautiful faces under wide, original hats, with a proud grace that was enchanting, they always crossed the establishment at noon, never stopping, since they had the luxury of their own bathhouse awaiting them, not looking around, speaking only to one another, as though the rest of the world didn't exist. In the water, they wore flannel bathing suits embroidered all over in red, straw shoes so they wouldn't hurt their little feet, and elegant big hats; and they went off with the swimming teacher, returning after an hour of exercise, all fresh and rosy.

The other girls in the establishment envied and hated those obnoxious and proud Altifredas, who were so rich, so beautiful, so elegant, so proud, and they made up stories about them. Naturally, said Enrichetta Caputo, with their pretensions, they would never find a crazy man crazy enough to marry them; imagine! They had no dowries, said Riccarda Galanti: their father spent everything he had on them, so they would make a stunning impression; they wore makeup, said the de Pasquales, biting their finely drawn lips; they would become two conceited prigs when they got married, said Caterina Borrelli, who always claimed to make profound observations, to her friend Annina Casale; as for Annina Manetta, she was immersed in the complete Buddhism of love: her friend Vincenzino Spanò had arrived and was sitting opposite her; they were looking continuously at one another, despite her mother's scolding. The Altifredas passed by, in the midst of a great silence, with their grand airs of superiority; behind them a new murmur arose: Signor Canavacciuolo, who never got up, had stood to let them pass.

The Galantis, too, went off for a swim with Enrichetta Caputo, since the double bathhouse was free; and again the piano tinkler began to play on the yellowish keyboard. Now there was going to be singing. The singer was a tall, thin, dark woman, with shiny skin that looked as though it had been oiled, big yellow teeth that were yellow like the piano keys, and a friendly smile: she was dressed in, or rather covered by, an ugly black silk dress all smooth and red at the seams, without a white collar, with a red coral horn as an ornament; on her thin hair, dyed brown, was a black straw hat, with a red feather that was combed and falling over; she wore no gloves. She must have been the pianist's mother, and she stood near the piano, in the romantic pose of an expressive singer, with her head somewhat thrown back, an ecstatic smile on her lips. In a plaintive, out-of-tune voice, she began to moan an old romance by Ciccillo Tosti:

> I think of the first time . . .

Caterina Borrelli, who didn't understand music, began to laugh right away, but Annina Casale, on hearing the sentimental refrain

> But you, you've forgotten it,
> You say that it was a dream . . .

grew very pensive. The singer, ugly, dirty, ridiculous, closed her eyes and warbled like an old off-key canary. Now, in spite of the singer's dirty appearance, her ridiculous air, and out-of-tune voice, the musical sentimentality of the Tostian romance made the girls in the room melancholic. Annina Casale was thinking of a law student from Cassino who had written her 120 love letters in forty days, had dedicated a number of sonnets and free songs to her, and had left her to marry the daughter of a provincial leather merchant; and her friend Caterina Borrelli, who pretended to be a woman in charge, felt herself falling prey to an indefinite melancholy, she who had never been betrayed, nor had ever betrayed.

Annina Manetta, the great martyr for love, the one who got slapped by her mother every day because of Vincenzino, looked at her beloved with eyes full of tears; Jovine, the little cripple, thought of a cousin who had gone away, who had loved her before she had had that misfortune with her leg and who had also "forgotten" her, like the man in Tosti's romance. Elena de Pasquale, who was twenty-eight and had had four broken engagements, had a reason to be sad; and her younger sister, Ida, had puffy lips, as though she was about to cry, making a face that she had learned from playing the part of the ingénue.

But the most attentive was a group of girls who until now had been having a lively chat in the corner of the room; at the beginning of the music, they had raised their heads quietly with an air of unhappy connoisseurs. They were the two Fusco sisters, fifteen-year-old twin girls who had been singing the part of the two Ajaxes in *The Beautiful Helen* at the Teatro Nuovo, who come onstage arm in arm, singing a verse, greet one another by doffing their helmets and withdraw to the back of the stage, to then wander through the operetta as walk-ons; and since they were pretty, they were almost always applauded for their youthful grace and had all the airs of prima donnas who earn millions singing in London or St. Petersburg.

There was Elisa Costa, a tall, thin girl with lung-colored skin, cursed with a round, prominent stomach, which made everyone take her for a pregnant woman and bothered her a great deal; Elisa Costa, who had been studying opera singing for ten years, destined for it, as she said, by her face and taste, and who never managed to get a contract, even though she bellowed in a loud, strident voice "Ecco l'orrendo campo" from *Un ballo in maschera* and "Pace, pace mio Dio" from *La forza del destino* to every impresario, theatrical agent, and agency secretary who happened through Naples. There was Gelsomina Santoro, who was studying singing at the conservatory, who barely knew how to read, who didn't know how to write at all, who had only the smallest thread of voice, who couldn't read music, but who certainly would be successful, because she was beautiful. This group listened to the music with the smooth eyebrows and the absorbed air of important people; the Fuscos pitied the poor singer, reduced to that occupation, when perhaps she might have had better luck, Costa made a scornful motion with her lips, and Gelsomina Santoro still wore her serene expression of a satisfied and attractive stupid woman. The singer ended without anyone applauding: she stood for a moment undecided, then went around with a tin plate. She asked for money smilingly, but without looking people in the face, averting her head, and she wore an expression that was somewhere between skeptical and humble, as though she was sure she wouldn't make much. In fact, even with so many people, she made only five cents. She threw them in her pocket without pride, but without looking at them; she shrugged her shoulders and went to sit in a corner, waiting to sing again.

Two cents had been given to her by one of the Cafaro sisters, some provincial girls from Picinisco in Terra di Lavoro, who spent five or six months a year in Naples. They were rich, very rich, with a three hundred thousand lire dowry each and then inheritances that no one in town or in the province dared ask them about.

There was a rumor that they had enormous expectations; no suitor dared present himself: they were getting older; the oldest was thirty, the second twenty-five, the third twenty-two; they were beautiful, elegant, very well educated, but seeing them all together—somewhat emancipated unmarried women who managed their own fortunes, with a certain mannish way about them, who decked themselves out in exaggerated hairdos and flashy jewels—fiancés ran away. They were generous and good, but of course, they envied those poor girls without a cent who got married at eighteen; they spent lots of money; they entertained, since they had no mother, but to no avail. Appropriately, Matilde Cipullo, whose married name was Tuttavilla, the great marriage broker, was with them: a beautiful middle-class woman who had run off with a penniless nobleman and who lived from hand to mouth, but who frequented the *aristocracy*. And so, through taste, kindness, laziness, by dint of gossip, she occupied herself busily with marriages; she always had two or three that were about to take place that she had arranged, and three or four in the planning stage; she dreamed of marrying off all the girls she knew with all the young men she knew and didn't know. Girls and mothers adored her; she spent the day in meetings, ran from one house to another, patched things up between couples who had quarreled, threw herself in the midst of every love affair, laid siege furiously to every bachelor. Now she wanted to marry off the Cafaro sisters, who were from her province, but without success; she had no respectable suitors to offer; those girls were too rich, while a poor girl was easy to pair off with a penniless suitor, and then one could always find a solution! And all the women knew Matilde Tuttavilla; everyone greeted her; she had stopped for a few minutes in every group; she had spoken in low tones with two or three mamas, with a wide smile, completely absorbed.

A cool breeze blew from the west: it was one o'clock; a sharp salty smell, the so-called smell of the reef, came into the room from the sea; things began to be less busy; many families had gone in swimming; there were empty spaces here and there. Signor Canavacciuolo had withdrawn to the far end of his little room where he could be seen through a raised curtain, gaily eating a plate of macaroni with tomato sauce, red and appetizing; one of his younger brothers took his place calling numbers, which were going up rapidly. The de Pasquales had gone in, Caterina Borrelli and Annina Casale, too; the two Fuscos with Costa and Santoro were getting ready; only Annina Manetta still remained, since she had a very high number, to her great satisfaction; her mother had already pinched her twice on the arm, since she could do nothing else; she had taken it without complaining; her sister was eating clams, throwing the shells in the sea. The curtains flapped in the breeze; few people were arriving now; the water must have been very hot; some young men still lingered, waiting for the young women to finish their toilette after swimming, and people were heard making dates to meet at the Villa in the evening. Signora Brown and Falco had taken in their carriage Enrichetta Caputo and her mother, who were happy to have a ride after coming on foot; the Altifredas had passed by again, happy after their swim, with their beautiful hair hanging loose on their shoulders, with very elegant Turkish cotton shawl towels on their shoulders, taking their time, making the other women angry. At that time the Sanges sisters arrived, quarreling among themselves, yelling, sweaty; they were five sisters, daughters of a city employee, rather ugly, ragged, noisy, wearing false jewelry, re-dyed cheap dresses, homemade lace, hats that had been remodeled four times, shoes dyed with ink to hide the cracks.

And they were all in love, and crazy; they robbed one another's
fiancés, fought like servants, smelled of cheap powder, went glove-
less, were enthusiastic dancers, atrocious gossips, and very poor to
boot. Finally, when they were about to buy a ticket, no one had any
money: after insulting one another, the five of them went to nego-
tiate noisily with Signor Canavacciuolo, who let them in, with
Neapolitan good humor.

II

Sweet to the senses, gentle to the heart, the September evening
had fallen over Naples. The stars sparkled, high and sharp, with a
lively shimmering; from the windows thrown open on the shadows, from the balconies, where white shadows were contemplating
the evening, streams of light poured out; from the terraces came
the amorous sounds of guitars and mandolins and singing voices,
with long sentimental refrains; everywhere there was a sharp, penetrating odor, of hidden flowers, of plants budding in the darkness,
of perfumed grasses; everywhere a warm, caressing breeze that
seemed the breath of a beloved person. And from eight o'clock on,
in the streets in Toledo, Chiaia, Chiatamone, among the shop windows glittering with jewels, which displayed feathered fans and
elegant hats, or along the shore of the poetic sea, on which the Chiatamone plane trees rustle, there was a slow movement of people
going to the Villa. Two lines of carriages were going down, like two
rolling streams; a full streetcar ran past every minute, whistling,
across Piazza San Ferdinando, carrying people continuously to the
Villa; but the sidewalks were packed with pedestrians who, on that
Sunday evening, were going languidly to the great Neapolitan
evening meeting place.

There was a constant parade of white or very light-colored
dresses, over which were sometimes thrown, more for appearances

than for protection from the autumn chill, little shawls of blue wool or a very soft pink; a constant parade of fresh young faces, with dark or blond bangs cut straight over the forehead, like the knights in Giorgione's paintings, thick braids gathered at the neck, held by tortoiseshell hairpins. Behind came the mothers, fathers, aunts, old cousins, male and female companions who were resigned and patient, dragging their feet: but really Sunday evening at the Villa belonged to the young, to the girls and young men for whom a bit of clear sky, a tree, a sad or happy note of music, a fleeting glance, a little smile is enough to be deeply happy.

And, at the open gate of the big public garden that Neapolitan youth adores and to which love owes so much, the surge of people dispersed among five straight avenues, dimly lit by gaslight. In the last avenue to the left went the solitary, melancholy beings, who were searching in vain for a soul that would vibrate at their own emotional pitch; in the second, the idylls that have already begun and are flourishing, under indulgent maternal eyes, loving couples who would perhaps marry, of course; everything takes place with this end in mind, it's only a question of time; in the meantime, they're young and it's beautiful to be in love when the stars and the glances of women are so soft.

Actually, that second avenue bears the name Lovers Lane, so naturally the couples who like to walk slowly go there, squeezing hands from time to time, exchanging those soft, brief words that are like a kiss, since they quiver with so much emotion; and behind them the male and female companions are chatting among themselves, keeping a somewhat watchful eye, not too much, wisely measuring out love to these pure, innocent beings, who are made happy by so little. In the big middle avenue walked the groups, two or three families together who plan to see each other every Sunday, who meet on the way, walk in line, girls with girls, mothers with mothers and the young men in the rear, with their top hats at a rakish angle, flowers in their buttonholes, walking sticks under their arms; and these groups follow one another endlessly, calling to each other, answering, in lines that stop now and then so that people can wait for one another and get back together again, thus having to walk in the big middle open avenue beneath the bright starlight.

In the first avenue on the right, where there is a double row of streetlights, walked everybody who wanted to be seen: the girls who were more vain than sentimental, more flirtatious than amorous, those who preferred the vulgar admiration of twenty passersby to the love of only one, the fresh brides who are inaugurating their first light-colored silk dresses, the hat with the trembling feather; the crafty widows who would like to marry again and can't make up their minds and who in the meantime are enjoying that transitional state that is so full of delights for female vanity; the men who want to attract attention and the people whom they think important. Only the last avenue on the right, called the Avenue of the Philosophers, small, narrow, dark, somewhat winding, was deserted; it is frequented only in the daytime, when the sun warms it. And, in all four avenues, among the trees, among the white marble statues that crown the fountains and from which thin streams of water flow into the basin beneath, amid the whiteness of nymphs, among the white marble seats that are already completely occupied, that whiteness of dresses went on passing, that graceful procession of feminine shadows that are the predominant feature of Neapolitan summer evenings at the Villa.

In the mild air, those skirts, those white ghosts, had something harmoniously young about their way of walking, and the poetry of night, of summer, of trees, of youth, of twilight surrounded them.

But the center of the Villa, where all those people were going, was ablaze with light. Beneath the statue of Giovanni Battista Vico, the pensive philosopher with the bent head, in a big luminous circle of adjoining candelabra, the musicians were placed, and around them, to the right and left, in groups, in the avenues, were the people, seated, on foot, waiting to be seen, or crowding together, according to their inclination and habits. And just as in Parliament it seemed that the two big opposing parties had formed voluntarily, each person taking his place, so it was at the Villa, with the left and the right: the right formed by older people, by very elegant ladies who were getting on a bit, who were already having recourse to some tricks of art in order to look as though they were still fresh, by unhappily married wives who came to console themselves at the Villa for the cruelty of their husbands, who refused to take them on vacation in the summer; by old coquettes who still dressed in white, with dyed hair and scarlet lips; by pretentious women who wanted to hold court.

Instead, the left side, a bit more democratic, was made up of girls who were really young and really beautiful, who had recourse to few resources of toilette, who were waiting for their fiancés or lovers or suitors, with the strong faith of those who believe in fate, of women who wanted to laugh and joke and have a casual conversation, of students who went there only to gaze fondly at their beloved and not to be seen, not so that people could admire the way their tie was knotted, but so that they could give a flower to their beloved without being seen. The right had a proud air and pretended not to see the left, though envying in fact its qualities of youth and beauty; the left, satisfied with itself, didn't even look at the right.

Mariano Vacca's café, a big glass-and-wood kiosk with two floors blazing with lights, was located in the middle of the groups that belonged partly to the right, partly to the left; in the middle walked the observers, the undecided, the incredulous, those who were idle in body and soul.

Old Signor Brown was sitting next to his wife, with his coat tightly buttoned, his collar up, his chin leaning on the head of his cane, plunged in the silence of the evenings of bad temper, when his young wife in vain gave him beseeching glances mutely begging him to speak, to smile, to be sociable. That evening, when the wicked old man had heard that Margherita Falco and her fiancé, Signora Brown's brother, were going to the Villa, he had said right away:

"Let's go, too, so that people won't say that I keep my wife at home."

And, with his vanity of an old man who had married a young woman, he had made her go out, though she refused to; he had made her wear a white dress richly decked with lace in which she looked stunning; he himself had put emerald and diamond earrings in her ears; he had knotted the light ties of a beautiful hat. She let him, almost resigned, rightly suspicious of this supreme kindness. In fact, as soon as they were on the big avenue and people turned around in the semidarkness to look at Signora Brown's beautiful face, as though fascinated, the old man was struck by black jealousy, and withdrew into deep silence. She bent her head, pale, mortified, lacking the courage to speak, and she looked enviously at her brother and Margherita Falco, young, good-looking, in love, and poor, who would marry and be happy. Tears rose to her eyes as she looked at that old man's frowning face. They had sat on the right, she a bit behind; the engaged couple was serene, talking calmly, full of the sweetness of that evening.

"Did you see? Did you?" Filomena Sanges was saying to the other four sisters, "Signora Brown is wearing a different pair of earrings this evening. Goodness! Goodness! How lucky that woman is!"

"Yes, but how disgusting that old man is!" observed Carluccio Finoia, the first clerk in a private bank and Carolina Sanges's fiancé.

"What does it matter?" said Carolina, shrugging her shoulders. "He's rich, that's enough!"

Carluccio Finoia was a bit hurt, he who had a salary of a hundred lire a month and would have to wait another four years to marry Carolina. And when he had been so generous that evening, paying fourteen cents a seat for the five sisters, their little brother, and himself!

For the Sanges girls, who went to the Villa every evening, whatever the cost, sitting down was a big problem; they borrowed from the grocery money, but often that wasn't possible, and they had to go looking for some dutiful suitor, and often they couldn't even find one and they walked around and around the whole evening, two by two, the last one with their brother, like carousel horses, tired, with sore feet, and they also had to walk back to San Giovanni in Carbonara, where they lived.

But that evening at the Villa gate, Carolina had latched onto Carluccio Finoia, who had had to play the rich man, so the five sisters strutted in the harsh light of the gas flames, so pompous in their percale dresses that had been washed and rewashed and ironed at home, displaying shoes that were coming unsewn and cotton stockings that cost fifteen cents a pair; they were dusted with powder, with bare brown throats and the idle air of ugly women who think they're beautiful. And since the crowd continued to grow around nine thirty, while the band was playing the Strauss piece "Libera la via,"* the Sanges girls, gossipy and ruthless, criticized everyone who passed by. The Galanti girls had arrived just then, in new pink percale dresses that went with their dark complexions and black eyes, and all three had their hair tied with pink ribbons.

"They look like flies in vanilla ice cream," observed Concetta Sanges, who was the ugliest of all.

*This probably refers to "Enjoy Life."

"The oldest is at least thirty-two," said Chiarina, who was twenty-eight. "It really suits her to wear a ribbon in her hair, as though she were a little girl."

"They're going to the café, that's where they're going, to eat ice cream; see how ill-mannered they are," murmured Carolina, who would have been happy to eat ice cream herself.

"They're so pretty, especially the one with the black curls," said Carluccio Finoia, who wanted revenge on his fiancée.

The latter looked at him fiercely: from that moment on, for the whole evening, Carluccio and Carolina did nothing but fight, now exchanging biting ironies, now indulging in serious insults; the sisters let them alone, as though they weren't there. Meanwhile, one of them, Concettella, turning toward the de Pasquale sisters' big circle, thought that she had made an impression on Pasquale Jacobucci, a young doctor, who perhaps would marry the youngest of the de Pasquale sisters in three or four years when he had a clientele; and Concettella, whose teeth were stained from scurvy, who was thin in a sickly way and whose hair was thinning, began to act the part of the romantic, making eyes, leaning her head on her hand, fanning herself slowly.

The de Pasquales were pretty, dressed in white, with black velvet bows and Alsatian bonnets with black ribbons, dyed eyebrows, and blooming lips as red as pomegranates, and as they chatted they lay back in their seats, laughing in order to inflate their white bosoms, as they did in the theater, while showing their little teeth. Just now Giovanni Laterza, a student from Calabria, very rich, whom those girls wanted to force to act in spite of his rough pronunciation, had ordered sour-cherry ices for everyone from Mariano Vacca's café, in order to make a good impression: and this display of generosity revolted everyone who passed by; the Sanges sisters were furious, no one ever offered them a glass of water. Only the circle around Jovine, the nice crippled girl dressed in white, maintained a certain serious reserve, deploring that lack of politeness; Malagrida, who was with Jovine that evening, all puffy, drowning in a blue silk dress, with a neck that was too short and a collar that was too high and too big, also thought that ice cream should be eaten in a café and not in public; and Enrichetta Caputo, who had worn blue ribbons given to her by Malagrida on her old white dress, was of the same opinion; she was always of the opinion of whoever took her about, in a carriage or to the theater.

Traffic was becoming difficult: the people who had already arrived never tired of walking around; those who were arriving couldn't find any more seats; it was a very thick, slow procession, passing between the two walls of seats, around and around: the young men making eyes at the girls, blowing the smoke from their cigarettes toward the vicinity of their hearts, the girls arm in arm, looking around with that marvelous visual power of the sidelong glance that only girls possess. The music was now a potpourri from the *Barber of Seville,* a lively piece, exuding happiness. Only Signora Brown was becoming more and more melancholy, a beautiful bejeweled victim, thinking of the scene that her taciturn husband would make when they got home. Since they had been sitting, an artillery officer opposite her could not stop looking at her, and the old man had noticed and had moved his seat in order to hide his wife's head; immediately, the officer had changed places: Signora Brown, without raising her eyes, trembled as though she were guilty; she wanted to leave but didn't dare say so; her brother and his fiancée were so happy! And, not wanting to look around, so as not to make the old man suspicious, she stared at a red spot among the trees, which sometimes grew pale, sometimes flared up, like a sputtering flame: the usual small eruption of Vesuvius, which no one in Naples notices.

Now, the music that was playing was one of the usual concert pieces, a mixture of variations on all the concert arias of Petrella's *Jone,* and the parading crowd moved as though it were synchronized in tune with Glauco's passion or the desolate lament of Nidia. The beauty of the evening had persuaded a number of people to come walking who hardly ever appeared; and the most standoffish families of Via Salvator Rosa, Sant'Eligio, Via Garibaldi, the Barriera Grande, and Largo Barracche had let themselves be lured there, among the plane trees and the gas flames, the iron seats and the municipal band. The people who were seated ended up losing their view; all they could see was a very thick procession of other people who were crowding in more and more and going slower and slower.

Matilde Cipullo, dragging her noble but penniless husband behind her, as well as two other young men whom she was supposed to find wives for, was annoyed by this delay: she was pulling along the gallant Arturo Aiello, a clerk at the prefecture, a handsome young man whom she wanted to marry to Enrichetta Caputo, a good deed, really the height of charity; Giovanni Pasanisi, a landowner from Salerno, whom she intended for one of the Cafaros, the rich women, followed her faithfully. She arrived in the group where Eugenia Malagrida, Jovine, and Enrichetta Caputo were gathered; after a profusion of kisses, in the midst of greetings and hugs, she sat down for a moment, so she could turn over Arturo Aiello to the Caputos, mother and daughter; but he, in order to look nonchalant, began to talk with Eugenia Malagrida, the big, awkward fat girl, over whose shiny face spread a look of great satisfaction, because it was so unusual for a young man to notice her. After ten minutes, since she couldn't stand it, Matilde Cipullo got up and left, taking Giovannino Pasanisi with her, looking everywhere for the Cafaros. The Sanges sisters were lurking around; they had quarreled with Signora Cipullo before she was married, and she had never wanted to make peace with them; she found them too ill-mannered and too raggedy; she would never be able to marry them off.

The Cafaros were seated back-to-back, beneath the statue of Gian Battista Vico, all dressed in light white muslin, very elegant dresses that were a bit light, perhaps, but which went very well with their rather strange big black-feathered hats. And they all had those distinctive things that mature unmarried women who are very rich permit themselves: all three had chains and watches, jeweled earrings, kid gloves that came up too high on their arms, always a bit of lipstick on their lips, and an air of nonchalance that was too unmistakable. Only one of them was talking with Peppino Sarnelli, a lawyer who earned a lot of money but who didn't have a cent of capital; he was courting her quietly, without too much show, in love perhaps, but not audacious, and Teresina Cafaro accepted it, one never knows, comforted by that wave of love, without thinking of the future; the two other sisters never intervened, as though it did not concern them, watching the crowd, without even talking among themselves, without exchanging a word with their old chaperone, who accompanied them everywhere; they were quiet, absorbed, their eyes fixed on the people who were passing by, prey to the masochistic state of mind of single women who want to get married.

And when Matilde Cipullo came up, flustered, with Giovannino Pasanisi from Salerno, the second sister stopped contemplating the passersby and began to converse, since she was the one who was supposed to marry Giovannino Pasanisi; and the third Cafaro sister, the youngest, remained isolated and silent, looking around with all her might, knowing perfectly well that no one would bring her a fiancé, since she was still twenty, and that she would have to find one herself, trusting only in her own capabilities.

Since they couldn't find any seats, Caterina Borrelli and Annina Casale passed the lighted round terrace and walked farther on, in the so-called little woods of the Villa, where there is only a big avenue and fifty little winding ones among the flower beds and groups of elms. There the light was dim and the scent of grasses and of night jasmine very strong; and wandering in that half darkness of trees were all those who wanted to flee the crowd, wanting silence, freshness, wide streets where one could breathe the light, fine air of that garden by the sea. The couples who passed did not even look at each other, each occupied by their own conversation, the man bent lovingly toward the woman, holding her by the arm in that great harmonious beauty of things, pulling her toward him, as though to protect her; the woman raising her head lovingly toward the man, drinking in his words, inebriating him with her smile.

The whole woods was full of this murmur of sweet words, of these amorous looks, of these luminous smiles; the whole woods of leafy acacias, of refreshing scent, of low black oaks was full of this great shiver of emotion that is love. And Caterina Borrelli, who pretended to be a skeptic, since she had read too many novels, let herself surrender to the soft, serene beauty of that evening: and her tormented face, which the glasses on her nose made more original, relaxed and became almost pleasing. Steeped in bad literature and idealistic poetry, she went along, repeating in a low voice some melancholy lines by Prati:*

She was twenty-four, that lovely girl . . .

Annina Casale listened, sighing, thinking of the law student who had betrayed her: but behind her another student, this time of medicine, was walking slowly along, step-by-step, smoking a fat cigar, whose tip Annina could see burning, by looking a bit to the side, and a new idyll was unfolding, with a certain slowness.

---

*Giovanni Prati (1814–84) was a prolific Italian nineteenth-century romantic poet.

Annina did not turn around too much; Caterina Borrelli had just finished preaching her a very rhetorical sermon on futile love.

The Fuscos, the two Ajaxes of the Teatro Nuovo, had stopped near the Temple of Virgil and were sitting on a bench with two young suitors who never missed coming to applaud them every evening from the orchestra at the theater; and they flirted, still very young but already skillful, talking of their dramatic triumphs, acting as though they were disgusted with marriage; and their mother, an angry, stingy old lady, sitting on the bench opposite, pretended to keep an eye on them while fanning herself spitefully, sleepily, obliged to be eternally vigilant. Signorina Costa wasn't there; she almost never went out in the evening, for fear of ruining her voice—and Gelsomina Santoro was on the terrace, since she didn't like to flirt, preferring to be admired by all those passing by to being courted by just one. As far as the loggia, as far as the other gate of the Villa on the Mergellina, there was a profusion of wandering lovers, the beautiful, simple, ardent, good-natured, and poetic love of Naples that takes place among the flowers and trees, overlooking the sea, beneath the stars, during the unforgettable evenings created for this love.

Only at eleven, while the musicians were playing the last number, "La Vague," Metra's famous waltz that every girl has danced to, did the crowd begin to thin out: the first to leave were the more middle-class families, the ones who took advantage of the bus that goes to Porta San Gennaro Sunday evening until eleven, and those who have to walk home and live far away. And the families left slowly; the girls tried to prolong their evening of love by walking slowly; their fathers and mothers walked sedately behind. Only Maria Jovine, the nice crippled girl with the big blue eyes, who left with her beautiful mother, had gone out by the middle gate, since she was tired of walking, and went back immediately to their carriage; she was comfortable only when sitting, in the carriage, at parties, and at the theater; all the amusing activities of the young were forbidden to her; this gave her a great melancholy appeal.

Elvira Brown, her husband, the sulky, nauseating old man, and her handsome brother with his sweet fiancée, Margherita Falco, were also leaving, the two lovers not arm in arm but walking side by side, with their hands touching; Elvira and her husband who took her arm were in back, silent, the old man striking the hard earth of the Villa vigorously with his cane, seized by a deep fit of jealousy, since behind them was heard the tapping sword of the officer, who was following them.

"We'll never come again to this Villa," old Brown had muttered, his voice whistling through his false teeth.

"Never again," his wife had answered, restraining the tears that were forming in her eyes and suffocating her.

And across the avenues, less numerous but continuous, the parade of women's white dresses began again. Annina Casale and Caterina Borrelli, who lived next to the Madonna of Succor, were also leaving, after buying pastries at the Caffè di Napoli and drinking water with sour-cherry syrup to drown their sorrows; they were reciting together lines by Aleardo Aleardi, "Mount Circello," where Corradino is mentioned—

A pale, handsome young man . . .

—especially as Annina's new student was a pale young blond.* The Fuscos, who had gone back to the lighted terrace, had met their friend Gelsomina Santoro again, the beautiful creature with the gray eyes and dazzling teeth, the silly little thing whom men were begin-

*Born in 1812, Aleardo Aleardi was an Italian poet of the neoromantic movement, who wrote about history and (in "Mount Circello") prehistory. As in the previous reference, we see Serao's literary interests reflected in those of Caterina Borrelli.

ning to go crazy over. And, as they walked away, the two sisters and their friend talked of their theatrical dreams, of the Teatro Nuovo; in the fall it would put on *Orpheus in Hell;* one of the sisters aspired to the role of Public Opinion; the other hoped to be given the role of Love; but both of them would have to wear skimpy little white tunics, a costume that was too short, and the two suitors were shaking, overcome by the jealousy that runs in Neapolitan blood; Gelsomina Santoro dreamed of being hired by the Italian Malta Theater, where all beautiful beginners who have no voice sing.

The de Pasquale girls were still there, laughing and fresh, used to staying up late because of the theater, unconcerned about the fatigue of their mother, who was a real bland and attractive figure, like the noble mother in comedies. They were able to have a discussion, now that that boring music that was always the same was over; Count Geraci, with his skeptical air of a young man tired of pleasures, had come to join Pasqualino Jacobucci and Giovanni Laterza. And they began a discussion of pizza, the traditional and popular Neapolitan focaccia, which Pasqualino Jacobucci disliked, since he had gotten indigestion from it, and which was unfamiliar to Giovanni Laterza, who knew only *scagliozzo,* a sort of sandwich filled with fried meat and sautéed mozzarella, which Count Geraci pronounced vulgar, although pizza exerted a strange attraction for his jaded stomach. While they were talking, the girls made eyes at them and threw back their heads slightly; it was then that it was decided on the spur of the moment to go to the *pizzaiolo* in Vico Freddo in Chiaia; the ladies consented immediately, for these little suppers, these nocturnal escapades, appealed to their humorous side. Their mother never said no; the girls threw rather theatrical red wool capes over their shoulders; Count Geraci, always correct, offered his arm to the old lady; the two young men did likewise to the girls, and the three couples set off through the soft shadows of the Neapolitan night.

Concettella Sanges was bursting with annoyance; she had thought that Jacobucci was looking at her; she had flattered herself that she was taking Elena de Pasquale's fiancé away from her; but it had been an illusion. Now, all the sisters were murmuring about the Galanti girls, who had held court all evening, showing off their gold leather shoes, shaking their little silver bracelets and making them tinkle, all of them brunettes but very attractive, especially Riccarda; Emilia Galanti had her surgeon next to her, whom she was going to marry the following year; Riccarda, who was the liveliest and the wittiest, was keeping two or three suitors at bay, and was perhaps secretly in love with a fourth; and the malicious Sanges had discovered that Mariannina, the youngest of the Galantis, was flirting with a little lieutenant stationed opposite her, who never let her out of his sight. And the murmurings increased, mainly Carolina: angry with Carluccio Finoia, she had become implacable.

"What do you care?" rejoined the latter. "The Galantis have military dowries."

"Who told you that?" she cried then. "How do you know? You've asked, haven't you?"

"I know," he answered curtly.

Carolina looked at him with such ferocious suspicion that he lowered his eyes, blushing. Mariano Vacca's café was emptying; at each moment another family got up from its seats and left; the chair man was going around putting his chairs in order. As they got up, the Galantis met Eugenia Malagrida and Enrichetta Caputo, who were also leaving; and since they were friends, they walked part of the way together.

The Galantis were wearing little black lace capes that made the Sanges girls turn pale with envy; Enrichetta Caputo had a white wool scarf that had been knit at home and already washed, but Eugenia Malagrida wore a short wool cloak embroidered with silver, very beautiful, that made her look more awkward than usual.

In spite of this, in order to look nonchalant, Arturo Aiello, the clerk who was there for Enrichetta Caputo, while watching the beautiful poor girl stealthily out of the corner of his eye, walked next to the coarse stocky one, falling in with Eugenia's goose step. It was a long procession of women: the three mothers, Signora Caputo, Signora Malagrida, and Signora Galanti, brought up the rear, chatting, Caputo as humble and vulgar as a servant, dragging along her misshapen ugly body, Malagrida, fat but self-assured, with the good humor of the shopkeeper who has gotten rich, Galanti, tall, strong, and very robust, with a slight mustache like her daughter Riccarda and a loud voice and imperious tone. In the avenue, Matilde Cipullo, whose married name was Tuttavilla, caught up with the procession and joined it, checked on how things were progressing between Enrichetta Caputo and Arturo Aiello—it seemed to her that they were going well—and immediately began to talk to Signora Galanti about a marriage prospect for Riccarda, a landowner from Terra di Lavoro, who would pass through Naples the next week. Signora Galanti listened, laughed, and answered that she left her daughters their freedom, that Riccarda especially had a capricious head of her own, that she would not be surprised to see her remain unmarried.

And the three mothers said in chorus that, if they were to live their lives over again, with the experience of existence that they had, they would never have gotten married, they always told their daughters so—but they were such obstinate creatures, they wanted to imitate their mothers; what could anyone do?

The three mothers nodded their heads, laughing among themselves, while Matilde Tuttavilla was scandalized: what was there better than marriage for girls? And, in spite of the privations that she had suffered with her husband, who was noble but poor, she spoke of marriage full of emotion and enthusiasm, like a convinced apostle who was constantly trying to make converts to her faith.

The Cafaros remained beneath the gaslight, almost forgetting the time: Teresina was touched, struck by the sweet nothings that Peppino Sarnelli, the eloquent lawyer with the bright future, was saying to her, feeling all the suspicions that a rich girl may have of a suitor who is too poor vanish with that delightful wave of love; Gabriella was listening to Giovannino Pasanisi, talking to him, scrutinizing his every intonation, his every intention, making him undergo that rigorous examination where the women examiners seem friendly, but are in reality ruthless; Carmela, the youngest, who was all alone, silent, already tired, but patient, let her sisters pursue their affairs of the heart, knowing perfectly well that their marriages would be advantageous to her. When they got up to leave, she put her arm through the governess's, letting the two couples go in front, calm in her expectations.

At a quarter to midnight, only the Sanges girls were still there, stubborn in spite of the fatigue of a day spent sweeping and dusting, cooking and ironing, since they didn't have a servant, shopping for dinner through the window, with a basket; and they were still quarreling about the Altifredas, those beautiful, proud girls who had gone to spend the fall in Switzerland when all the other middle-class girls, whether rich, comfortable, or poor, stayed in Naples. The Sanges girls were bent on staying; their little brother was grumbling, when Carluccio Finoia, in order to make peace with Carolina, finding that he still had a lira in his pocket, proposed to go eat Indian figs, white, red, and yellow, which cost a penny for three; they would find them in Piazza Municipio, going toward San Giovanni in Carbonara, where the Sanges family lived. And they were seized with a frenzy to eat these Indian figs, since no one offered them refreshments at a café, and while the four sisters were quarreling among themselves, Carolina went off with Carluccio, bursting with pride over her lover's splendid generosity.

Now, at midnight, the Villa was empty, and the gas lamplighter came and put out the flames, leaving one for every eight, a very dim light. The starry night, deep and soft, widened its domain in the garden of love: alone, in the shadows, breathed Vesuvius, now pale red, now fiery, nearly ablaze.

III

It was a great big square room, without draperies, painted simply in pale yellow; there was no rug on the gray brick floor, which was always dusty in spite of the water that Signora Caputo was always throwing on it. Along the wall there was a sofa covered in worn-out crimson wool; the two armchairs were also in crimson wool, covered with pieces of crocheted lace, which was Enrichetta's specialty; there were two or three shelves of painted black wood, on which lay some ugly old knickknacks, an album of old photographs, cardboard boxes covered with shells, faded satin candy boxes; a little round table on one side with a white marble top that was already spotted with yellow, with no cloth, on which stood two lamps; a very small upright piano with a chair covered in tattered and faded red silk; about forty mismatched straw chairs, some lower, some smaller, some with red backs, some with black backs: this was all the furniture. In order to get to this big room where they were to dance, one had to cross an antechamber where the only furniture was a big table intended for coats and hats, another big, dark, unfurnished room divided in two by a curtain, behind which were hidden the mother's and daughter's two shabby beds; the antechamber was lit by a disgusting, smoky old lamp hanging on the wall; the room that one passed through was perfectly dark.

The whole power of illumination was concentrated in the dancing room, two gas lamps on the little table, an oil lamp on a bookcase, two

candles in the candlesticks on the piano; but the candles were
unlit, so that they wouldn't burn down too early. At eight, behind
the curtain in the bedroom, Enrichetta was sewing some lace that
had been washed and ironed to her old red satin bodice, and she
still had her hair rolled in paper curlers; she was wearing a white
slip, with one leg crossed over the other, and she was responding
sharply to her mother's sharp voice and brusque tone.

"He's going to have to tell me his intentions, do you understand? I'm tired of seeing him around the house."

"So am I, I assure you: send him away if you like; I don't care."

"Why does he always go to the Malagridas' house?"

"Because I'm there, he says."

"Oh, indeed? The way he acts makes me suspicious: I'm thinking some ugly thoughts!"

"What thoughts?"

"Arturo is leaving you for Eugenia."

"Eugenia's too ugly."

"But she has money; she has money; she has money!" the old
lady sang out on three notes as she tried to fasten a worn-out corset.

Enrichetta bowed her head at those words, which were destined
to crush her her whole life long. Someone knocked at the door; the
two women looked at each other in embarrassment; they were half-
naked, neither of the two could go to the door, and they had no
servant. They were afraid that it already might be some early guest.

"Perhaps it's the colonel's wife," the old lady grumbled; "she's
always out of something."

She resigned herself, wrapped herself in an old shawl, and went
to the door, dragging her slippers. Enrichetta was slowly combing
her hair, looking at herself by candlelight in a greenish mirror, like
a girl who is weary of her lot in life; these weekly Saturday parties
tormented her, in that bare, dirty house that the government's pity
generously bestowed on the officer's widow and orphan, in that

great madhouse that is the Pavilion of Divine Love, since she had never felt her poverty as she did that evening. Just then her mother returned, grumbling.

"What did the colonel's wife want?" asked the girl.

"She wanted the four chairs that she lent me; she has visitors."

"Wonderful! There won't be enough chairs; where will people sit?"

"The young men don't need to sit down," answered her mother, pinning a batiste camellia in her hair.

"And did you put gas in the lamps, Mama?"

"I did, but they need a little more; they're not full."

"And what if they go out?"

"So they go out! . . . At midnight I'm going to send people away, I am!"

"Then it would be better not to have them come."

"No, my dear; every week people dance at the Galantis' house, at the Malagridas', and at the Falcos'; I don't want to be left behind. Do you understand?"

"But they have money," murmured the girl, powdering her bare throat.

It was the eternal refrain that the mother threw in the daughter's face, and the daughter threw back in the mother's, from time to time. This embittered them, made their private conversations a continuous war. Enrichetta looked at herself in the mirror, satisfied that she was whiter than the Galanti sisters, thinner than Malagrida, rosier than Falco, more attractive than Borrelli, taller than Casale, the most beautiful, in short, of all the girls who came to dance at her house on Saturdays.

"Is Gaetanino making up to you?" her mother asked suddenly.

"A little bit: he's not doing it anymore, for fear of Arturo."

"Arturo, Arturo! . . . We're going to have to break off this Arturo business; I'll talk to Matilde Tuttavilla this evening."

"And who's going to play the piano? I won't go near it, you know, Mama."

"Ciccillo de Marco, the hunchback, will play it; that's why I invited him: I'll say nice things to him; he'll go into ecstasy and play all evening."

An hour later, the big dancing room was already filled with people: the mothers, Signoras Galanti, Malagrida, Falco, and Borrelli, sat in the places of honor on the sofa and in the two armchairs, fanning themselves, each singing the praises of her own daughters. The girls sat next to one another, in a line, all of them still composed, because they weren't dancing yet; they were playing a little music first, and the young men were standing behind the girls' chairs, talking to them in low voices, while Signora Candida Scoppa, six months pregnant and enormous, with the fatigued face of a woman with child, was singing Denza's romance "Giulia" about a dead girl. Malagrida, the daughter, was wearing for the first time a black velvet dress that made her look less fat and ugly; what was new was how slim her waist looked; surely she must have been wearing a corset from Paris; she had always measured seventy centimeters around her waist; that evening she wasn't more than fifty-eight: true, she was standing very straight, like a petrified trunk, and she went pale from time to time, since she couldn't breathe. Enrichetta Caputo had gotten a bit sad again to see her so elegant: actually, she liked Arturo Aiello and she wouldn't have liked to lose him in this way. But she had distracted herself, since she had to receive her friends, by taking their coats and scarves and putting them on her bed; she was tireless, trying to make them forget the poverty of the room, the meager light of the lamps, the lack of chairs, with her smile of a beautiful girl who has nothing else. And no one seemed to notice that poverty, those girls and young men who had come there only to have fun and make love, and to dance, they who would have danced in the square to the sound of a fife.

They were dying with laughter at a song by Gaetanino Ceraso, who was singing or declaiming a scene in dialect, "The Signora's Hand," in which a young man in love, while following his beloved in church in semidarkness, seizes the mother's hand instead of the daughter's, and the old lady immediately offers to marry him. Gaetanino Ceraso, an engineer of bridges and roads, was cultivating comic singing very successfully during these weekly dances, but this kept him from making conquests: girls loved men who were melancholy or at least serious, those who didn't make everyone laugh; Enrichetta Caputo also felt that way: she preferred Arturo Aiello's seriousness, and the ineffable air with which he passed his hand through his hair. Even poor Elvira Brown was laughing, who that evening had worn a new red brocade dress and a pair of very beautiful ruby earrings; next to her the jealous old man wore a brand-new red wig, and his false teeth gleamed in their gold frame; as long as there was no dancing, the old man enjoyed himself, keeping his wife at his side: that evening he was tender to the point of holding her hand; she bowed her head in humiliation and confusion, not daring to look people in the eye.

She felt, yes, she felt in those who met her, pity, cold curiosity, condemnation, scorn; she felt the differing judgments of people fall on her, on her who, beautiful, young, and poor, had willingly married a disgusting, rich old man, and those who were kindest pitied her, yes, but they didn't think that she was so unhappy, with all that money, and those who were most severe accused her of greed and thought that she had sold herself in marriage. She was well aware that she had done it through compassion for her own family, that was immersed in respectable but increasing poverty, for her parents who were old and tired of privation, for her good and clever brothers who needed money in order to go into honorable, lucrative professions: but to whom should she tell all this? And also, why should she tell it? She allowed people to regard her as the most venal of women, who had given herself to a cadaver in exchange for the jewels and fabrics with which he covered her, and she made the noble sacrifice of her life in silence, under the unjust opinion of the public.

Arturo Aiello had appeared on the threshold of the room, in his buttoned-up Sunday coat, with a white camellia bud in his buttonhole, and he was looking around the room to see who was there; cleverly, without looking as if she were doing so, Enrichetta Caputo had slipped among the groups to arrive at his side, while Federico Pietraroia, the amateur actor, declaimed Armando Fusinato's "Family Dinner."

"Is that camellia for me?" asked Enrichetta in a low voice.

". . . It's for you," he said, removing it from his buttonhole and giving it to her, after, perhaps, a slight hesitation.

She went back across the room, this time gloriously, wearing her camellia in triumph; it began to be noisy; the chairs were pushed back against the wall; the girls and young men were conversing in a lively fashion; people were starting to dance. Gennaro Mascarpone, senior clerk in the house of Maquay Hooker, which deals in cod, was the master of ceremonies and had been calling out for five minutes:

"*Waltzer, en place.*"

The couples were forming, first two or three, timidly, then as many as six or seven, standing straight, waiting for everything to be in order. Enrichetta Caputo had gone up to the hunchback, Ciccillo de Marco, and by smiling at him and making eyes at him, tried to convince him to play that waltz, just that one, a few twirls, just to begin. And the malicious hunchback let her flirt with him, let her beg him, looked unhappy, shook his head, and said no; Enrichetta had to promise that she would dance the quadrille with him, or he wouldn't play. The first strident notes of the tune out of the piano were exhilarating to the girls and young men, who were keeping time to the music and nodding their heads, overcome by their youthful passion for dancing.

"The waltz, the waltz!" shouted Gennaro Mascarpone.

Enrichetta looked around for Arturo to dance the waltz with her, as they had established, without his having to invite her any longer; all the girls danced the first dance with their lover or fiancé; it was the rule. Emilia Galanti was in place with her surgeon, Mariannina was leaning on the arm of her lieutenant, who had asked her to dance as prescribed, Margherita Falco was dancing with Elvira Brown's brother, Annina Casale with Federico Pietraroia, who was courting her. So where, then, was Arturo Aiello? Surely, he, too, was looking for Enrichetta, to open the dancing. And as the hunchback began to pound out the music on the piano, the couples began to whirl around, and Enrichetta saw Arturo dancing with Eugenia Malagrida, without ever looking in her direction, as though he were ashamed: she saw that Eugenia wore in her hair, which was rather thin but which had been artificially done by the hairdresser, a white camellia blossom similar to the one she had taken from Arturo.

A very sharp pain made her go pale, while, together with the couples who were dancing, making the floor shake with the gaiety of thoughtless youth, it seemed to her that the whole room was spinning around. Gennaro Mascarpone, a handsome young man with a soft French pronunciation and a pretentious air, asked her to dance; he was the master of ceremonies in the room; he acted like a tyrant, grabbed girls, and generally danced more than the others; she refused by a shake of her head, since she didn't have the strength to speak, still watching Eugenia whirling around, big and solid as a tree trunk in her new black velvet dress, with Arturo Aiello, whose melancholy air went to the girls' hearts. Gaetanino

Ceraso, the engineer who sang funny songs, had an intuition of that intimate drama; he went to Enrichetta and asked her in a low voice:

"Why aren't you dancing the waltz?"

"Because I don't like it," she answered in irritation.

"Come, come; be nice, take a turn with me," he went on softly.

She looked at him, moved for a minute, guessing that he had guessed, and she was on the verge of accepting, as revenge against Arturo. Gaetanino waited, but she saw him before her, as he had been a moment ago, simpering and ridiculous, as he made the guests choke with laughter when he sang "The Signora's Hand."

"No," she said, "no, I don't want to dance."

She went on standing straight, watching those who were dancing: the Galantis, so pretty in their new dark green wool dresses; Margherita Falco, stunning in her simple outfit of white wool; Annina Casale, who was making her short black silk train swirl out; Caterina Borrelli, quite pompous in a gray wool dress with bands of black velvet; even Eugenia became bearable in her Parisian corset and her dress made by Madame Ricco; all of them were happy to dance with the person whom they loved or liked. She felt the whole shame of her old cream-colored wool skirt, of her old red satin bodice, of her washed lace: she felt the whole shame of that empty, dirty, badly lit room, the roof that had been given them by charity; she felt the whole isolation and abandonment of daily poverty, unending and invincible—a wave of bitterness coursed through her blood.

The couples were walking around to rest themselves; the mothers had pulled their feet back, so that they wouldn't be stepped on, and were smiling at their daughters, with whom they were satisfied; Signora Caputo was talking to Matilde Tuttavilla with great emphasis, and the latter was listening to her with great concern. Enrichetta was keeping busy: she had taken Riccarda Galanti into the kitchen for a drink of water: a bare little kitchen with quite a few utensils; on a small table was a plate of cold macaroni and a small piece of Swiss cheese, Enrichetta's supper; the water was drunk out of a greenish glass and came from a pail standing on the floor; disgusted and pitying, Riccarda would have liked not to drink the rest, but she was afraid of offending Enrichetta. Then, Emma Froggio, a big, aggressive blond, had two buttons pop off her dress from dancing so much: Enrichetta had to take her into the dark room, behind the curtain, carrying a candle that she had taken from the piano, among the two unmade beds, the basins full of dirty water, the clothing strewn around, and the scattered slippers in order to find a needle, thimble, and thread to sew Emma Froggio's buttons back on. When they came back into the big room, a monster quadrille was being formed of sixteen couples, such as had never before been seen in the Caputo house. Gennaro Mascarpone was acting like someone possessed, brutalizing his friends and abandoning himself to ferocious delaying tactics. But they were short three to make up these sixteen couples, so Signora Galanti had already gotten up to get people to dance.

"Will you dance the quadrille with me?" whispered Arturo Aiello to Enrichetta, as she passed next to him.

"No, I'm taken," she answered, without even turning around.

And she went to choose a partner. They were still one couple short: Gennaro Mascarpone, with the insolence of the master of ceremonies whom nobody must disobey, went to invite Signora Brown, even though he knew that it was the worst compliment that anyone could pay her; everybody knew about the old man's jealousy. And while she, being a timid woman, was feebly resisting, three or four couples surrounded her and begged; without her, they wouldn't be able to dance; her husband looked around, as though it didn't concern him, pretending not to see the looks with which she asked his permission to dance—and she finally gave in and got up, so beautiful on the arm of a triumphant Gennaro Mascarpone, while the old man turned green with bile. At that moment people noticed that Ciccillo de Marco wasn't there and that there was no one to play the piano. There were two or three minutes of great confusion, of despair. Mascarpone was furious, grumbling that he wasn't used to directing the music in houses where there wasn't even anyone to pound the piano; finally Matilde Tuttavilla sacrificed herself in order to amuse all those young people, went to the piano, called out that they would have to be satisfied with some old tunes adapted as best she could for a quadrille. Now they were dancing, all three exclaiming in low tones over Enrichetta Caputo, who was dancing very nonchalantly with Ciccillo de Marco, the hunchback.

At eleven thirty, the girls surrounded Gennaro Mascarpone, begging him, beseeching him, to let them do a cotillion; but he resisted, saying that it was impossible to dance the cotillion without the necessary things: bouquets of flowers, scarves, and decorations. The girls protested: it didn't matter at all that they didn't have any of these things; he was full of imagination; he would invent steps; they would be satisfied with anything, as long as they could dance the cotillion; their mothers wanted to leave right away; he shouldn't go on being mean. Gennaro Mascarpone gave in and went to talk in secret with Signora Concetta Caputo and Enrichetta, so as to have at least a few indispensable items.

Mother and daughter pretended to be nonchalant, but they were upset: a chair belonging to the major's mother-in-law had been broken during a galloping dance and would have to be replaced the next day so that they could give it back to her; the candles were only four inches high; the oil lamps were growing dim; Matilde Tuttavilla had broken two wires on the piano because she had pounded too hard; and at midnight the colonel's widow would certainly appear at the window to yell about all the nocturnal noise they were making, as she had done the Saturday before, when Arturo Aiello had had to go over and mollify her. Still, the two women put up a good front with Gennaro, who asked them for a cushion, a mirror, and a candlestick with a lighted candle. While they were beginning to dance, Enrichetta searched for all these things: first she took a dirty, dull brass candlestick to Gennaro, which contained the stub of a candle. Two partners, bearing the names of two flowers, Rose and Gardenia, were presented to a lady: she chose the gardenia and danced with the partner who bore this name; the other, with the rose, carried the candle behind the dancing couple; the whole room laughed behind his back—he, too, pretended to laugh, to look like a witty person, but the unlucky man was brooding over that injustice of fate. Gaetanino Ceraso, carrying the candle behind Margherita Falco and her fiancé, whom destiny had reunited, simpered and made a variety of faces to express his bitterness; the guests died laughing; the waltz went on and on; Ciccillo de Marco was playing like a madman, so happy to have danced the quadrille with the most beautiful girl at the party.

After two or three other steps, Enrichetta took Gennaro Mascarpone a pillow from her little bed: it was thin, with a pillowcase of dubious whiteness, and the fascinating Kneeling Figure began, to the amusement of all. The lady who was to dance took this pillow up to every seated partner, put it at his feet while looking at him out of the corner of her eye, and the partner's goal was to kneel down in one motion so as to fall on the pillow; the lady's goal was to immediately pull away the pillow so as to make the partner fall on the floor on his knees. Everyone was eager to see the double craftiness of the men and women, who had to study one another, guess what the other was going to do, and rely on his or her wits; and the partner's angry face when he fell on the floor on his knees, or the dull thump of the man who fell triumphantly on the pillow and the woman's irritated face was great fun. Gennarino Mascarpone was declared to be the god of masters of ceremony. Caterina Borrelli, nasty as a fat monkey, which she slightly resembled, made all of her partners fall and didn't dance with anyone; Federico Pietraroia succeeded in dancing with Elvira Brown; Eugenia Malagrida refused to carry around the pillow because she didn't like making her partners fall down; Enrichetta was nervous because a disk in a candleholder had exploded, and the candle was burning down; Matilde Tuttavilla was chatting with Signora Malagrida now, raising her eyebrows at something surprising that the large signora was saying.

Enrichetta had now given Gennaro Mascarpone her greenish mirror for the great Final Figure. A lady sat in the center of the room, holding the mirror and a handkerchief in her hand: one by one the partners came to look at themselves; the lady cleaned the mirror for the ones that she didn't want to dance with; she gave it a quick cleaning, as though she were putting a line through a word or erasing it, and she put down the mirror for the one whom she wanted to dance with. It was the big final choice, in which every attraction manifested itself ingenuously, the declarations of mutual love, of nascent affection, of preference made public, clearly and simply: and the partners acted like skeptics; they didn't want to come look at themselves; they had to be dragged. If the love affairs were known or suspected, there was a low murmur among the guests; everyone laughed indulgently, as though giving them friendly encouragement to love each other. But everyone fell into a profound stupor when Eugenia Malagrida—who had a dowry of one hundred and fifty thousand lire, who was big, fat, stocky, and had a shiny face—after dusting off the mirror for all the potential partners, put it down for Arturo Aiello, the poor clerk, who was reputed to be the official fiancé of Enrichetta Caputo. Everyone looked at Enrichetta: she was laughing nervously; the disk under the other candlestick had broken.

In the kitchen, in the smoky light from the lamp in the foyer, Signora Concetta Caputo had been complaining for a quarter of an hour about all the mishaps that had occurred that evening (whose only consequence would be to provoke gossip that would reflect badly on them when it got around); she enumerated the broken chair, the broken wires, the gas that had been consumed, the exploding candlesticks, grumbling unceasingly. Enrichetta, who was still wearing her old red satin blouse, looked at the plate of cold, greasy macaroni that she was supposed to have for dinner and cried.

IV

You entered through a large courtyard in a big gray building on Rua Catalana, where you could make out the outlines of seven or eight carriages for rent, without horses, with their shafts in the air; the courtyard also served as a storage room. You went up a staircase that was large, but muddy and poorly illuminated, to a second floor, where the door was wide open; you entered without being announced into a foyer where the open umbrellas left puddles of rainwater on the ground and coats were drying on the chairs. It was the apartment of Don Giuseppe Froio, ex-captain of the National Guard, where people had danced every Sunday during Carnival and now would be coming on the first Sunday of Lent for the breaking of the pinata. Don Giuseppe Froio had always exercised the profession of usurer, but he did only small loans, never big ones, because he feared losing capital, and slowly he had gotten rich; at fifty he was a captain and a notable person in the neighborhood of the port.

For a long time, he had lived with Franceschella, his servant, but the latter had also lent money at interest so successfully, and with such a hard head, that her admiring master had opened a pawnbroker's shop for her that, under Franceschella's marvelous management, had had a return of a hundred percent, with the result that Don Giuseppe had decided to marry Franceschella, who had become Signora Franceschina after the marriage; she had turned the public business over to a niece, but she continued to lend money at interest privately, at home. Now, Don Giuseppe and Signora Franceschina had no children, and they knew how to conduct their business: they weren't stingy, and they were tormented by the desire for honors, tortured by the vainglory of entertaining at home. Every Sunday during Carnival, people went to dance at their home; the three rooms were full of people whom they knew and didn't know, friends of friends of other friends, sisters of the relatives of close friends, whole families with the addition of fiancés who had been brought by other families: Don Giuseppe and Signora Franceschina asked nothing, as long as people came, danced, and filled the house. The house was large: three reception rooms, one living room, but the furniture was heterogeneous, a strange jumble: a red sofa, a blue armchair, a rococo clock that was stopped, a small table of sculptured wood, a brocade curtain, a fake Smyrna rug; all the chairs were mismatched, none of the candlesticks were alike; there was an enormous mirror without a frame, religious paintings that were very smoky, a marble Venus with broken arms, all in a jumble as in a junk shop. And if you knew the story of the master of the house, you understood that those things had been pawned by unfortunates who had not been able to redeem them; it was furniture that came from so many different houses that had been carried away, forgotten, abandoned—grieved over perhaps by the owners who had been, however, unable to save them from ruin. If you looked at Signora Franceschina, she looked like the house;

her head, neck, ears, hands, arms, waist, chest were covered with jewels, all of which were mismatched: earrings, pins, rings, bracelets, chains and small chains, malachite and jewels, pearls and crude gold, down to a medallion that contained a delicate miniature, the portrait of a woman—a family memento, perhaps, or a love token. But those who came to amuse themselves in the Froios' house didn't come to observe all this; it was such a pleasure to find a house that was big and well illuminated, where it wasn't even necessary to greet the hosts as you went in and out! Don Giuseppe still wore the cap of the National Guard on his head, in memory of his old honors; Donna Franceschina, through long force of habit, constantly went around refueling the adjustable lights, and the couple smiled at everyone, as though they were old acquaintances, happy to see their house bursting with people.

That evening of the breaking of the pinata, it was hard to move around; everyone had come hoping to win a prize. The de Pasquale girls, in provocative black silk dresses that were cut low with a square neck, with sheer black sleeves that left their white arms visible, and blond hair on their shoulders, had brought along their whole tribe of admirers; even Count Geraci had deigned to come, in spite of the fact that he usually frequented the salons of the nobility: and without paying attention to anyone, they held court as though they were at home, laughing and chatting, all sweetness and liveliness, a bit made up, a bit melancholy underneath it all, seeing that they weren't getting married, despite all this attention. The Fuscos, Elisa Costa, and Gelsomina Santoro were standing around a piano, passing sheets of music to each other, with a knowledgeable air, still talking about music; a rumor was circulating: Maria Fusco was getting married, to the tenor of the Teatro Nuovo, the one who played Angelo Pitou in *The Daughter of Madame Angot* and Maraschino in *Giroflé-Girofla;* the other sister had tried to kill herself over a student who had abandoned her.

Annina Manetta was radiant: her mother, having given up beating her so that she wouldn't love Vicenzino Spanò, had finally consented; Vicenzino had proposed; they couldn't get married for another five years, but in the meantime he accompanied Annina everywhere; now the scenes were starting with Adelina, the youngest, who had gotten it into her head to fall in love with a shoemaker's son. The mother was desperate and slapped Adelina daily; even that evening the shoemaker's son had managed to come to the Froios' house, where he had been brought by a friend. Caterina Borrelli and Annina Casale, the inseparable, were walking through the rooms arm in arm, Caterina with her glasses on her nose and her lovely gray wool dress with the bands of black velvet that already looked old because she was so slovenly; Annina decidedly in love with Federico Pietraroia, who was supposed to come to the Froios' house that evening; he went everywhere. Emma Froggio had lost a heel of her boots on the stairs, and she sat sulking in a corner, unable to move, with her foot hidden under the chair.

Fortunately, they weren't dancing that evening; it was Lent, and Signora Franceschina was observant.

The Sanges girls, all five—with the faithful Carluccio Finoia next to Carolina, with Rocco Marzolla, a harpist in love with Gaetanella Sanges, who was afflicted with a strange deafness and who was waiting to be accepted by the Orchestra del Fondo so that they could get married—were mad with curiosity to know what was in the two pinatas that were to be broken. Every time that a friend or acquaintance passed by them, they called to him in a loud voice and grabbed him by the arm to find out the great secret from him. So, was it true, what they were saying, that the pinata for the women contained a gold bracelet for the one who broke it and a number of other lovely gifts? Was it true that the one intended for the men contained a nightcap as a prize and a number of humorous gifts for the rest of the party? Who would put the blindfold on the women? Federico Pietraroia, that affected imbecile, who divided his time between making love to the de Pasquales and being the silly lover of Signorina Casale? Who would put the blindfold on the men? Gelsomina Santoro, that flirt, to say the least? They would see some strange things! And the excitement grew and grew among all those girls, all those young men, those mothers and old aunts; there was tremendous impatience; they couldn't stop chatting and fidgeting; there were more and more questions, more and more answers, when Don Giuseppe Froio, with his National Guard beret pulled proudly over his ear, with his attractive gentleman's smile, an old reminder of his usurer's dealings, walked through the rooms, saying softly:

"Signore, signorine, let's go into the living room for the breaking of the pinata!"

He himself offered his arm to Signora Clementina de Camillis, of the marquises of Latiano, a proud, grumpy old lady whom everyone worshipped, whom they respectfully called *La Marchesa,* as though there were only one in the world, and who gave an aristocratic air to Don Giuseppe Froio's rooms.

In the living room, the chairs were arranged as for a cotillion, in couples of men and women, but people were no longer thinking of conversing, or making love, or flirting, or secretly pressing another's hand; the girls were distracted, overcome by curiosity and desire, burning with the desire to break the pinata in order to obtain the famous bracelet. In the middle of the big empty circle, where all eyes were fixed, Federico Pietraroia and Mimì Falabella, Donna Franceschina's man Friday, carried by the handles a large reddish brown pinata of the kind that are baked in the ovens of Sessa Aurunca, together with the pots used by every Neapolitan; the wide mouth was stopped up with a piece of white cloth tied with a string. The two young men pretended to make an effort when they picked it up; a murmur sprang up:

"It's heavy, it's heavy, it's heavy!"

Gelsomina Santoro, looking very elegant in a dark green dress, all embroidered in gold at the wrists and neck, like an officer, waited with a red silk handkerchief and a broom handle in her hands. The first man to be blindfolded was Don Giuseppe Froio, who joined in willingly: he was blindfolded and made to walk around the room; he was given the broom handle, then he was left alone in the vicinity of the pinata lying on the floor:

"Careful, Don Giuseppe!"

"Turn to the right, Don Peppì!"

"Watch out, watch out!"

"Careful, Don Peppì!"

After testing the ground for a bit, he raised the broom handle with both hands as though it were a club and struck a blow, but he missed by a hair and only the handle of the pinata was broken. There was an explosion of laughter, applause, protests, and comments; the women were particularly excited. Mimì Falabella, the other master of the house, as he was called, had himself blindfolded at some length by Gelsomina so that all five of the Sanges girls snickered:

"Mimì, you can see, you can see!"

"Hit hard, Falabella!"

"One, two, three!"

But Falabella, who must have known that there was a joke in the pinata, struck a great blow that fell on the ground, to one side: it was better to make people laugh at a hit that fell short than at a prize they would have to put up with. And the men's turn followed; all of them bent their heads, under the white hands of Gelsomina Santoro, who tied the handkerchief behind their necks: in the middle of the circle some hesitated, trying to orient themselves, then finally gave a blow that landed far from the pinata, amid the snickers of the guests; some made up their minds right away, struck a great blow in the air, and tore off their masks right away, as though they wanted to see the pieces of the broken pinata; some struck two or three short, furious blows, breaking the rule that permits only one blow; some struck skeptically, just to get it over with, shrugging their shoulders. And the noisy gaiety of the spectators increased; Donna Franceschina was splitting her sides laughing noisily; when Gelsomina tied the red handkerchief around the hunchback Ciccillo de Marco's big head, there was a minute of complete silence, sudden and strange: the hunchback didn't wait; he didn't take aim; he struck one fast, successful blow, hit the pinata in the middle, and broke it in two. A cheer greeted the victory of Don Ciccillo, who was all smiles, flattered, and there was a triple prize: a knit nightcap with a white tassel, a wide cardboard snuffbox, and a gold-tipped walking stick, which was really a cheap penny stick that had been crowned with a tomato. The hunchback bravely put on the nightcap, took up the snuffbox and the amusing stick, picked up the two pieces of the pinata, and went around offering the other gifts to the men. There were dried fava beans wrapped in gold papers, as though they were choice sugared almonds; there were cabbage stalks carefully rolled in blue, pink, and silver tinfoil, of the kind that are used for chocolates; there were small pieces of pasta tied with colored ribbons; there were roasted chestnuts wrapped in curly papers; there were silk purses full of dried beans, and eggs filled with flour that broke in your hands. And although some may have cried out, or protested, or laughed, or joked about his gift, everyone agreed on Don Giuseppe's and Donna Franceschina's wit: it wasn't possible to do things better than this; it must have taken two months to prepare all those surprises. And, as for that tomato on the walking stick that Ciccillo de Marco was parading around with so proudly, it was enough to make you die laughing, wasn't it? Concettella Sanges, very excited, tried at any cost to win de Marco's favor, but the latter turned his back on her;

his choice had already been made, since Carnival; Concettella couldn't get anything from him; she had to be satisfied with touching his hump with her hand, as though by chance, for good luck. As the guests stood aside, the pinata intended for the women was carried respectfully to the middle of the room by Federico Pietraroia and Mimì Falabella; and they pretended to carry it effortlessly, as though it were very light. The women, who had advanced to the front, having pushed the men to the back, did not take their eyes off it, as though it contained their fortune.

"It's empty, it's empty," murmured the men teasingly.

All the women dreamed of the gold bracelet with a sapphire, they said, no, with an emerald, and they were afraid that one of the first ones would break the pinata. In fact, the first was Donna Clementina de Camillis, of the marquises of Latiano, the ill-tempered old woman who got angry at Federico Pietraroia because he tied her handkerchief too tightly, who felt around with the broom handle where there was no pinata and nearly broke Mimì Falabella's head by hitting him with the broom, who looked at the assembly with the frown of an offended sibyl and went back very unhappily to her place. Nor did the second one, Donna Franceschina, break the pinata, but she hadn't intended to break it, out of politeness, since she was the hostess; she must have seen very well where the pinata was, said the Sanges sisters; Mimì had blindfolded her so loosely! The first Fusco sister struck the pinata, but the blow was too weak; it didn't manage to break the clay.

"You need iron, an iron cure, Signorina!"

"Or quinine, an extract of quinine!"

The second sister only cracked it; the pinata seemed to be made of iron; everyone praised the pinata's solidity. Emma Froggio failed to strike a blow because of her missing heel; she limped unhappily back to her place, almost in tears; Caterina Borrelli asked Federico Pietraroia not to tie the blindfold too tightly—in any case, she was nearsighted; she couldn't see anything without her glasses—and she struck an unsuccessful blow that was so violent that the broom handle broke in two; they had to get another one. Understanding, Donna Franceschina ran to the kitchen.

As the pinata still remained intact under the women's blows that were too strong and missed the mark or too close but too weak, anxiety increased: there was a terrible fight between the five Sanges sisters and Federico Pietraroia: one claimed that he had hurt her eye; another said that he had pulled the hair on her neck; the third was suffocating under the blindfold because she was used to breathing through her nose; they all said that they would have been able to break the pinata very easily if it had not been for the ill will of Federico Pietraroia, who had his favorites: the dispute grew serious. Carluccio Finoia and Rocco Marzolla had to intervene. Finally, there remained only Annina Casale and the two de Pasquale sisters; as he put the blindfold on Annina, Federico murmured something in her ear, but she didn't understand and turned to the left, struck the back of a chair and broke it. Federico made a gesture of disappointment; the Sanges sisters kept an eye on them; finally the words were whispered clearly to the last one, the younger de Pasquale, a very pretty little blond with an ingenuous air:

"Donna Ida, keep to the right."

The pinata made a cracking noise and broke in two; the men applauded. Ida de Pasquale, almost dancing with joy, seized a white paper package, the prize; it was a silver bracelet covered with black enamel, with the word *memento*, a cute little trinket, but one that was worth twenty francs. But they all craned their necks to see the sapphire, emerald, jewel, or pearl; and the little blond carried around the other little gifts, which were mysteriously wrapped and carefully sealed. There were little paper fans that cost half a franc apiece, change purses made of artificial Russian leather, velvet pincushions, tiny carved wooden eggs with a white metal thimble inside, picture frames made of painted cardboard for photographs, little blue glass jars for toothpicks, packets of rice powder, small bottles of perfumed essences: all the unsold merchandise of a department store, which made those girls go into ecstasies. As she carried these gifts around, Ida de Pasquale showed off her silver bracelet, with a gracious air; all the women thought it was beautiful and regretted that they hadn't gotten it, in spite of its little value. The Sanges girls were bursting with envy, for one had gotten two artificial gold cuff links, another a box of tooth powder, the third a small calendar, the fourth a picture of the Savior, the last, finally, a pack of scissors with steel blades—were they being made fun of? Hadn't they seen that Federico had told Ida de Pasquale the secret word? And hadn't Ida given them the rejects on purpose? What kind of a way was that to treat people? But, over all this happy or angry—though always tumultuous—discourse, a tray of homemade cookies was passed like a peace offering, followed by a tray of glasses filled with Lacrima Cristi, the wine that was made in Don Giuseppe Froio's big Ottaiano vineyard; and with people's spirits calmer, the Games of Forfeit began, from the calm and serious game The Key Turns to the rowdy, uproarious one of Post Office, with the great, galloping finale: The Train Leaves for the Devil's House.

V

The rumbling of Vesuvius began on the day of April 22, 1872,* at one in the afternoon. It was a dull, subterranean noise, but continuous, accompanied by the unceasing shaking of the windowpanes. The day was very clear, of great springlike sweetness; the Neapolitans crowded into every street where Vesuvius could be seen, went

*Sources vary on when the eruption began—some say April 24.

up on every terrace, climbed onto every roof, appeared at every
attic window. On Vesuvius rose a long, thick whitish cloud, in the
form of a pine tree, colored pale pink at its base where it touched
the crater: one could see nothing else. But the rumbling did not
stop, so that all the houses in Naples began to shake, from Posillipo
to Borgo Loreto, from the Vomero Hill to the Via di Porto; the roar
seemed to come from the bowels of the earth, beneath the pedestrians' feet. The director of the Normal School entered the second-
year class, where Annina Casale and Caterina Borrelli were students,
and said that, due to exceptional circumstances, school would close
that day at one instead of three; they could all go home.* At the
door in Via di Gesù there was a confused exodus of 180 girls
returning home, astonished at this vacation, and they met groups
of students who were coming from the university, where the rector
had canceled classes two hours earlier than usual. In the Church of
the Madonna of Succor, where, since it was Wednesday, the Sanges
sisters were listening to a sermon in honor of Mary the Immaculate, the preacher stopped, shortened his words by at least half, had
the women say the prayer that is said on the occasion of lightning
and earthquakes, and sent them all home. In the artificial-flower
workshop, where thirty florists worked under the direction of Signora Malagrida, terror spread: one of the girls' mothers lived in
Sant'Anastasia, a village beneath Vesuvius: she screamed, cried,
and became agitated; it wasn't possible to keep the workers any
longer, so they had a half holiday and went home; Signora Malagrida returned to her apartment in Via dei Fiorentini, very upset.
In the half darkness of the Teatro San Ferdinando, the de Pasquale
sisters, Federico Pietraroia, Giovanni Laterza, and other amateur

---

*Sic. Interestingly enough, Caterina Borrelli and Annina Casale are still in
school in this last section, whereas in the first part of the story at the beach
they have graduated! Serao, who was a prolific writer, obviously did not have
time to revise all that she wrote.

actors were rehearsing *Lucia Didier, or Honor for Honor* in front of half a theater full of personal friends; but when the roar began, many of the spectators went outside to find out what was going on. The Teatro San Ferdinando is very close to the Maddalena Bridge; the roar could be heard much louder; the girls felt that they were drowning in its shadow, and the rehearsal was canceled. In the Jovine household, where the sweet crippled girl lived, there was a party that Wednesday; since it was the grandmother's name day, the beautiful Altifreda sisters were there; the Galantis were arriving; for a while they joked about the eruption, the roar, the earthquake, and the rain of ashes, while ice cream was being passed around and people were still presenting bouquets of flowers; but little by little the conversation fell off; everybody listened; the dance of the windowpanes got on the crippled girl's nerves; she shook nearly as hard as the windows did; the guests began to leave, trying a few last jokes, but reluctantly; everybody wanted to be in her own home. When everybody had left, Maria Jovine went to bed with her head among the pillows so that she wouldn't hear the shaking of the glass panes. Everyone—businessmen, employees, laborers, the idle—seemed to have been seized with a great desire to go home; on the street they greeted one another hurriedly, exchanged a few brief bits of news, left one another with a gesture of farewell, as though serious business drew them elsewhere. Thus, public and private offices remained deserted, some voluntarily, others forced to close.

The afternoon seemed very long; only when night came could they gauge the progress of the eruption: bad news was circulating, two new mouths had opened on the volcano; Cercola and Sant' Anastasia were lost; there were rash victims who had tried to climb Vesuvius the evening before. It was whispered that covered stretchers had arrived in Via Forcella, in which there were terribly burned human bodies wrapped in sheets, but still alive, agonizing amid horrible spasms: the bell at the door of the Hospital of the Pilgrims, where the wounded were taken, never stopped ringing on that afternoon, constantly announcing new disasters.

In the evening, all of Naples poured into the streets, gathered on terraces, on balconies, on streets from which the volcano could be seen. Three great lava flows, of dimensions that had never been seen before, were pouring from the mouth of the crater: one of them fell on the opposite slope, threatening the village of Ottaiano, and its widest spread could be seen on the slopes of the mountain, where it illuminated the sky in the background. The second, in an almost horizontal line, went down toward the sea, cutting the whole width of Vesuvius, covering the earth in front of people's very eyes. The third, very wide and majestic, spread out magnificently along the slope of the mountain, widened in the Atrium of the Horse, descended like a river of flame, threatening Resina, Portici, Naples. The white cloud had vanished completely; the very clear starry sky was red in the reflection on that spring evening, up to the zenith; the Tyrrhenian Sea, completely still in both the gulf of Castellammare and in that of Naples, was red up to the Ovo fort. The mountain, sea, and sky were aflame, and at the same time, there was a profound peace in nature; there was not a breath of wind, not a noise from the waves; as a matter of fact, the sea was full of boats, motionless in the incandescent reflection. Only the bowels of the earth were writhing and shaking, never stopping.

At the marina on the San Vincenzo Pier, which the Neapolitans call the Wharf, the Sanges sisters were among the crowd; they were ecstatic as they contemplated the marvelous spectacle, experiencing from time to time a shiver of terror, when they heard the words that ran like a refrain through the crowd:

"The third lava flow threatens Naples."

In vain did Carluccio Finoia and Rocco Marzolla beg them to leave, since they had already seen enough; in vain did they both offer to pool their resources and take them to the café in Via Principessa Margherita for an ice: they resisted, overcome by astonishment; they forgot to squabble, transfixed by that immense glare. Rumors of victims were running through the people: a beautiful woman, a doctor, two fiancés, and then a group of students, a group of peasants, two guides. What were their names? The names weren't known; the newspapers hadn't yet come out.

Annina Casale and Caterina Borrelli were leaning on the railing in Via del Gigante among people who had been standing for two hours, watching the visible progress of the eruption: Annina Casale had a lorgnette; she even saw the trees burst into flame for only a minute, like a match being lit, even before the lava touched them; Caterina Borrelli was reciting in a low voice a passage from *The Last Days of Pompei* by Bulwer Lytton; but they too were beginning to feel worried deep down, since the phrase was being repeated continuously around them:

"The third lava flow is threatening Naples."

The Malagrida family—father, mother, daughter, along with Arturo Aiello, Eugenia's fiancé—were at a rich uncle's house, on a balcony in the Vicolo d'Afflitto, on a straight line from the Via Santa Brigida, from which all of Vesuvius could be seen; they had gone to that uncle's as though they were going to the theater, to "see the mountain," but the magnificence of the phenomenon, all that fire reflected in the sky and sea, and the sense of danger, had struck that family of fat, happy people. Eugenia, holding her fiancé's hand tightly, bowed her head, as though she were overcome by melancholy, and he spoke to her softly, to cheer her up: there was no danger, and then, wasn't he there, he who loved her so much, and had for so long, since last summer, since the first evening that he had met her? The fat girl, to whom no one had ever said such sweet things, was trembling; her face was burning; she felt as though all the flames of the eruption were in her; she no longer heard the words that the old people in the Malagrida home were murmuring:

"The third lava flow is threatening Naples: we should display San Gennaro."

A crowd of guests thronged the great terrace of the Hotel de Rome in Santa Lucia, which overlooks the sea; the owner of the hotel, a practical man, wanted to take advantage of the publicity that the mountain was bringing him. Little Count Geraci had secured invitations for the de Pasquales and their retinue, and the girls had settled in a corner, showing off their Mephistophelean black velvet capes, lined in red, but they no longer felt like laughing or chatting; that fire had left them bewildered. In vain did Jacobucci, Laterza, and Pietraroia try to joke and give scientific explanations; they weren't listening; they were very pale under the heavy powder that they wore on their faces, with their big, sad eyes full of melancholy, no longer thinking of acting or of love. At a certain moment, while they were talking about that immense third lava flow that was surely and inevitably coming down toward Naples, Ida murmured, trembling all over:

"Why don't we display San Gennaro?"

The musical girls, the two Fuscos, Elisa Costa, and Gelsomina Santoro were together in the house of their teacher Pantanella, who wanted them to sing a funny chorus, but the teacher's house was up over the Chiaia Bridge, with a balcony from which the whole gulf could be seen; from the piano where they were gathered, along with other girls, the immense glare of the eruption was visible; they couldn't sing, and were continuously distracted; attracted and fascinated, they wanted to run to the balcony. They sang, but their voices died in their throats; the Fuscos had a cousin in Resina; Signorina Costa pitied that poor Don Giuseppe Froio, whose vineyard in Ottaiano was ruined: they had met him in the afternoon, pale and upset, tears in his eyes, followed by Donna Franceschina, who was crying. And Gelsomina Santoro, hearing that there was danger for Naples, was asking everyone:

"But why don't they display San Gennaro's relics?"

The Galanti sisters were on the bank of Chiatamone, near the Hotel Washington, along with Maria Jovine: they had taken her from her home, where she was having constant convulsions, telling her that, after all, it was best to be able to see. They surrounded her while she bowed her head in fear and nervousness; and her mother tried to calm her: listen, if the danger grew worse, they would leave the next day for Rome or Florence; good heavens, it wasn't as though they were living in the time of Pompeii; they could escape. The Galantis were also a bit upset; they, too, said that they wanted to go away to the country for a bit, not because they were afraid, but to get away: Naples wasn't pleasant, with those mountains spewing lava everywhere. And they were so immersed in this reverie that it didn't occur to them to speak ill of the Altifredas, who were passing slowly by in their carriage through Chiatamone, going toward the Riviera, enjoying the whole eruption.

At a little window in Capodimonte, Annina Manetta was in an agony of impatience, waiting for Vicenzino Spanò, who hadn't arrived, so that she could go out; in the Pavilion of Divine Love, the *Pungolo** had arrived with the news. Enrichetta Caputo, who was feverish that evening, had read it, cried out, and fainted. Her mother and Ciccillo de Marco were taking care of her; the hunchback had read the paper and turned pale, thinking that now Enrichetta was his, out of gratitude; he had prevented her from climbing Vesuvius the evening before with the people who had come to get her. And in a villa in Posillipo, the two newlyweds in

*"The Goad"

love, Peppino Sarnelli and the oldest daughter of the Cafaro family, who were handsome, rich, and good, were watching the eruption with their arms around each other, unafraid, since nothing frightens lovers who are embracing.

The *Pungolo* gave the first list of the victims:

Vicenzino Spanò, medical student; his body was recovered.

Guido Castelforte, age twenty-four, doctor of medicine; his body was recovered, embracing that of his fiancée.

Margherita Falco, age eighteen; see above. (One had to die so as not to leave the other.)

Elvira Brown Castelforte, age twenty-five; she had gone farther than anyone else; her body has not been found. A liquefied piece of metal was found: perhaps her gold choker. She is supposedly buried under the lava.

Nevermore!

I

The enormous Piazza del Mercato was overflowing with people. The crowd thronged not only the vast square, leaning against the booths of the street artists, the tents of the itinerant ice vendors, and the little yellow and red carousel, but it was growing thicker along the Corso Garibaldi, around the amphitheater and the courthouse, and thronging the many balconies and terraces that overlooked the piazza. It was not only the twenty thousand inhabitants of Santa Maria who had left their houses on that mid-August evening, to attend the great fireworks display in honor of the Assumption of the Virgin Mary, but also those of nearby villages and cities, who were drawn by piety and curiosity. In the crowd of common people, leather tanners from Santa Maria rubbed elbows with greengrocers from San Niccola la Strada, silk spinners from San Leucio, *torrone* makers from Casapulla, farmers from Maddaloni and Aversa, and the pale prostitutes who loll on sofas and languish for an entire season on the banks of the lakes; on the balconies lit up with little colored balls, the middle class and the aristocracy of Santa Maria were entertaining the middle class and aristocracy of Caserta and Capua on the occasion of the Assumption.

On the terrace of the Military Society, festooned with Chinese lanterns, Giorgio Lamarra, the handsome blond artillery lieutenant, the dream of the romantic young girls of Santa Maria, was celebrating noisily with a group of cavalry officers from Nice who had come from Capua; from her aunt's small balcony, Clementina Riccio, a languid, melancholy brunette, didn't take her eyes off that terrace and Giorgio Lamarra; on the balcony of her godmother, Donna Peppina Cannavale, Paolina Gasbarra, nearsighted, lively, and witty, leaned on the railing and laughed loudly so that Giorgio Lamarra could hear her; on one of the five balconies belonging to the newly married Rosina Sticco that were full of light and people, Grazia Orlando, the loveliest creature in Santa Maria, pretended to chat with Caterina Borrelli, her Neapolitan cousin, but in reality she was watching the terrace and Giorgio Lamarra—not one of them was looking at the eight pyrotechnical machines lined up on the right side of the piazza, or the castle, which would figure in the finale where they were to see the triumph of the Ascended Madonna in the sky.

On the large balcony of the town hall, the two Roccatagliata girls, the mayor's daughters, both ladylike slim brunettes, were bustling around the three Capitella sisters, the daughters of the mayor of Caserta, who had arrived in their carriage accompanied by their father and brother, who was to marry Cristina Roccatagli-ata: this marriage seemed logical to all the girls of Cristina's age, eighteen, and irregular to all those who were twenty-three to twenty-five, among whom was Emma Demartino, who considered Cristina too young. The three Capitella sisters each had a dowry of a hundred and fifty thousand lire; Clelia Mesolella, who had been married for a year, had brought two hundred thousand to her marriage; half a million had awaited Felicetta de Clemente when she had wed her young husband, so that the balcony of the town hall, the richest in dowries, past, present, and future, was the object of much sighing on the part of males and females. The two brides, Clelia and Felicetta, were glittering with jewels.

The balcony of the Marquis Tarcagnota also displayed three large dowries of a hundred and fifty thousand lire, in the persons of the three Tarcagnota sisters, who had attended the leading boarding school in Naples and were proud and aristocratic; but the three girls were afflicted with such enormous, increasing corpulence, their fatness was so oppressive and ridiculous that all the fine wits of Santa Maria made fun of them. On this evening they were all proud to entertain the old duchess of San Demetrio, who had come from her castle in Recale, and their balcony shone nobly, lit up with twelve adjustable lamps. From time to time in that brightness, one could make out the form of an awkward person, or a fat, almost swollen cheek; or the powerful curve of an a shoulder stood out; or a short, fat arm, that looked as though it would split its sleeve, gestured: it was one of the Tarcagnota girls moving about.

But the greatest stir was on the five balconies belonging to Rosina Sticco, the new bride. Rosina, the oldest of the seven Astianese sisters, had married Vicenzo Sticco, a grain merchant, the week before and had brought him fifty thousand lire; the father of the Astianeses was very rich, but he had seven daughters, who ranged in age from twelve to twenty-five. Sticco was the richest man in town; he had the finest house, with five balconies overlooking the piazza, which he had had furnished by a rug merchant from Naples, and Rosina, with legitimate pride, was entertaining guests in her home for the first time. She was wearing the rose-cut diamonds that her husband had given her, eight or ten heavy, gleaming bracelets, and she was proud of herself, of her red and gold living room, of her blue and white bedroom. She was showing all these things to everyone, men and women, without concealing her pride.

The house was full of unmarried girls and of brides. First, there were the six Astianese sisters, like stair steps, brunettes, blonds, and tawny haired, one for every taste, of all sizes, who were everywhere, so much so that it seemed as though there were twelve of them, each with her suitor in the piazza, or on some balcony, or at the windows of the Garibaldi Society; then there were Grazia and Maria Orlando with their young cousin from Naples, Caterina Borrelli; then Lucrezia Piccirillo Sticco, Rosina's sister-in-law, the wife of a landowner from Casapulla; then Luisa Ciccarelli, the ugliest girl in town, who was stupefied by her ugliness, with her mouth that was always slightly open and her big hands hanging at her sides; then Carmela Barbaro, the county clerk's young wife, who came from an Albanian village in Calabria and was half Oriental and half mountain dweller; she was very dark, smoked constantly, and seldom spoke. Finally, there was Rosina's good friend and contemporary Emma Demartino, the tall, pale, gracious one, slightly anemic, the sentimental girl with brownish large eyes and a languishing head.

As people arrived, Rosina Sticco grew more and more serene and affectionate, with the natural, calm good humor of young brides; as people arrived, she would call her husband with increasing sweetness:

"Vicenzino? Vicenzì?"

The girls looked at everything curiously, upstairs and down, from the balconies to the living room, the foyer, and the bedroom, with enigmatic smiles, slightly disturbed by that matrimonial atmosphere that was the reality of their dreams. Certainly there were not six young men like Vincenzino Sticco in Santa Maria, but the six Astianese sisters were sure that they would make better marriages than the oldest: Emilia dreamed of living in Naples; she was ambitious and daring; she would give up rose-cut diamonds and diamond bracelets, but she wanted to go to Naples; Grazia Orlando, who actually did have twenty thousand lire, a military dowry, was thinking about her fine blond officer with the squeaky sword, who was so much handsomer than Vincenzino Sticco;

Maria Orlando, calmer and not as dreamy, calculated that she would be courted by Ciccillo Mosca, the oldest of the Mosca brothers, who would occasionally walk beneath her windows on the hot afternoons at La Croce; Caterina Borrelli, who was still too young, had the nonchalant, conceited air of Neapolitan girls, who pretend to scoff at marriage; Luisa Ciccarelli, the stupid one, was touching the materials to see whether they were silk, wondering whether the lace on the curtains could be imitated by crocheting, reading the visiting cards that had been sent in congratulation, besotted, bereft of ideas or dreams. Emma Demartino, Rosina's contemporary and best friend, was following her everywhere she went, as though she were in a dream, and when Rosina would say, in her sweet, melodious voice: "Vicenzino? Where is Vicenzino?" Emma would experience an emotion that was like a stab of tenderness.

Suddenly, a flood of brightness made everyone, men and women, run to the balconies, but it was a false alarm: flares were being lit at the Military Society; Giorgio Lamarra was holding two in his outstretched hands, and he was fantastically illuminated with red. Clementina Riccio was waving her handkerchief from her balcony, as though she were fanning herself; Paolina Gasbarra, the lively shortsighted one, was shouting, "Bravo, bravo!" unable to restrain herself—and Grazia Orlando was very moved to see her handsome officer in all that red light, like Faust or Mephistopheles. In that light, it could clearly be seen that ices were being carried around on the balconies of city hall; the Roccatagliata girls were coming and going, offering them to the guests, while even in the Crocco house the windows had been opened, since the light made them think that the fireworks were beginning. The two Crocco sisters, dark-haired and skinny, all decked out in trinkets, steel pins, and paste buckles, leaned out, showing their angry faces of old maids who were stubbornly intent on finding husbands. The two Caputo sisters, who were faithful friends, leaned out, too, coiffed and dressed in the fashion of fifteen years earlier, but completely calm and laughing, patiently tolerating the forty years that they had been available; and finally, Lady Irene Moscarella, the prehistoric old maid, leaned out, she whom everyone remembered as an old maid from time immemorial, the spinster who was no longer angry or laughing, but who had lapsed into apathy, into the near immobility of life.

Emma Demartino had remained on the balcony, thinking, while two bands, one on the right and one on the left, were playing first the royal march, then the hymn of Garibaldi. She was happy, very happy, for her friend Rosina, but she was thinking that if Carluccio Scoppa, who was studying law in Naples, hadn't failed two subjects, she, Emma, would have gotten married before Rosina: Carluccio was in Naples studying for the makeup exams; in November he would graduate, and perhaps they would marry the following August. What a shame that they had to lose a year this way! True, she was already twenty-five, and this gave her a latent feeling of melancholy that was like a hint of bitterness: she felt pale and wan, as though she had lost her bloom, while Rosina Sticco at twenty-five was abloom with rosy color and smiles. With what grace Rosina went around serving sugared almonds and marsala wine, pleased with her big silver trays, her little glasses from Bohemia, the sweets that had come from Naples, and the wine that Vincenzino had ordered from Sicily! If only Carluccio had had better luck on his exams! Now it would be she, Emma, who would be giving her friends almonds to celebrate her marriage. And she declined to eat the ones that Rosina offered her. A deep melancholy had descended on her soul.

Meanwhile, the firing of mortars announced that the spectacle was beginning: one of the machines began to fire off three-colored fireworks, rotating pinwheels, and rockets. The people of Santa Maria applauded; the whole crowd swayed in satisfaction. Emma shook herself, shrugged her shoulders, tried to free herself from melancholy: in the final analysis she wasn't the unhappiest of all. It was true that those Astianese sisters had a dowry of fifty thousand lire, but there were six of them: they were a regiment, an army corps; they frightened young men; who knew if they would get married? And the three admirers of Giorgio Lamarra were three silly little things: neither Clementina Riccio nor Paolina Gasbarra had a military dowry, and Grazia Orlando's father would never give her to an officer—and he, Giorgio, was fooling all three of them; he had a sweetheart in Florence, as everyone knew; he would marry only her.

The tricolor pinwheels burned gaily, showering sparks, while the peasants from Altifreda, Curti, Centauro, and Cancello Arnone looked on with open mouths; the hearts of the Astianese girls and of Don Juan's three admirers were on fire, but what remained? A bit of smoke, a great shadow, a painful flashing in people's eyes.

But another machine lit up immediately: there was a volley of rockets that mounted very high in the sky, where they opened with a weak explosion, like a flower opening, and divided into many delicately colored stars. The Capitella girls were very rich, but for this reason no one dared to court them: they had extravagant expectations; there wasn't anyone in the province who could satisfy them; would the Capitellas get married? And the Roccatagliata girl also, the youngest, was wrong to marry before the oldest: it's bad luck, and in the provinces people pay attention to this. As for the Tarcagnotas, with all their money, they were too fat; they couldn't marry; Luisa Ciccarelli was too ugly, too much of an imbecile. In spite of the delicate rockets opening softly in the sky on that mild August evening, in spite of the ecstasy of that crowd dazzled by the light, in spite of the gaiety of all those young men and women scattered on the balconies, Emma felt a wave of bitterness come over her: life for her and for the others seemed a long, joyless path, a hard one without rewards or anyone to help them along the way.

It happened that, beneath the bright yellow light of a golden shower that sparkled like a fountain of fire, the two windows of the Crocco household displayed their gallery of old maids. The two Croccos shook their beribboned heads, shiny with pomade, and leaned over to see whether a large supper had really been prepared in the Tarcagnotas' dining room; they showed their yellowed dentures in grimaces that they thought were ironic smiles. The two Caputos, with their hair worn low over their temples in two bands, their long, flat bodices, their black silk aprons, were admiring the Feast of the Assumption for at least the fortieth time and were smiling meekly, while Lady Irene Moscarella, dressed in gray green wool, her thin hair gathered into little rolls over her temples, kept her bland, expressionless face, her indifferent air of one who is dead to everything human.

Emma saw these five women, all either pale or livid beneath the great golden shower of fireworks, and she seemed to see in that group a whole vision of the future: it struck her that she and all her friends were destined to grow old as spinsters, that they would become angry and mean like the two Crocco sisters, meekly resigned like the two Caputo sisters, or indifferent, like Lady Irene Moscarella. Yes, perhaps one of their fiancés would die like Chiara Caputo's, two days before the wedding; another would end up an old maid because of her father's terrible avarice, like Margherite Crocco; someone else would not marry due to a passing fit of mysticism, like Vincenzella Crocco; and another, who could know? Perhaps she, Emma Demartino, would remain an old maid for no reason at all, because of a whim of fate, like Lady Irene Moscarella. And the power of suggestion was so strong that she already could see herself at fifty-five, dressed in gray green wool, with her thin

hair that no longer covered her yellow skull, with her bland wrinkled face that no longer showed any emotion, in that egoistic
supreme separation from all things.

But after it had applauded the fountain of fire, the crowd fell
silent. The last part was beginning. First, there was a big tri-
umphal arch made up of paper lanterns, on which "Long Live
Mary" was spelled out on the pediment; then four explosions of
fireworks in the form of a square, with a bunch of flowers, rockets,
and large and small pinwheels. When the arch was completely illuminated, in the space within, the statue of the Virgin began to rise,
with her head against the sky, her white hands open and extended
so that she seemed to be saying good-bye to the earth. She went up
very slowly, as though she were being liberated; the powerful
machinery that was lifting her was invisible. She was dressed in
her red tunic with her blue cape, and she was smiling at heaven and
saying farewell to the earth. The bells of the cathedral, San Carlo,
the Croce, and Sant'Antonio were playing the Gloria. The incandescent fireworks were burning, throwing flames, showering
sparks, disgorging stars; flares had been lit on many of the balconies. The people in the piazza were kneeling, praying, and cheer-
ing the beautiful Mother, who had been assumed into heaven.

II

The new mother leaned her head and shoulders against a big pile
of pillows, with the finest pillowcases decorated with embroidery;
her two pale white hands were stretched out on the wide piece of
antique lace that formed the edge of the sheet, nearly touching the
blue damask bedspread. She was wearing a batiste nightgown
frothy with lace; on her dark, wavy hair she wore a formal cap; and
her fingers, wrists, and ears were adorned with many jewels. She
moved but little, spoke little, and was a little pale, but beatifically

smiling; from time to time she half-closed her eyes, as though she were falling asleep.

From the morning on, the house had been full of people coming and going; she was dazed by so many questions, so many congratulations; finally, at around two, she had kissed her baby, who had been brought to her in his baptismal gown, and everyone had gone to the cathedral: now she was breathing quietly, resting, since the coming and going would begin again in a little while. Emma, who was sitting at the foot of the bed, was talking to her softly; she hadn't wanted to go to church.

"Rosì, why name him Gaetano?"

"That's what Vincenzino wanted," said the new mother, moving just one finger to mean that there was no way to oppose him.

"It's an ugly name."

"Ugly, yes, but the baby is beautiful."

"All your children are beautiful," murmured Emma.

"This one is the most beautiful," said the mother placidly.

"When you have your fifth one, you'll say that he's the most beautiful."

"I suppose so," agreed the new mother with a smile.

There was a moment of silence. Rosina Sticco was smelling a bunch of herbs, the herb dear to women in childbirth.* Emma was lightly tracing the damask of the bedspread with her finger, as though she were caressing it; and her dark eyes were more languid than ever; her anemic pallor had a slightly yellowish tinge that was not yet noticeable.

"Your sister Giannetta didn't come from Caserta?" asked Emma.

"No, poor thing: her mother-in-law is ill. Maria sent me a telegram from Piedmont, and Costanza wrote me from Verona."

*Rosemary

"Costanza has two children?"

"Yes, two."

"And Maria?"

"One, and Giannetta has one."

"And you have four: your mother is already a grandmother eight times over."

"Yes, eight, but she still has three daughters to marry off. I'm not talking about Olimpia and Teresa, but Assunta is already twenty-eight; it bothers me, you know . . ."

A slight blush rose to Emma's forehead.

"What does it matter?" she murmured. "Women don't have to get married."

"Don't say that, dear. Any bad marriage is always better than none."

"Why?"

"Because of the children, Emma," the happy mother said softly, gravely.

A veil of tears trembled for a minute in Emma's eyes.

"Children, children," she said. "What are you going to do with these beautiful children?"

"For now, I'm going to enjoy them . . . They're so little! But Vincenzino is full of ambitions for them."

"You always talk about the children, the two of you."

"Always."

"And do you like the future?"

"It's not mine that interests me, it's theirs."

"It's true," Emma affirmed.

Again, they were quiet.

"How late they are," murmured the new mother. "They must have taken the long way, or Mama has detained them."

"Grazia is the godmother?"

"Yes, Grazia Orlando, and her husband is the godfather."

"Remember, Rosina? It seemed that Grazia was crazy for Giorgio Lamarra, and then she got over it and married Attorney Santangelo."

"She did the right thing: what's the point of loving a scoundrel like that?"

"Clementina Riccio also got over it and married her cousin, the cripple . . . What admirable constancy!"

"What's the point of these loves that go on for so long, Emma?"

"When you love someone, who notices time?"

"Vincenzino and I got married after being in love for six months."

"But there's only one Vincenzino, and he's yours." And her intonation was somewhere between spiteful and humble.

An expression of real pity appeared on the sick woman's face. But she had no time to say a comforting word to Emma. Caterina Tarcagnota, whose married name was Savarese, was entering, enormous in a black dress, with shiny red cheeks and arms that looked like colossal sausages. And immediately, she exclaimed with a sigh:

"Oh, my dear Signora Sticco: some of us get so much, others nothing!"

"You have time, my dear baroness. You'll have twelve."

"If only an angel could fly over and say 'amen,' but I don't count on it; everything depends on your constitution."

"So they say, but who knows? Hasn't Signora Roccatagliata had some, even though she's so thin?"

And while they were talking, other women arrived for the customary visit. Clelia Mesolella, with a new dress and a pair of new earrings, two large emeralds; Felicetta de Clemente, five months pregnant; Carmela Barbaro, whose Oriental eyes had grown weaker and weaker due to the low atmospheric pressure in Santa Maria;

Lucrezia Piccirillo Sticco, who had come here expressly from Casa-pulla: sitting in a circle around the bed, speaking in discreet voices, they discussed children, pregnancy, horrendous and strange cases, whims, smells, surgeons, and midwives.

Everyone showed the greatest interest in finding out from Rosina how the birth had gone, and she retold the same story: how she hadn't suffered at all; everything had gone very well; the handsome boy was in a hurry to be born. And the listeners nodded their heads, satisfied, smiling, and one after the other they delicately redirected the conversation; each one would tell her own little motherhood story, and in the meantime the others listened with extreme courtesy, following all the details, making observations; they all supported one another, or when someone disagreed, a friendly discussion would begin.

The atmosphere was full of these touching voices, of this sweet and solemn talk, which may seem frivolous but which sums up a woman's whole life: these recent brides who were already mothers, or were going to be, or deeply wanted to be, gave in to the affectionate impulse that sprang naturally from their open hearts.

Already pink, Rosina listened, nodding with approval or disagreeing by moving her hand: she, the happy mother. Straight, motionless, leaning against the head of the bed, Emma, the only unmarried woman in the room, was listening. All that maternity flowing from their words, smiles, voices, expressions, certain intonations, all that happy wave of love, came to her, penetrating her soul; it was as though she were drinking in all that sweetness; and in the spasm produced by that too-strong impression, her pale face became waxen, and her large dull eyes became sadder and dreamier than ever.

From the road came a faint noise of wheels: the new mother's thoughts wandered, her eyelids closed, and she remained as though absorbed in her thoughts; the ladies waited in silence. A loud bell echoed through the whole house; the new mother's face was transformed. And in the foyer there arose a gentle clamor of servants and family:

"He's back, he's back! May Saint Gaetano bless him! May he grow up healthy! May he grow up healthy!"

The small being came forward, solemnly carried in the arms of Grazia Orlando Santangelo: his long white baptismal dress, covered with lace and embroidery, hung down on one side; his little head was resting on a lace-covered pillow. His slightly red face, with its delicate skin, was framed by the frills of a ceremonial cap; his open eyes had the very serious stare of newborns; his mouth opened from time to time, with that adorable movement of birds trying to peck; and a tiny little hand moved its fingers slightly, as though the new-born were thinking to himself. Grazia Orlando Santangelo, in a brocade dress that she had ordered expressly from Naples and a hat sparkling with pearls, very dignified and attentive, held the baby in her outstretched arms, as though he were on a tray. Behind her the midwife, Donna Mimma Scaletta, showed off her pea green silk dress, white crepe shawl, black hat laden with red roses, and a mosaic pin depicting the Roman Colosseum; she was fat, as midwives traditionally are, with their air of good-humored indulgence and their gravity of important persons. After came Vincenzino Sticco, the happy father, and Ciccillo Santangelo, the godfather, in tailcoat and white tie, and the whole procession of old aunts, Signora Astianese with her three still-unmarried daughters, and Emma, Ferdinando, and Carluccio, Rosina's three children.

A large circle of people standing formed around the bed, and in the middle, Grazia Santangelo went up to the new mother: she said, in a slightly quavering voice, as she handed her the baby:

"My dearest friend, I give you back a little Christian."

The mother took the little Christian in her arms, leaned over him, and kissed him at length. Perhaps she said something to him silently; perhaps a fervent maternal blessing fell on the little Christian, giving him a store of love that would last throughout his existence. A deep silence, filled with emotion, reigned in the room: Grazia Santangelo clasped a pearl-and-emerald bracelet on Rosina's wrist, the godmother's gift; Ciccillo Santangelo had placed on the bed a red leather case that contained a little silver place setting and a glass, the godfather's gift to the baby. Then Rosina handed the little Christian back to Grazia; the two women kissed, and the baby was carried around in Grazia's arms.

First he was taken to be kissed by his father, Vincenzino Sticco, who barely dared to brush his cheek, for fear that his big mustache would make him cry; then to be kissed by his grandmother, who made the sign of the cross on his forehead and chest; then to the Astianese girls, who were his young aunts, and around to all the women. The new mother followed this introduction with her eyes, smiling a bit and bowing her head, at each tender phrase that all those people were murmuring to the little Christian. And it was like a concert: the little one with his tiny face, his barely formed little nose, the slight grimace that he made with his mouth, that soft blond fuzz that stuck out on his forehead from beneath his little cap, the delicacy of his tiny restless fingers, moved all the guests. They kissed him very gently, so as not to hurt him or make him cry; they spoke to him with words of love, those little names that the female heart invents; the young women looked at him curiously, as though he were an object.

Tommaso, the servant, was going around with wine and sweets; sugared almonds were offered jokingly to the solemn little Christian, and godfather Santangelo wanted to make him drink some marsala, to get him used to it early on, he said. And there was a spurt of small-town jokes about which marsala little Christians prefer, while the nurse,* Olimpia, a peasant from Cascano, stood in a corner, very lovely beneath the white batiste handkerchief that was kept on her head with large hairpins, in her skirt of shimmering purple silk, her yellow silk decorative sash, and her black silk bodice trimmed with gold.

Finally it was the children's turn: Emma and Ferdinando had followed Grazia Santangelo around step-by-step, as she carried their little brother around in her arms; Emma touched his baptismal gown from time to time; Ferdinando stood on tiptoe but couldn't see anything; Carluccio clung to Ferdinando, since he was only two and still in a girl's skirt. When everybody had kissed the baby, Grazia Santangelo sat down, and the three children stood contentedly in a circle around her. The little Christian was in the middle, with his eyes wide open, yawning with his little mouth; the three children looked at each other in silence. Only Emma, the little woman, kissed him: Ferdinando put his arm around his head, on the pillow. And since the little Christian was waving his hand, Carluccio gave him his small finger, and the newborn baby's little hand closed around that finger.

The evening shadows fell over the room. The weary new mother leaned her head against the pillows. The room was empty. She turned, searched next to her with her hand, and called in a weak, gentle maternal voice:

"Gaetanino? Gaetanì?"

The baby looked at his mother with his bright little eyes. But behind a curtain a light sob was heard: Emma Demartino was crying.

---

*Wet nurses were not uncommon in wealthy households in nineteenth-century Italy and France.

III

She measured the work that she had done with an experienced eye and saw that the stocking now came down to the end of the calf: she would have to begin a series of double stitches to make the stocking narrower at the instep. She was counting the stitches carefully, with her thumbnail grazing the needles, when a very soft whistle rang out in the quiet afternoon air, in the vast summer small-town silence. Immediately Emma raised her eyes and looked between the slats in the green blinds: Federico Mastrocola was at his place in the small window of the barn, showing his dark head, which was a mass of curls, and twirling his sprouting little mustache. Emma looked down again and began to recount the number of stitches that she had to decrease; her pale, anemic spinster's face had grown increasingly colorless with the years.

Her eyes had lost the brightness and languor that used to make them so attractive; they had become rather dull and opaque; two bags of yellowish loose skin with a hint of blue had formed beneath her eyelids; her lips had gone from red to pink, from pink to a very pale, delicate purple. Her cheeks still kept their elegant delicacy, and the skin on her temples, near her ears, was as white and transparent as porcelain; but what aged that face hopelessly wasn't her poorly disguised sparse hair or her thin neck: it was those two bags of loose skin, which were already tinged with the colors of decay and decomposition. Her hands working on the stocking were still beautiful, but her wrists already had some faint wrinkles that made the skin look shriveled; her waist was still slim, but an unmistakable sign of age was the cut of her dress, which was loose and flat over the chest, short-waisted, and wide over the hips, that very strange but very characteristic cut of old maids; another sign of old age were those black leather square-toed shoes, tied with black silk ribbon, with wide low heels, that made no noise when she walked.

Again, Federico Mastrocola's whistle rang out softly; it was answered by another whistle: on Chiarina Oliver's veranda, a small blond person had appeared, in a flood of sunshine, her blue eyes blinking: it was Emma Sticco, whom everyone called Mimì because of her sweet beauty. Behind her, Chiarina Oliver could be seen sitting, bent over her embroidery, a large bedspread completely covered with stars; she could be seen, intent only on her work, uninterested in what her friend Mimì Sticco might be doing beyond the veranda. Actually, the blond Mimì also held an embroidered star in her hand, but she wasn't working, as she smiled at Federico Mastrocola. The distance between Mimì's veranda and Federico's barn was short, since both extended into the Olivers' big garden, which was green with fig trees; next to it was the Tarcagnotas' garden, but the other two fat ladies had gotten married, one in Nola, one in Naples; the oldest one had died in childbirth; all the windows were shut up; so that there remained only Emma Demartino's balcony from which the maneuvers of the two lovers could be seen. But the green blinds were never raised; the old spinster was never seen; she stayed behind the slats knitting stockings. And in that hot peace of a summer afternoon, in that silence of a sleeping small town that is digesting its macaroni, the two lovers would chat, under the sleepy supervision of Chiarina Oliver, who pretended not to hear.

"Why didn't you come to Mass this morning?" said the little blond, trying in vain to look severe, while her eyes shone with love.

"I had to go with my aunts, the Caputos, to the station."

"Did they leave?"

"Yes, by now they're already at the convent in Mondragone."

"I'd like to go there, too, Federì," exclaimed the sweet girl with a laugh.

"Wait until you're sixty-five, Mimì, and there's no longer a soul around who loves you."

For a moment the spinster Emma Demartino's hands froze on the needles as though immobilized. Then she passed one hand over her forehead, as though she were wiping away a cloud: her hand was cold, and her forehead was freezing.

"After the station, where did you go?" the implacable blond inquisitor began again.

"I looked for you in the piazza."

"That's certainly not true."

"I swear."

"It's not true: don't tell a lie."

"Then ask Luisa Ciccarelli and her husband: I was with them."

"I will: I saw Luisa at Mass; she was wearing a red hat that was very unbecoming; she was yellow, and horrendous."

"She did look horrendous, but her hat was green and her face was the color of dirt," exclaimed the lover in a triumphant voice, avoiding the trap that she had set for him.

Mimì Sticco, the clever girl who had set the trap into which Federico hadn't fallen, was laughing; Chiarina Oliver was also laughing softly; but behind the green slats no smile touched Emma's purple lips. She was concentrating on putting the double rows on the right and left of the needle, identical so that the stocking would come all the way down to the heel. She heard everything that the two young people were saying, that day as she had for two months, over the flowering pomegranates in the Tarcagnotas' garden and the wide, thick foliage of the fig trees in the Olivers' garden; and the chattering of the two lovers, alternately merry and sentimental, was accompanied by the shrill cry of a type of cicada; and the west wind sometimes carried a bad smell of tanned leather or rotting hemp; sometimes it carried the scents of the Astianeses' garden, where the tangerines were in flower. But the blond Mimì and Federico were unaware of what was going on around them, whether stench or perfumed odor, the song of the cicada or the low buzzing of flies; they were unaware of what went on behind the green blinds.

"Oh, Mimì, who did you go to Mass with?"

"With Mama and Aunt Lucrezia Piccirillo."

"Is it true that they want to make you marry Antonio Piccirillo?"

"I prayed to Saint Emma this morning not to let that happen."

"Will Saint Emma protect us, Mimì?"

"Let's hope so," murmured the little blond, joining her hands together.

"Let's hope so," repeated Federico, who had grown thoughtful.

Behind the blinds, the spinster looked at the white knit sock without seeing it: she distractedly pricked her cheek with the fourth needle. The loose skin gave in to the pressure of the needle, but not a drop of blood could be seen beneath that withered anemic skin. Recalling the words of hope that the two young people had pronounced, she bent her head at the memory of dead hopes, worrying her bloodless cheek, stirring up her dry, silent heart.

"But is there really a Saint Emma?" Federico asked, trying to play the skeptic.

"You're a heretic, Federico," Mimì Sticco observed gravely.

"She's not on the calendar."

"Read the French calendar, read the Book of Martyrs: you'll see."

"If there's not a Saint Emma, we'll canonize you, Mimì."

"Of course, because of my patience with you."

Their idyll nearly turned stormy. The little blond was furious, because Federico didn't have an ounce of seriousness in him: he joked about everything; no one could be sure of anything with him; Federico was angrily chipping off pieces of plaster and hurling them savagely at the snails in the Olivers' garden. Chiarina Oliver had to intervene; at a certain point in the day, she always had to intervene between the two lovers.

"What have you got against snails, Federico?" Chiarina asked, laughing.

"Nothing: it's Mimì who's bedeviling me," he muttered.

"All right, dear Federico: leave me alone."

"I will."

"Find someone else."

"I will!"

"What a shame that Aunt Assunta Astianese, the spinster, married the old court clerk last year: you could have had her."

"You're right, but I'll write to Lady Margherita Crocco in Teano, to ask for her hand."

"Ask for both their hands, Margherita's and Vincenzella's, with the vineyard and the money, who have fifteen thousand ducats and fifty years between them."

"Yes, yes, of course, I should."

And they scowled at each other, Federico pulling nervously at his long curls, Mimì tapping her small fist on the balcony railing. Chiarina watched them with an affectionate malice in her eyes, holding her embroidery aloft and playing with the thread.

Federico had lit a cigarette and was smoking and looking up in the air.

Behind the blinds, Emma Demartino was watching the two quarrelsome lovers: wasn't it like this, perhaps, that she used to argue so sweetly with Carluccio Scoppa so long ago? Her limp hands, pale against her brown wool dress, had fallen into her lap, and the spool of thread had fallen on the floor: the cat, the old, fat red cat, who was curled up sleepily and egoistically, did not even deign to play with the spool.

"Mimì," called Federico.

She shrugged and didn't answer.

"Don't be mean, Mimì; you know that I love you." And he said these last words softly, looking around.

"Shh!" she said, touching her lips with a finger; however, her features were already calmer.

"Why?"

"People can hear you."

"Who do you think will hear me? Everybody's asleep at this time."

"If Mama finds out that I talk to you every day from here, she won't let me go to Chiarina's anymore, and she'll lock me in my room."

"Please, what will we do?"

"We'll die," the little blond exclaimed tragically.

"Come on!"

"Sure, I'd be capable of throwing myself in a well, as they say Paolina Gasbarra did for a blond officer."

"But she didn't die."

"She didn't die right away; she was still alive when they got her out, but she caught bronchitis and died three years later of consumption. I'll die of tuberculosis, too, Federico, if I can't marry you!"

"Don't say things like that; you make me sad."

And they looked at each other with such melancholy, and they were so young, so healthy and good looking, that Chiarina Oliver burst into fits of laughter.

"But why is your mama so mean?"

"Mama is kind," the blond replied, "but she says that we are too young, that it's a youthful whim, that you're not serious, that we must wait. I'm sixteen: Mama wants me to become an old maid."

And hadn't she also been sixteen once, the woman who was listening and no longer knitting, behind the green blinds? When, in what sweet and faraway time of life? And hadn't she thought then that her youth would never end?

"Are you coming to Maria Orlando's wedding?" asked Mimì.

"As you like, Mimì."

"Yes, come; Maria Orlando wants to have a big party now that she's managed to bury two husbands one after the other, the two Mosca brothers: now she's taking her third, and all the wealth of the Mosca family will go to the Orlando family. Come; we're going, Godmother Grazia wants to introduce you to Mama: try to please her; don't say anything, but be serious."

"Can I flirt with Godmother Grazia?"

"No sir, you insolent boy!"

"Then with your Aunt Olimpia, who's so nice?"

"Of course not, Mr. Scoundrel!"

"So what will I do? Who will I talk to, so that you won't get mad? Shall I attach myself to your godmother, Mimì? She's old enough, don't you think?"

"Be quiet!" said the blond, looking at the window with the green blinds.

But the godmother didn't move or give any sign of life; she didn't even flinch at the cruelty of those two lovers. Hadn't she, too, perhaps, been cruel in her happiness so long ago, in the past that had fled so quickly away?

"What shall I say to your mama, to please her, Mimì?"

"Talk to her about her children: that's all she's interested in."

"I'll talk to her about you: I'll tell her I love you."

"You're crazy, Federì: talk to her about the boys."

"Who does she love most?"

"She loves them all."

"Doesn't she prefer Gaetanino?"

"No, no, she loves us all equally. Talk to her about Ferdinando, who's at military school in Naples; he was first in his class last week, or talk to her about little Carlo, who's the best looking of all . . ."

"You're the best looking of all . . ."

". . . Don't interrupt me. Congratulate her on Gaetanino, who was so miraculously cured of smallpox; tell her how cute Paolino and Petruccio are. In a word, remember that she doesn't care about anything but us or love anyone but us."

"And Papa?"

"When women have children, they don't love their husbands anymore," the little blond said solemnly.

"And do you intend to act like that, too?"

"Yes, I do, too."

"Then I'd rather not have children."

"Don't let Mama hear you say that."

Mechanically, Emma Demartino had reached into her pocket, had taken out her rosary, and began to say it to herself, so that she wouldn't have to listen to that conversation any longer. It was a prayer that rose monotonously from her soul, a prayer without energy or ardor. She had nothing more to ask, either for herself or for others. However, from long habit, she added a Prayer for the Dead to each Our Father, since Carluccio Scoppa had died of cholera in Naples; and when she said this prayer, which asked for peace for the poor dead man, who was buried in a cemetery without flowers, under an unmarked stone, a faint, melancholy surge of life welled up again in her heart. No, the poor dead man hadn't loved her: he had stayed in Naples, where he had married a Neapolitan woman; she, Emma, had remained unmarried, for no rhyme or reason—but now she was without remorse, just full of a great sadness, as though everything were moving away from her, in a great, slow funeral cortege. In fact, the faint striking of a bell, the death knell, was heard from the Church of the Cross.

"Who died?" Mimì asked.

Emma listened.

"Lady Irene Moscarella," answered Federico. "She was ninety, or maybe a hundred and twenty. Who will take her place now?"

And maliciously, without speaking, with smiling eyes and gesture, Mimì the blond pointed to the balcony of her godmother, Emma Demartino.

Emma had seen everything: that glance, gesture, and smile, and they had reached her heart, without causing her to flinch. In truth, she now dwelt in a state of supreme spiritual inertia: nothing human could cause her hope or regret.

»»» «««

The State Telegraph Office
(Women's Section)

I

As Maria Vitale closed the door of her house, she was struck by a chilly morning breeze. Her rosy plump cheeks grew pale from the cold; her chubby young body shivered in her cheap dress of black light wool: she pulled around her neck and chest a flimsy shawl of blue wool, which took the place of an overcoat. In the small Piazza del Bianchi, not a soul was around: the blacksmith's shop was still closed, the *Pungolo* printing press's iron grate was still down: from the small streets of Montesanto, Latilla, Pellegrini, and Santo Spirito that led into the little piazza, there was no one to be seen. A clear gray light fell over the old houses, on the windowpanes wet with frost, on the filthy little streets: the sky had the cold brightness, the fine metallic glint of a winter dawn. Then, as she started out, Maria Vitale, surprised by the silence and the solitude, was struck by a vague uneasiness.

"Perhaps I'm leaving too early," she thought.

She tapped her foot on the ground in anger. They didn't have a clock in the house, and she had to be at the office by five minutes to seven. So, in the morning, the problems started: her mother woke up very early and called from the other room:

"Mariè?"

"Mama?"

She would go back to sleep, the sound sleep of healthy, untroubled girls. After five minutes her mother would call again, in a louder voice:

"I hear you, Mama, I hear you: I'm getting up."

But since drowsiness lured this big, robust girl back to her little bed, her mother gave up and grew quiet, and her father, the cabinetmaker, intervened with his loud voice:

"Mariattella, get up: if you don't, you'll have to pay a fine."

Then she made up her mind, and got up in one motion, yawning, not daring to look around at the bed, for fear of falling back on it, next to her sister, Serafina: she walked quietly, in her blouse and skirt, so that she wouldn't awaken her two brothers, Carluccio and Gennarino, who slept in the same room, behind a curtain. She went to the kitchen to wash her face; instead of coffee, which her family didn't drink, she ate a piece of fruit left over from the evening before and some stale bread, while she dressed in a hurry. Careful as she was, she had arrived at the office after seven four or five times, because she didn't have a clock; the director had noted this tardiness in the register, and Maria Vitale had paid a one-lira fine. What would happen was that her ninety-lire monthly salary, between the six that the government took in taxes and the other two or three that were paid in fines, would be reduced to eighty in a flash. So, every morning she was overcome with fear, and sometimes she went out too early.

"What time can it be?" thought Maria Vitale, saddened by the idea that it was very early.

In the Alley of the Bianchi, which leads to Via Toledo, she met the itinerant coffee man, who went around with his little stove with the coffee machine buried in hot ashes and three or four little cups hanging from his fingers.

"Galanòt, what time is it?" she asked.

"It's five thirty, signorina. Will you have a drop of coffee?"

"Thanks, I don't want any."

An hour—it had to be a whole hour—she had gone out an hour early! She went along with tears of vexation in her eyes, thinking of that good hour of sleep that she had lost: an ingenuous, childlike pain mounted to her lips from her heart, as though she had been done a great injustice, as when she was a little girl and she had been punished for something she hadn't done. What should she do in that hour? Oh, how she would have loved to go back home, back to snuggle in her warm little bed, with her cheeks buried in the pillow and her arms wrapped around her waist! That was useless now: she had left too early; she would never get back that beautiful hour of lost sleep. Where should she go? The cold breeze bothered her as it threw in her face the dust of Via Toledo, which had not been swept yet; she couldn't walk around at that hour, alone like a madwoman, among the fruit sellers who were coming down from the orchards to the central streets of Naples, among the garbage trucks that were lumbering gloomily along the pavement. Should she go pick up Assunta Capparelli, who lived in Ventaglieri? Assunta worked in the afternoon; that day she didn't have to get up early; certainly—lucky her—she was sound asleep. Should she go get Caterina Borrelli, who lived in Pignasecca? Nonsense! Caterina Borrelli was a shameless sleepyhead who got up at a quarter to seven, dressing in six minutes and arriving at the office at a run, laughing, yawning, with her hat askew, her braid undone, her tie inside out, and answered the roll call: "Present!" Bitterness spread through Maria Vitale's good soul: it seemed to her that she was all alone in the great world, condemned to sleep too little, condemned to be always cold and sleepy, while all the others slept in warmth, in the intense, deep happiness of sleep. And in her bitterness there was also a sense of abandonment, disgust with poverty, childish pain. Bowing her head as though in resignation, she entered the Church of the Holy Spirit automatically, seeking refuge and comfort.

Immediately, that holy semidarkness, that soft, humid air that wasn't cold calmed her. She sat down on one of the painted wooden benches, the ones for the poor who didn't have the money for straw seats, and she rested her head on the back of the bench in front of her. Then she prayed quietly, saying one Gloria, three Our Fathers, three Ave Marias, and three Requiems, as is prescribed for those who happen to enter a church when there is no service. Then she prayed to God to protect the soul of her grandmother, who had died the year before, and the health of her mother and father; she named her brothers and sisters, her godfather, her superiors at work, travelers at sea during stormy weather, the souls of the abandoned. She asked nothing for herself: in that physical torpor she felt no spiritual, personal desire; no need took shape in her soul. She only, confusedly, would have liked to ask the Madonna to let her sleep until nine in the morning: a wonderful happiness that she had never enjoyed. She only felt a stubborn sleepiness enter her head and then travel down her neck and spread slowly through her body: she slept, with her face in her hands, her hat over her forehead, her legs motionless, and her trunk bent over in discomfort; as she slept she heard the sexton coming and going, moving the seats, sweeping the marble floor. Suddenly a voice murmured in her ear:

"Vitale? Are you asleep or crying?"

"Here, Mama," murmured Maria, awakening.

Giulietta Scarano, a girl with beautiful chestnut hair and a small head on a fat body, with bright eyes that were always ecstatic, was smiling mildly beside her, looking toward the high altar, where the Holy Spirit was shining in a golden halo.

"I fell asleep. Did you mistake the time, too?"

"No, I leave early, because I have to come on foot from Capodimonte. I always come in this church as I pass by."

"Shall we go?"

"Yes, it's time."

They set out, Maria Vitale feeling sore and very cold all over, her legs asleep, and Giulia Scarano moving wordlessly, like a sleep-walker.

"What's the matter?" asked Maria.

"Nothing," said the other, in a melancholy young voice veiled by sobs.

"It's still Mimì, isn't it?" Maria insisted, with the wise, compassionate air of an invulnerable young woman.

"Yes, it still is."

"You'll ruin your health over him."

"If only I could!"

"Don't say such terrible things. Oh, what an awful thing love is! That's why I've never wanted to have anything to do with it."

"Of course, people always talk that way when they're not in love with anybody. It's because Mimì is sick; I can't see him and I feel as though I'm going to die," the other girl burst out, unable to stand it anymore.

"Oh, the poor thing! Let's hope that it's nothing," murmured Maria, immediately growing serious.

Going down Via Monteoliveto, they had nearly reached the fountain, Giulietta Scarano absorbed in the misery of her love fixation, Maria Vitale shaking her head over human sadness. She was not an intellectual type like Caterina Borrelli, who was always writing a novel in a great big notebook; she couldn't write poetry like Pasqualina Morra, but she understood that love is a great trial.

"I can't see him," repeated Giulia Scarano.

"Write him a short letter."

"I've already written him three since yesterday, each one four pages long, but I don't know how to send them. Mama has fired Carolina, the servant who liked me and helped me . . ."

"Mail them."

"I don't have the money for stamps, and I'm ashamed to send them without any. Who knows, perhaps Galante, the cleaning lady, could help me . . ."

They were in front of Palazzo Gravina, an austere gray building made of old travertine stone, with very simple architecture. It looked, and was, very old: behind its thick walls it had certainly seen a succession of happy and dreadful events, love feasts and ambitious plots, sweet human affections and ferocious human passions. Now its ground-floor rooms, hermetically barred on the street, were open to the public under the portico and inside the courtyard, and were used as a post office. Around its high, wide windows, on the corners of its dark walls, was a vertical flowering of white mushrooms, the porcelain telegraph insulators, from which branched out all those very thin wires, ten or twelve on one side, three on another, four or five on a third, a light network that spreads out over the world. On the middle balcony, behind a large metal shield on which was written STATE TELEGRAPH OFFICE, a man was smoking, leaning against the metal bars, looking at the morning sky.

"Who's that?" asked Maria Vitale.

"It's Ignazio Montanaro: he probably worked last night."

On the wide staircase, Cristina Juliano caught up with them, greeting them without stopping. She looked like an ugly man dressed as a woman, with her big, deformed body, too large in the shoulders, too long in the bust, with no hips, large hands, knotted wrists, and enormous feet. She was still wearing a white straw summer hat, drawn down over her forehead in order to lessen the effect of her frightening white blind eye and to accentuate the marvelous wealth in her two large black braids, an abundant richness of hair, the weight of which pulled her head backward.

"It's hopeless, I just don't like this Juliano," said Vitale.

"She's not a bad person, though," answered Scarano, with the mildness of one in love.

They were joined by Adelina Markò.

"What cold!" she said in her soft, seductive voice.

With her fingertips she smoothed her very blond, wavy hair that the wind had blown out of place. But the wind had brightened her beautiful mouth with the lips delicately raised at the corners and had given pleasing color to her blond's fine golden complexion. The lithe, lovely eighteen-year-old was well protected in a warm, elegant coat of deep green cloth. A white feather waving on a green felt hat gave her the look of a young amazon, the appearance of an aristocratic English girl ready to mount a horse. Adelina Markò was neither poor nor lower class: she was one of the two or three fortunate young women who worked only to have dresses made or to buy linens for their trousseaus. When she came into the office, Adelina Markò, with her benevolent smile, her rhythmic footstep, her fine, expensive clothes, her eccentric hats, and her exquisite perfumes, looked like a young duchess who deigned to visit this place of work, a royal infanta, kind and human, who enjoyed spending a day among the humble telegraph workers.

They were still talking about the cold, in front of the white door on which was written WOMEN'S SECTION. Gaetanina Galante, the cleaning lady, came to open the door, showing her pointed, olive-colored face, like that of a crafty fox.

"Has the director come?" the three assistants asked, almost in a chorus, as they came in.

"Of course not! She's still at Mass," answered the other, sneering with the insolence of a spoiled servant.

They took a breath. It was always better to get there before the director, in order to demonstrate zeal and love for the office. As they entered that dark foyer, bureaucracy seized the minds of all the girls; office jargon, ungrammatical and conventional, sprang to their lips. Those who had already arrived—some seated, some near the window, in order to have a little light—were already talking about lines, breakdowns, blockages on the direct circuits. The large room was dark, and they instinctively lowered their voices. The only window looked out on the narrow Vicolo dei Carrozzieri; the darkness in the foyer was increased by the huge wardrobe that was divided into many little wardrobes, in which the assistants kept their hats, umbrellas, and coats; the poorest kept their lunches, which they had brought from home; those not so poor kept their embroidery or their crocheting; the most studious or romantic, their notebooks. In the middle of the large room, there was a big mahogany table; on one wall, a canvas sofa; there was no other furniture. In the free spaces on the walls, enclosed in thin black wooden frames without glass, hung an alphabetical list of the assistants and day workers, internal regulations, the latest directive from management, and a geographical and telegraphic map of Italy. Nobody read this dusty, fly-specked print anymore: what they were all interested in was the piece of paper that was being passed from hand to hand, which gave each of them a particular line for that day. The director, with her round handwriting, all flourishes, wrote on one side in a column the number of the line, and opposite the name of the assistant who had to work there that day for seven hours. As soon as they came in, everyone looked eagerly for this paper while they were still taking off their hats and unbuttoning their coats. And since there were good lines and bad lines, lines with no work and lines with a lot of work, lines that demanded infinite patience and lines that demanded particular speed, so there was a corresponding cacophony of exclamations.

"It's true that I'm a silly thing and that I still don't know how to receive well," murmured Maria Vitale, "but to put me every two days on Castellammare is unbearable. If I do fifty telegrams in seven hours it's amazing: I'll learn fast at this rate."

"You should thank God," said Emma Torelli, a big, tall, pale blond, with a strong Piedmontese accent. "I wish I didn't know how to receive, like you. Today they've given me Salerno, that dreadful line: it's Saturday, and there will be the lottery tickets that the people from Salerno play in Naples. One hundred and eighty dispatches, just like that! I've got a headache; you'll see what an argument I'll have with my correspondent today, if things don't go right!"

"But what is the director thinking, to give me Avellino?" exclaimed Ida Torelli, the second sister. "I can't work with that old man: imagine, dear Markò. A sixty-year-old mummy who can't stand the women's section. When you call him, he doesn't answer; after an hour, he calls you all of a sudden and throws a tantrum. He interrupts every word that you transmit; he asks explanations for every dispatch. He's irascible, pigheaded, and insolent: it's a line that makes you want to kill."

"I'm on Genoa," answered Markò, in a voice like a song, "which isn't fun. The line is so long that the battery doesn't last long enough; the current fluctuates: sometimes it's very strong, which blends and mixes up all the signals, sometimes it's so weak that the signals can't get through. When you call the correspondent, he doesn't hear you; when he calls you, you can't hear him. Things go well for ten minutes, and you begin to breathe. Of course, after eleven minutes the line breaks down. There are more and more dispatches; they're always three hours late."

The unhappiest of all were the *hughiste*, the best assistants, who had learned how to work on the Hughes printing machine. Two people work on this complicated machine that looks like a cymbal, and both workers must be able and pay attention. Now, when she made up these couples, the director never paired off two friends, in order to avoid excessive chitchat; she always paired off a skilled worker with a less skilled one. Therefore, there was no love lost between these pairs: one treated the other with contempt, and the other felt the contempt. These slaves did not complain aloud, because of their pride, but each one stayed sulkily in her corner, without talking to or looking at the other. Maria Morra was rehearsing the part of Paolina in *Our Good Peasants,* in which she was supposed to act an amateur role at the Theater of San Ferdinando; her friend Sofia Magliano, a brunette with a long goatlike face, exuded vexation as she crocheted a star; Serafina Casale, small, cold, proud, pale, and quiet, was taking some iron citrate in a wet wafer for her anemia; and Annina Pescara's beautiful round face was very distressed at the idea of having to work with that boring Serafina Casale.

In a dark corner, Giulietta Scarano begged and implored the servant, Gaetanina Galante, to do her this favor, for the love of the Madonna, to send someone with a letter to Mimì. Galante said no, protesting that she didn't want to get mixed up in these affairs anymore, that she had had too many problems, that the assistants were too ungrateful, that she, the servant, was worth a lot more than so many who were proud of themselves because they worked on machines and then had to humiliate themselves to her for every sort of favor. Giulietta Scarano grew pale; her voice shook before this servant who was torturing her with an insulting refusal, drowned in a stream of triviality: she went so far as to take her hand pleadingly.

All at once, over the angry, complaining voices, drawled in boredom, over the explosions of amorous complaints and office jealousy, a hiss was heard: the director was coming in. Immediately, in a chorus of voices that ranged from soft to loud, sharp, slow, quick, and tardy, these words were heard:

"Good morning, Director."

She nodded her head, with a friendly smile on her lips the color of dead roses. Her fine ash blond hair was pulled back precisely, not one hair out of place: her entire face had the soft plumpness, the ivory pallor of old maids of thirty who have always lived in a convent or girl's boarding school, in a natural chastity of temperament and fantasy. In fact, there was something of the cloister about her; in her black cashmere dress, in the white lace collar, in the cautiousness of her footsteps, in the lowness of her voice, in the softness of her hands, which seemed as though they should join only in prayer, in the unexpressive transparency of her gray eyes, in the way she bowed her head to think. She took off her cape and gloves, quietly, and looked at the girls, noticing that Ida Torelli was not wearing her usual girdle, that Peppina de Notaris was wearing a man's ring on her little finger, that Olimpia Faraone was wearing too much makeup. The assistants looked nonchalant, but they were conscious of being under that cold stare, and they grew nervous. She was the first to enter the machine room, and she sat in her place behind the desk, writing slowly in some of her notebooks with her head bowed, as though she were doing homework.

"A storm's brewing in the director's office," said Caterina Borrelli, insolent and nearsighted, pushing her glasses up on her pug nose.

The assistants were still in the foyer, since it was five minutes to seven: every minute that the electric bell rang, someone arrived. There was Peppina Sanna, very thin, very English, in a dress of little black-and-white checks, in square-toed boots without a heel, a big blue veil around her hat and head, with an umbrella, a little black leather handbag, and a Tauchnitz edition always under her arm.* There was Maria Immacolata Concetta Santaniello, a big, fat white girl who swayed like a duck as she walked, whom everybody made fun of, who was full of religious scruples and who invoked

---

*Bernhard Tauchnitz was a German publisher who started *The Library of British and American Authors*, a series of inexpensive paperbound editions, that was very popular in nineteenth-century Europe.

the names of Jesus and Mary before sending a telegram. There was Annina Caracciolo, very dark, with curly black hair, a mouth that was red and open like a carnation, big, languid eyes, and the indolent bearing of a Creole: she was a lazy worker, whom no reproach or mimicking could awaken. They chatted in groups of two or three, glancing furtively toward the director, who was still writing, looking like a schoolgirl handwriting expert; as soon as she heard a voice that was too loud or a laugh that was too shrill, she raised her head and went:

"Shh!"

Then, the bell rang, and the liquid voice of the director was heard:

"Ladies, let's go in the office."

In silence, they filed in front of her desk and headed toward the machines. In the bright light of the big room, illuminated by three windows, could be seen the sleepy faces of those who hadn't slept enough, the wan faces of those who had caught a chill, the pale faces of the sickly; and from all flowed a feeling of peaceful resignation, of indifferent boredom, of apathy that was almost serene. Their workday was beginning, without laughter, everyone mechanically busy in those first transmissions: bent over the machines, some were unscrewing the little steel needle that imprints the signals, some were putting in a new roll of paper, some were using a brush to moisten the revolving cushion with ink, some were testing the springiness of the keys. Then, in the morning quiet, there began the tapping of keys on anvils, and every once in a while, these phrases rang out monotonously:

"Director, Caserta doesn't answer."

"Director, everything's fine with Aquila."

"Director, as usual, Genoa's asking for a spare battery."

"Director, Benevento wants to know the exact time."

"Director, Otranto has a dispatch of four hundred words, in English."

The winter sun was now entering the office. No one raised her head to see its thin rays on the windows.

II

All of a sudden, in the quiet of the machines that seemed to sleep, in that holiday afternoon repose, a light telegraphic signal was audible. No one heard it: the few assistants, who were unfortunately condemned to come to the office from two thirty to nine on Christmas Eve, were doing other things. Maria Immacolata Concetta Santaniello, with her hands hidden in her lap under her office smock, was silently saying the rosary; Pasqualina Morra, the poet, was reading a small volume of verses by Pietro Paolo Parzanese, a book permitted by the director; Giulietta Scarano was writing quickly on a sheet of telegraph paper; Adelina Markò was drowsing with her hands in her muff, and a little fur around her neck; Annina Caracciolo, the lazy one, was looking up in the air, with her expression of distraction that enabled her to work less; and the others were either napping or whispering with their neighbor, or pretending not to hear so they wouldn't have to move. But the call continued, louder: it came from a solitary machine in the corner of a small table. Concetta Santaniello interrupted one of the Sorrowful Mysteries and said in a prayerful tone:

"Foggia's calling."

But she didn't move: she didn't do anyone any favors, and she never moved unless ordered to by the director, with the placid egotism of a thoroughgoing bigot. And as the calls became more and more frequent, the assistants, in order to say something, to interrupt that annoying silence, to make noise, each said:

"Foggia's calling. Foggia's calling. Foggia's calling. Who will get Foggia? Who will answer Foggia?"

"Quiet, quiet, here I am," said Annina Pescara, entering from the foyer and running to the Foggia machine. "What a nuisance, Foggia!"

And she began to receive, holding the piece of paper with two fingers of her left hand and writing the telegram for Naples on the white paper. After the first words she called her inseparable friend.

"Borrelli, come here."

Borrelli folded up a literary paper called *The Butterfly,* which she was reading in secret, put it in her pocket, straightened her glasses on her nose with that instinctive motion of the nearsighted, and ran to her friend. Borrelli now was also reading the piece of paper attentively:

"What an imbecile!" she exclaimed, all of a sudden.

"Excuse me, I think he's not an imbecile; he's very much in love with his girlfriend," answered Annina Pescara, offended in her sentimental proclivities.

"Yes, but a man shouldn't humiliate himself like that," Borrelli retorted, in a learned manner.

The love telegram went on; it was fifty-nine words long; it came from Casacalenda and was addressed to one Maria Talamo in Naples, on the Riviera of Chiaia. It was a very sweet telegram; the man gave vent to his love on that family holiday, pitying himself for his unrelieved solitude, desiring a word of affection from the beloved, swearing that nothing would make him give up this love, neither the wars of men, nor the adversity of destiny, nor even the scorn of her, the adored woman. All this was read by Maria Morra, who had also run up, by Peppina Sanna, who had stopped as she was passing by, by Caterina Borrelli, and by Annina Pescara, who was still receiving.

"What a lot of rhetoric!" exclaimed Borrelli.

"This telegram is from Casacalenda?" asked de Notaris, moving closer.

"Yes, yes," was the answer.

"Oh, it's the usual; one comes almost every day; I've gotten them, too," said de Notaris.

"He's the one who's so sentimental," yelled Ida Torelli from her place. "Wait, I want to read it, too."

They were standing in groups of ten around the Foggia machine. Annina Pescara proudly drew her small body up on the cloth armchair and repeated those passionate words in a solemn tone. The girls all listened intently: Ida Torelli, the skeptic, snickered; Caterina Borrelli, the wit, shrugged her shoulders, as though she was fed up with so much foolishness. But the others were rather moved by this incandescent telegraphic prose and were already whispering about their own loves, for better or for worse. Adelina Markò, the beauty, had two or three admirers whom she couldn't stand; instead she loved a high-placed employee of the telegraph office, a widower with two sons who was too old for her, whom her parents would never let her marry; and she tormented herself with this love, unable to ever speak to him or write him. Peppina Sanna thought about her handsome naval officer, with the blond mustache and curly hair, who was then sailing in the waters of Japan and who would not be back for two years. Maria Morra, the amateur actress, had loved faithfully for five years a clerk who was awaiting a promotion in order to marry her and who in the meantime was consoling himself by rehearsing with her Marenco's *Celestial One* and the farce *A Cold Bath*. Annina Pescara, as she finished reading the dispatch, thought of her second-year law student, who then had two more years to study in order to get his bachelor's, two to become an attorney, and four or five more to wait to get some customers or a position as a judge in some small town in Basilicata. These humble, respectable, ardent loves surged in these young souls on this holiday that they had to spend in this big room full of machines, far from the people that they loved, far from simple family pleasures. But discussion immediately ceased. The director had come in from the other machine room, where she had been to confer with the shift foreman of the men's section.

"What is this crowd, ladies? Back to your places, back to your places; you're not allowed to leave the machines. Look, Torelli, Naples–Chiaia is calling you and you're here talking! Sanna, have you finished copying that file that I gave you? De Notaris, here's a telegram for Potenza: send it. Markò, are you leaving your place, too? What a plotting mania!"

"Director, there was a telegram," said Caterina Borrelli, with her usual impertinence.

"What telegram?"

The director caught up with it in front of Annina Pescara and read it. The assistants, who had returned to their places in complete disgrace, looked at her to see what impression that love telegram had made on that nunlike face. But she revealed nothing and, turning around, went and threw the telegram through the hole in the door that divided the men's section from the women's. On her way back, she stopped in the middle of the room and said severely:

"Ladies, I've always thought that I directed an office of serious girls, of hardworking employees who forget in this place the thoughtlessness and the rashness of the young. I see that I was mistaken; I see that a trifle, a bit of foolishness will distract you, absorb you, and make you forget your work. If you're not careful, things will go badly. Remember, ladies, that you have taken an oath not to reveal the secret of the telegram: the best way is not to show any interest in what private individuals write in telegrams. So much for the next time."

There was a profound silence: no one dared answer. She had spoken slowly and dispassionately, without looking at anyone, with her eyes lowered. She wasn't cruel, but she felt her responsibility deeply, and she was constantly nervous lest her section look bad before her superiors. There was a profound, uncomfortable silence: everybody was thinking; they didn't go back to work, as though they were in a trance. Only de Notaris's keys clicked, transmitting to Potenza the words of the dispatch.

"What time is it?" asked de Notaris.

"Five thirty," murmured Clemenza Achard, her neighbor.

And then:

"Five thirty-one," yelled Ida Torelli.

"Thanks," said de Notaris and wrote the time on the dispatch being transmitted.

Five thirty. It had been night for half an hour, and yet there were three and a half more hours until nine. The gas lamps had been lit, but since there was no work, the director had ordered that they be lowered: the men's director always preached gas economy. So it was hard to read or embroider in that half light: the shadows of the machines flickered strangely on the little tables, with the wheel where the paper unrolled, with the little movable steel arm, with the power key that looked like the crosslike hilt of a sword. There was a glimmer here and there: the glass bell that protected the little lightning rod, the pad of a key, Olimpia Faraone's crystal earrings, the black hairpins that Ida Torelli wore in her blond hair. A deep silence: unable to read or write or embroider, the girls were thinking.

"So what did Naples–Chiaia want from you, Torelli?" asked the director from her post.

"Nothing, Director: we exchanged banalities."

"Did she speak to you afterward?"

"Yes, she said that it was Christmas and she was bored."

"I hope you told her to be quiet!"

"I didn't answer her, Director."

"All right."

Conversation on the lines was severely prohibited, except for urgent office business. They made allowances for tardiness, for mistakes, for lack of ability, but for conversation with the correspondent never. Whoever was caught in the act of talking was punished first with a warning, then with censure, a serious punishment: an angry letter was written to the correspondent from the director's office, telling her that this must never happen again. And yet this was the most frequent transgression, committed with the greatest gusto, because it was the most dangerous. In fact, even in that silence, in that half light, Annina Pescara was talking in a very low voice with the correspondent in Foggia. The latter, after transmitting the love telegram, had immediately exclaimed:

"What an oath we have to take, don't we, signorina?"

And Annina Pescara had immediately answered that it didn't bother her to take the oath, that love was a beautiful thing; the correspondent had answered that love makes three-quarters of humanity unhappy. The sentimental discussion on the line grew more intense: Annina Pescara, who guessed her correspondent's words, from the simple noise of the needle that makes the signals, didn't need to let the paper run; then, so that her answers could not be heard in the office from the noise of the keys, she had tightened the screws of the keys hard, so that they wouldn't make noise. Plunged in shadow, with her shoulders leaning against the armchair, she seemed to sleep, with one white hand stretched out motionless on the keyboard: her friends and colleagues saw that she was talking to Foggia, because they had done it themselves on other occasions; but who would have dared to betray her? Over there, Olimpia Faraone was talking to Reggio, as usual, but being more careless and less expert; she let the paper run, tearing it off piece by piece and putting it in her pocket: for twenty days she had been talking every day with the Calabrese correspondent, who had already written her two love letters. Holidays were just made for forbidden correspondence: the male employees got bored in their solitary offices, without any work, and they felt the need to chat; the girls were bored, too, and talking with a stranger like that, at such a distance, stimulated their fantasy. This took place quietly; but on the sinner's face could be read her satisfaction at the little deception she was committing.

"Pescara?" called the director.

"Director?" the latter said with a jump, frightened as she pressed her hand hard on the keyboard, to make her correspondent be quiet.

"Well, are you sleeping?"

"No, Director."

"Ask Foggia if it has anything."

Annina Pescara smiled in the shadows. After a minute, in a monotone:

"Director, nothing with Foggia."

But Caterina Borrelli, who always had some trick up her sleeve, said to Olimpia Faraone:

"Faraone, ask Reggio if it has anything."

"All's well with Reggio: there's nothing."

The director didn't notice anything. She was writing a letter to a school friend of hers, who was a country school teacher in a small village in Molise. She was wishing her a happy new year, recalling the good old days in the convent, telling her that she was happy with her post, and yet the letter was melancholy. Poor woman, she, too, was falling under the same spell as all those girls, brought together to do nothing in a big room in the semidarkness, in front of a silent machine, on the sacred day of Christmas, while their relatives, friends, and dear ones had assembled at dinner, to play bingo and have family dances. Even she, who no longer had any relatives and was alone in the world, was seized by homesickness, by a nostalgia for those she had loved. She raised her head and looked at all those motionless girls, some dozing with their foreheads in their hands, some talking with their neighbor in low voices—and she stopped scolding them, feeling the sadness of those long, cold hours falling over their youth; she stopped scolding them, for there arose in her heart a deep pity for them, and for herself.

Maria Vitale sneezed twice.

"To your health," said Clemenza Achard in a very light voice.

"Thanks," and she blew her nose hard. "Are you here? I didn't even see you. Aren't you on the other shift?"

"I changed places with Serafina Casale, who preferred to come in the morning, since it was Christmas."

"And so you made a sacrifice?"

"It wasn't a sacrifice."

She was a very delicate creature, thin, rather ugly, frail, and timid, who wasn't good at the work and who always remained silent on the worst lines, gifted with angelic patience, never complaining, never raising her voice, trying to remain in the background as much as possible. She rendered her friends a number of small services, as a matter of course: she brought a tapestry design for slippers to one, a fashion card to another, a novel to a third, a piece of music to a fourth; she sat at a line that was going badly, exchanging with a nervous colleague who couldn't stand it anymore; she was always ready to change shifts with one, to remain in service two or three hours longer for another, even to give up her holiday, which fell every two months, to anyone who asked her; she lent her umbrella and went home in the rain; she lent her shawl and went out shivering with cold. All this without pretense, in gentle silence, with such affectionate naturalness that her colleagues were no longer grateful. They knew that they only had to say, in order to obtain any one of these sacrifices from her:

"Oh, Achard, please, please do me this favor . . ."

She couldn't resist; she would say yes, immediately. Sometimes they became rude with her, who was always very well mannered. In fact, the day before, Serafina Casale had said to her:

"Achard, please let me come in the morning, tomorrow. It's Christmas; we're having a big dinner at my house, and then we're going to the theater. You're surely not going anywhere, and you don't care about Christmas: change places with me."

Of course, the gentle creature had not dared to answer that Christmas was very important to her and that she had been planning to go to the opera at San Carlo that evening for a month, and she had done the favor for the person who had asked her so untactfully. When the director had found out, she had said:

"Poor Achard! You take advantage of her."

So Clemenza Achard was there, next to Maria Vitale, who had a red nose and a runny eye because of a bad cold. Maria was giving vent to a childlike bad mood, physical and spiritual, because she couldn't breathe and because she had to be in the office on Christmas.

"Imagine, dear Achard, that I barely had time to listen to the three Christmas Masses at the Church of the Pilgrims; then we went with Mama, my sister, and Gennarino to my godmother's, Donna Carmela's, who's a baker and has a lot of money. She served us coffee: but what coffee! I thought it was poison: I can't taste anything with this congestion, and then the thought of having to come to the office at two thirty! I had dinner alone, at one thirty, on a corner of the table: a little dish of pasta and a bit of stew, then some fruitcake that my godmother gave me. My whole family had dinner together at about three; then they went to the theater in the daytime, to the Fondo: they're doing *Madame Angot's Daughter*!

Lucky them, who can have a good time! By nine, they'll already be home asleep, they who've had the good luck to enjoy Christmas."

"If your papa comes to get you at nine, why don't you have him drive you to the theater?"

"What, at that time? Much as I'd like to, I'll be so tired that I'll have only one desire: to sleep. Oh, Achard, I've always liked to work, also to bring money home, to relieve Papa, who has asthma, from having to work too hard, to comfort Mama, who lost her health with her children, but this is too hard a life. When everybody's enjoying the holiday, we're in the office: God the Father rested on the seventh day, and we never rest. If we get sick and don't come to the office, they subtract those days at the end of the month, as they don't even do with servants; if we're absent on purpose, they don't pay us and they scold us. We no longer know what Christmas, Easter, and Carnival are. Do they give us eighty-four lire at the end of the month? And all this work? This is nothing but slavery."

"Why didn't you teach school?" asked Achard with a sigh.

"I was too stupid," said Maria, bowing her head. "I always made spelling mistakes in my Italian homework, and I didn't understand arithmetic."

"So what can you do about it, then? You must have patience. Christmas or another day, isn't it all the same thing? And then, some suffer for one thing, some for something else."

"Poor Achard, you must have problems, too. Does your stepmother treat you badly?"

"No, no," said the latter immediately, but in a trembling voice, "my stepmother is kind."

"Don't you have a brother who's in the military?"

"Yes, yes, in Pavia."

"Did he come home on leave?"

"He couldn't get one."

"So he probably spent Christmas alone, too, poor thing. Are you unhappy because of him?"

Clemenza Achard shook her head, as though to say no, but tears slowly flowed down her cheeks, without sobs. Maria Vitale, seeing her cry, was saddened for herself and for her colleague; suffocating from her cold, she began to sob loudly.

"What's the matter, Vitale? Why are you crying?" asked the director.

"Nothing, nothing," the former mumbled between sobs, grumbling, coughing, blowing her nose.

"What do you mean, nothing? Why are you crying? Tell me."

"I'm crying because I have a cold, there," said the other, with childlike irritation.

"Lucky you, if you don't have any other reasons to cry," murmured Giulietta Scarano. "Breathe ammonia and you'll get better."

"Nonsense! A nice cup of tea is better," suggested Peppina Sanna.

"Don't listen to them, Vitale," called Ida Torelli. "Get under the covers and try to sweat tonight: tomorrow you'll be cured."

"Vitale, don't do anything they say, my girl," said Caterina Borrelli, laughing.

There was a stir in the office. The prefect of Naples had communicated a circular to the central office that said that the prefects and subprefects of the kingdom were advised to seize issue 358 of the paper *The Spiral,* since its article entitled "The Monarchy," which began with the word "Until" and ended with the words "in a pool of blood," contained opinions against the actual state of things, insulted institutions, and incited revolt. Immediately the gas flames were raised; the keys began to hum. Campobasso, Avellino, Cassino, Pozzuoli, Castellammare, Salerno, Caserta, Benevento, Reggio, Catanzaro, Aquila, Foggia, Bari, Bologna, Genoa, Venice, Ancona, Cosenza, Casoria, Potenza, Sora, Otranto were ready to receive the notice of the seizure: for five or six minutes, the office became animated once again, the din of transmission spreading through the two rooms, like a cheerful rebirth of activity. Then there was a minute of pause and silence, then a metallic screeching of needles; the correspondents repeated everything to Naples, the number of the telegram, the title of the paper, the issue, the title of the article, the words with which it began and ended, in short, the most important things, to avoid mistakes. A voice asked what time it was and was answered: it was seven. The flames were lowered, the assistants leaned back again in their chairs, resuming the thread of their conversations or of their thoughts. The correspondent from Catanzaro had immediately said to Maria Morra, after the telegram concerning the seizure:

"Was it worth all that bother for so little!"

"What do you mean? Are you joking? Who knows what was in that article?" Maria Morra had answered.

They talked about politics: Maria Morra hated the Republicans, calling them "rags"; the correspondent was a Socialist. The correspondent from Cassino condemned the telegram, too, telling Clemenza Achard that she had had to answer so fast that she had swallowed a glass of liqueur the wrong way and now she was coughing like a madwoman. Clemenza Achard was completely bewildered, not daring to engage in a conversation that was forbidden and yet afraid of seeming rude to the correspondent, if she didn't answer her. Not knowing what to do, she tapped one little tap on the keyboard, just one tap, very timidly, and Cassino, seeing that the conversation was not renewed, fell silent. At that moment, there arose from the Piazza della Posta, where already were heard the first explosions of Christmas fireworks, a long, very soft whistle. Peppina de Notaris, in spite of her presence of mind, blushed with her delicate brunette's complexion, and all of the assistants more or less either jumped or smiled. They all knew the passionate legend of Peppina de Notaris's lover. He was a young man who was dark and thin like her, a clerk at city hall: he adored Peppina. He stayed at the office until five; and if she was free in the afternoon, he went to her house and stayed there until seven, her dinner hour; he went back immediately after dinner. But when she was working afternoons, he ate a quick lunch and went and ensconced himself in the little Caffè della Posta, opposite Palazzo Gravina. Every half hour he gave a long, low whistle, as if to say: here I am, I'm here, I love you. There was never anyone in that little café, and Peppina's lover stayed there three or four hours, reading all the papers, talking with the owner, the waiter; he had made friends with everybody. In the summer, he sat in the doorway and talked with the tram drivers, who were waiting for passengers to leave for Posillipo. And he never forgot to whistle punctually every half hour, as though to say: cheer up, my beauty, I'm here, I love you, I don't have the heart to go amuse myself while you work, I'm waiting for you, have faith, be patient. The gentle romantic legend made the rounds of the women's section, and they all waited for the whistle, as if it were their own romantic interest. At nine, Peppina de Notaris was the first to leave, saying good night quickly; outside she would find her father, who was waiting to drive her home; but down a ways, under the arches of the walkway, in order not to attract attention, walked the lover. They exchanged a "good evening" in low voices, and the three of them went off, softly discussing what had happened that day in the women's section and at city hall. He looked neither tired nor impatient at having waited so long, alone in a café, doing nothing: she looked at him with infinite tenderness, without thanking him.

"Ladies," warned the director, "don't fall asleep, because the Signor Director will be here in a moment."

Those who were doing embroidery put it down, wrapping it in a little piece of newspaper; those who were reading closed their books. Pasqualina Morra took back the little volume of Aleardi's poetry to the director, who had lent it to her: she was the favorite, because she didn't talk or move from her place and because she had published verses "To a Violet" in a religious collection. Maria Immacolata Concetta Santaniello, known as "the high-spirited," in order to gain favor, began to read the Petersburg Convention for the international telegraph service. The first to move from her place to go see the director was Cristina Juliano.

"Director," she said, leaning on the desk and staring at her with her round, white, squinting eyes, "since the Signor Director is coming, tell him to let me go half an hour early."

"And why?"

"It's Christmas: I have to go dancing."

"Are you going to a party?" asked the director, looking at her dress of very cheap gray wool and the red chenille scarf at her neck.

"We're dancing at my house," answered the assistant very proudly, "since we rent rooms to some students . . ."

"When the director comes, I'll tell him."

Cristina Juliano went back to her place, swinging her long masculine body. It was Caterina Borrelli's turn:

"Director, since the Signor Director is coming, tell him that I'd like to leave half an hour early."

"Are you going dancing, too?"

"I have to go to the Sannazzaro, to Marini's first performance."

"What is she performing?"

"Cossa's *Messalina*."

The director frowned.

"I'll tell him," she answered then, in a dry voice.

"Can Annina Pescara come, too? I don't go anywhere without her."

"It seems to me that you're asking too much, Borrelli."

Two or three others went to ask for this half hour, a miserable thirty minutes begged for like a favor. Adelina Markò was going to San Carlo; Olimpia Faraone was going dancing, too. The director promised to tell him, to intercede: she couldn't do any more, but there were too many requests. All of those who had made them kept looking toward the door where the Signor Director usually came in. He was a stern Piedmontese, who was sometimes difficult, who ran the female assistants like a platoon of soldiers, and whose cold temper and northern strictness frightened the bravest among them. He dined like a real Piedmontese, at the Wermouth of Turin in Piazza Municipio, and afterward always dropped in at the office for the evening inspection: he would take them by surprise, coming up behind them; he would only greet the director, and going around the telegraph tables, he would see every lateness, every mistake, every negligence, the blue printer's ink dirtying the machines, the keys that were too high, or too low, the registers that were badly kept, the disorderly sheets of telegraph paper. In a low voice, looking the assistant straight in the eye, he made his observation in few words: the assistant lowered her eyes without answering, tried to repair her mistake. At first, some had tried to excuse themselves, but he turned on his heel, turned his back on them, and walked off, as though he hadn't heard, not admitting in principle that anyone could talk back to him. In the daytime, in the sun, the director did not look as terrible; but in the evening, in the half shadows, with those proud, black inquisitor's eyes, with his flitting among the machines, with that deadly quiet voice that would not permit an answer, with the way he unexpectedly grabbed hold of the register, of the keys, of dispatches at a standstill, there was something unreal about him; he was terrifying. In the daytime, they called him "the Pope," because of his infallibility, or they called him "Mammone," who is the boogeyman of Neapolitan children; but in the evening, they only called him "the director," and those three syllables, whispered rather than spoken, made their blood freeze. But they got to the point of desiring his presence, at least to gain half an hour!

"What do you want to bet that tonight the director won't come, and we'll slave here until nine," said Caterina Borrelli to Annina Pescara.

"Where can he be if he doesn't come?"

"He's probably celebrating Christmas by having dinner with the assistant director."

"Borrelli, you're nasty."

"What do you mean, 'nasty'? They're getting married: didn't you know?"

Annina Pescara immediately confided the news to Ida Torelli; the rumor circulated in a low voice. The topic of discussion was this: can the assistant director keep her position when she gets married? According to the rules, the assistants could not; but did the rules extend to the director and the assistant director? There were those who thought so, and those who did not.

"You'll see, you'll see, she'll get married and stay here," argued Olimpia Faraone. "We'll have quite a good time, between the husband and the wife."

"What are you talking about? The assistant director is a bit nervous, but she's not mean, you know," said Peppina Sanna.

"She's really kind," added Caterina Borrelli. "You have to know her well, to appreciate her: I've been on her shift, and I know."

"But she won't stay here, after she gets married," said Peppina de Notaris. "There will be a competition, among the most able, for the position of assistant director."

Who could the winner possibly be? Whose new will would they have to submit to? Perhaps Serafina Casale's: proud, disdainful, arrogant? Or if Adelina Markò won, so beautiful and kind, that would be a great pleasure for everyone: but she wouldn't accept; she was supposed to get married any day now; she was a temporary employee, just passing through. Caterina Borrelli? Quick, intelligent, but too animated, too rowdy; she made too much fun of her superiors, they would never nominate her. Pasqualina Morra, the poet? Too young, soft, bland, lacking in energy and prestige.

"Ladies, ladies, quiet, please."

It was eight fifteen: this last hour, from eight to nine, seemed interminable. Those who had asked to leave early were seized with nervous trepidation: no, the Signor Director wasn't coming, and they would have to agonize until nine.

"Oh, Director, when is the Signor Director coming?" exclaimed Borrelli in a desolate tone.

"Here he is: do you want something?" a voice asked, at her shoulder.

In spite of her impertinence, Borrelli remained speechless. The director twirled his mustache as though waiting, watching her coldly, with the tranquil domination of men who are not vulnerable to women.

". . . Nothing, thanks," Borrelli murmured stupidly.

As usual, the director walked among the tables, with a slowness that made those who wanted to leave early tremble with impatience: he read the registers, at length, as though he were studying them; he read the time of all the telegrams at a standstill because of the office's holiday closing. Markò, Borrelli, Juliano, Pescara, and the others looked at the women's director beseechingly, as though begging her to leave her place, to join the Signor Director, to ask him that blessed favor. It was eight thirty. The director didn't understand, or pretended not to understand: she knew that she shouldn't interrupt the Signor Director in his inspection. Those minutes that were passing seemed eternities. At a certain moment, they began to despair: the director took a telegram that was being transmitted on the Terracina line and went to the door of the men's section.

"He's leaving, and he hasn't given us permission to go," they thought.

It was a false alarm: he returned immediately, and this time he went straight to the women's director's desk. He spoke to her in a low voice, without gesturing, but with an evident force and intensity: she listened, concentrating, with her eyes lowered, one very white hand stretched out on the desk, the other propping up her cheek: from time to time her eyelashes fluttered, as though she approved. But she didn't answer, and he went on talking, energetically, without raising his voice. The girls who had asked permission to leave were trembling, as though that last quarter of an hour represented their salvation. Every time the director opened her mouth, they gave a start: but she would say two or three words, as though she were making an objection, which the Signor Director would immediately counter and begin his peroration once again. At ten minutes to nine, unable to stand it any more, Caterina Borrelli said in a low voice:

"To the devil with it all!"

"Aquila says good night," said Adelina Markò loudly.

"Tell them right away that their clock is wrong, that it's ten minutes to nine, that according to the rule, they are no longer permitted to say good night and that they must wait for Naples to say it," retorted the Signor Director.

Eight fifty-five. Now the great final exhaustion had struck all the girls, the aridness of seven hours spent in the office doing scanty, thankless work. They were motionless, with no longer even the strength to get up and leave: they had intensely desired the hour of nine o'clock, they had worn themselves out in that desire, and now, exhausted, apathetic, dead tired from waiting, boredom, and pointless chitchat, they no longer wanted anything else. Those who were supposed to go home were thinking of supper and bed, feeling a completely animal need to eat a bite and to lie down; those who were supposed to go to the theater or dancing were finished, spent, bone tired; they no longer had any vanity nor felt any motivation.

"I'm staying here until midnight," grumbled Borrelli to Annina Pescara.

"And why?"

"Because I feel like it."

"Naples–Chiaia says good night."

"It's three minutes to nine. Wait," answered the Signor Director, with great severity this time.

Finally came the liquid voice of the women's director:

"Nine o'clock: ladies, by all means say good night."

The telegraph workers filed out one by one, saying a leisurely good night only to the director, since the Signor Director did not wish to be bid good night. In the foyer, lit by a flickering gas flame, in front of the open wardrobes, they put on coats, wound scarves around their necks, silent, their faces concentrated and closed in indifference, in a spiritual brutishness. Olimpia Faraone, in front of the mirror in the middle, brushed powder in her blond hair with a powder puff and the others didn't envy her; they looked at her, a bit astonished that she still felt like getting herself up. But her vanity, of the languid variety, thrived on that state of dejection. Adelina Markò had brought along a black velvet vest to wear after work; but now the desire to do so had past, and she had taken two white camellias from a glass of water and was attaching them to her chest, on a rich lace tie; and her entire beautiful person, from her soft, languid fingers, which couldn't manage to attach a pin to her lovely, blond, lithe neck, exuded an infinite fatigue. They went out, saying good night faintly, without kissing, as though stupefied, their faces relaxed in fatigue; outside, mothers, fathers, brothers waited to drive them home.

"What's the matter?" Giulietta Scarano's mother asked her.

"Nothing, Mama."

"Do you feel bad?"

"No, I'm tired."

Maria Vitale left with her father, wrapped in the mantilla that Clemenza Achard had lent her: Maria Vitale bent her head under the heavy weight of her cold and breathed deeply to overcome the congestion in her chest. The assistants went off by way of Via della Posta, Via Monteoliveto, Via Nuova Monteoliveto, and Via Trinità Maggiore, wrapped in coats, shadows vanishing into shadow, slightly bent, as though struck unexpectedly by old age.

III

The Signor Director's proclamation, in the form of a letter to the director, was as follows: The general political elections were scheduled for Sunday, April 8, and the second ballot for Sunday, April 15. In that two-week period, but especially on Saturday, Sunday, and Monday, there would be an overflow of telegrams on all lines, important and unimportant. Therefore, it would be left to the assistants' zeal as to whether they would work two, three, or four hours overtime, in addition to the seven hours' normal service. All those who gave proof of their devotion to their work should sign the paper below; they were left in complete liberty in this matter, since they were not under the slightest obligation. This proclamation was read in a solemn manner before all of the assembled assistants, in the presence of the director and the assistant director. The girls listened absentmindedly, feeling as though they had a bad headache, unable to make up their minds: they still had two days. And there immediately arose a ferment of rebellion; it developed in the office, in the street, at home. No, they didn't want to do overtime. Even ordinary work was martyrdom, oppression. Should they do more? Of course not. Why? For whom? They were treated like so many beasts of burden, with those three miserable francs a day, whittled away by taxes, fines, and sick days, when almost all of them had high school diplomas and served the telegraph office like men, as second-class employees who made two hundred lire a month. Could they protest that? Of course not! Who would listen to them? They were not appointed by royal or ministerial decree but by a simple decree of the director general, which could be revoked from one minute to the next. If the telegraph assistants proved failures, they could all be sent home, without any right to complain. The future? What future? They were "beyond the pale"; they didn't have the right to expect a pension: in fact, according to the rule, the government fired them at forty without further ado; that is, if they had the misfortune to remain telegraph workers until forty, the government put them out on the street, old, dazed, unable to do anything else, in poor health and penniless. All these unvoiced complaints that lurked in these young souls, who were unable to tolerate the bureaucratic yoke, rose bitterly to their lips and tried the spirits even of the most serene: all the little wrongs, all the little injustices, all the little sufferings, found a voice, were rekindled in memory, depressed spirits lifted in that river of words, those phrases that were repeated twenty times over, those complaints that were as monotonous as a refrain. At Caterina Borrelli's house Annina Pescara, Adelina Markò, Maria Morra, and Sofia Magliano discussed; at Olimpia Faraone's house Peppina Sanna, Peppina de Notaris, and Ida Torelli plotted. The friends met in order to come to an agreement. They argued everywhere, between the radicals and the conservatives: between the aggressive rebels who advised not going to the office at all, in order to leave their employers in a tight spot, and the passive rebels who intended just working a normal schedule. Relatives, fiancés, and friends took an interest in this great question, some taking sides for a complete rebellion, some for a moderate attitude; no one advised overtime. The assistants felt that it was management that was asking them; they felt they were in the stronger position; they wanted to show that they had character.

But when the day and time came to sign, on that big white sheet, a curious psychological phenomenon took place, a complete revolution in these spirits. And in a procession, silently, with a decisive air and a proud demeanor, each of them went up to write something. The first, Rachael Levi, a Jewess, small, very ugly, always bedecked with jewels, wrote that she would work one hour more every day. Grazia Casale, the plump brunette, perfumed with musk, wrote that she would work both for herself and for her sister Serafina, who was an invalid. Adelina Markò would stay during the day until five and every evening until midnight. Emma Torelli: she would do five hours overtime every day. Ida Torelli: like her sister. Peppina de Notaris: she would come at seven, leave at noon, come back at four, and leave at midnight. Peppina Sanna: she would do a double shift, from seven in the morning until nine in the evening; she asked only two hours for lunch. Maria and Pasqualina Morra: they would come from seven in the morning until midnight; they asked two hours to go to lunch. And so on with all the others, from both shifts, without exception, who went from offer to offer, until the last, Caterina Borrelli, expressed in her big, crooked handwriting her complete devotion: "I am at the disposal of management." But beneath these last words was attached a brief letter: Maria Vitale wrote from home, where she had been kept in bed with bronchitis for the third time, that she was feeling better and that she would do everything possible to come do her duty.

What a day Sunday, April 8, was! In the morning, in poured, thick as hail, telegrams from the candidates to the important voters, to the labor unions, to the communal secretaries, begging: the last fervent, pious entreaties—humble, impassioned telegrams, full of reckless concessions and desperate promises. Then there was the latest political circular from the minister of the interior to all the prefects and subprefects of the kingdom, in figures, 472 groups of numbers, an immense labor, so that there was the constant fear of a numerical error, which would have destroyed the meaning of the telegram: and for every wrong number the employee pays a six-lire fine. But it was at noon that the telegraphic fever reached its zenith. From all the large and small towns, from all the provincial capitals, from all the subprefects and prefects, arrived the results of the hamlets—to the minister, the newspapers, the candidates, the candidates' friends, the party heads, the political associations: and immediately afterward came private telegrams of commentary, lack of confidence, encouragement, moribund hopes, victory, congratulations, expectation, oaths, bitterness, skepticism. At three in the afternoon, the fever became white-hot. In the men's division, four lines to Rome were functioning, two more than usual, and there was a delay of three hours; there was such an overflow of telegrams to Florence, Milan, and Turin that they were being counted in series of ten. All the machines, Morse, Siemens, Hughes, double Hughes, and Steele, were operating: the two shift foremen were present, going back and forth like sleepwalkers, with burned-out cigars and a bundle of telegrams in hand. The door that communicated with the women's section was half-open, which was a novelty, but no one turned around. In the women's section, all the assistants were present, each one at a machine; the women's director came and went. The women's assistant director, tiny, short-haired, with the attractive little head of a quick shop boy, ran from one machine to the next, adjusting the timer, adding the toner, fast as a squirrel, with ready hands, a lively eye, and a loud, quick voice. The telegrams came out of nothing, poured out, emerged from every line; there was a three-hour delay on every one; the telegrams to be sent mounted up, formed stacks, platoons, heaps; while one was being transmitted, five arrived to be transmitted; while they finished transmitting a series of ten, fifty-two remained "stopped." The assistants caught the fever, which was rising by the hour. Tall, sitting on a big chair, her dress covered with a big black apron, Adelina Markò worked nimbly at the Hughes machine, on the Genoa line, transmitting with the quick fingers of a veteran pianist, making the whole mechanism creak rapidly, charging the machine with powerful kicks of her right foot, her hair up on her head so that it wouldn't bother her neck, her sleeves rolled up so that she could transmit more easily; next to her, Giulietta Scarano barely had time to record the telegrams. Maria Morra also sat on a tall stool, on the line with Bari: a lock of hair fell down over one eye; she had a spot of blue ink on her chin, her collar unbuttoned because she felt as though she was suffocating; from time to time, Emma Torelli took her place so that she could rest a bit, recording and classifying the telegrams, doing all the secretarial work. Between the two Hughes operators, who were both equally responsible for the line, these brief dialogues took place, although they didn't stop transmitting or writing.

"How many more are there?"

"Forty-three."

"And how far behind are we?"

"Two hours and fifty minutes."

"For God's sake!"

On the line, then, with the correspondent:

"How many do you have?"

"Sixty-four," was the firm reply.

They grew pale. The telegrams had multiplied miraculously; everybody was telegraphing now. They had had to install a fifth line with Rome and—an unhoped-for honor—it was being run by the women's section, which until then had never corresponded with the capital. On that line, on the Morse machine, they only received: Borrelli had been assigned it, because she was the one who was best at receiving. With her glasses firmly planted on her nose, one leg crossed over the other like a man, her mouth moving nervously, without ever raising her head, without moving or turning, she continued to receive, guessing the words from the first syllable, finishing writing the telegram before the correspondent had finished sending it. After receiving fifteen or twenty, she would ask:

"Are there many more?"

"A great many."

"How many?"

"About seventy."

"Go on."

And she began to receive again, her mouth dry, her fingers dirty with ink up to the tips. Then, seized with a sort of telegraphic delirium, she said to the correspondent: "Transmit faster. I can receive." He would hurry the transmission, so that it was very fast, of almost unbeatable speed, and she would urge him on, spurring him, as a jockey does a racehorse, saying to him from time to time: faster, faster, faster.

On the Naples–Salerno line, there was a wonderful sight to behold in a different way. The Salerno correspondent was the best employee in that office, and he was corresponding with Peppina

Sanna, one of the strongest, if not the strongest, of the women's section. In the morning, they had exchanged a joking challenge, like brave champions; they had greeted each other like two top-rank fencers, and the tournament had begun. They alternated the transmission and receiving of a telegram: as soon as the correspondent put his signature on his telegram, Peppina Sanna had her hand on the key to add her own. There were alternate noises: now the very fast, skipping key from Naples, under Peppina's firm hand, now the needle that received the transmission from Salerno, which danced and danced, with an infernal tapping. They egged each other on: "What a tortoise you are!" exclaimed Peppina Sanna. "Ah, so I'm a tortoise?" shouted the correspondent, and he sped up like a madman, trying to scare her. "Do you think you can scare me?" she exclaimed and increased the speed of her own transmission to the point where it didn't seem possible that he could keep up with it.

"Faster, ladies, faster," shouted the assistant director.

"We're far behind," murmured the director, wandering among the tables.

The men's director came and went, but mutely and seriously, without a word, pacing like a lion in a cage. He said nothing, he saw everything: the pale face of Annina Pescara, who had been sitting for ten hours on the Reggio line and who shook her head from time to time, as though she couldn't hold it up; the angelic patience of Clemenza Achard, who was struggling with seven small offices on her line that all had telegrams and that all wanted to go first; the suffering of Ida Torelli, who was condemned to the Naples–Ancona–Bologna line: she had sixty telegrams, Ancona and Bologna wasted time fighting among themselves; the skill of Peppina de Notaris, who managed to guess, rather than read, the transmission of the correspondent from Catanzaro, a fool who didn't know how to transmit. He paced up and down like a lion, but he said nothing: the assistants were all quick and intelligent that day; that atmosphere, that excitement had brought out brand-new qualities in them. They affectionately helped one another to ink, pens, and paper; those who were the least inclined to correspondence recorded, put the time on the dispatches, counted words, put on rolls of paper, gathered up the telegrams that had been transmitted. There were no more distinctions of shift, of personal dislike, of moral values: they helped each other in a sisterly way, driven by the desire to do well. At eight in the evening that Sunday, the telegraphic assistants, all present, without having had lunch or dinner, went on transmitting, in Hughes, in Morse, between a pile of telegrams that had already been done and a pile still to be done, with bright eyes, braids undone, nervous hands that pressed the keys hard, and husky voices that asked from time to time:

"Is it still jammed?"

IV

After a very mild October, with a tepid spring sun and a great blooming of roses, on November 1, All Saints' Day, a white line of clouds had covered the sky, and in the afternoon had come the fine autumn rain, the rain that always dampens the pious pilgrimage of people going to the cemetery on the Day of the Dead. And it rained continuously the whole first week of November, with a few intervals in which the rain stopped, as though it were tired; but gradually, after half an hour the little drops began to fall again, slowly, sparsely, then growing thicker, coming down for two or three hours with a monotonous noise that put one to sleep. In the foyer of the women's section, open umbrellas shiny with water dripped from the tips of the ribs leaning on the ground; on the back of the canvas sofa and on some chairs wet capes were drying, and some shawls that the rain had discolored; even on a Hughes machine that was used for instruction there was spread out a blackish raincoat, flecked with large black spots of water. The most cautious changed their boots as soon as they came in, putting on old pairs that they kept in the closet; at the end of their shift, though, it was difficult to put on again the ones that had shrunk from being damp. Since the rains had come, a snack for those who could pay for it was no longer lemon ice, which melted into a tart, greenish liquid, in which they dipped a penny roll; when November came, they drank hot chocolate, a blackish, heavy, very hot drink that burned the tongue and the stomach. Gabriella Costa, the Little Lavalière, so nicknamed because of her white, oval, melancholy face and because of the blond curls on her forehead and temples, complained softly that there was ground brick in that hot chocolate.* This matter of the snacks was an eternal subject of argument between Gaetanina Galante, the servant, and the assistants: the latter didn't pay day by day; they kept an account. They ate cookies and pastries; at the end of the month, when the servant gave them a bill for ten or even fifteen lire, they made faces: the best mannered said nothing; the most gossipy said there certainly must be a mistake, they couldn't have eaten all that stuff. But it was hard to win with Gaetanina Galante; she was so insolent and ill-bred, for she had made a nice nest egg from the snacks; and she had lent money to some of them, with interest—not much, twenty, thirty, fifty lire, which she had them pay back in monthly installments of five or ten lire, according to the amount. The day on which the monthly salaries were paid by the administration she stayed longer in the office to collect. It was

---

*This is probably a reference to Louise de la Vallière (1644–1710), the mistress of Louis XIV and the basis for a character in Alexandre Dumas's novel *The Vicomte de Bragelonne.*

impossible not to pay her, so great was the terror that one of the directors would come to know about this debt; and she took advantage of this terror to exercise a certain dominion over those who owed her money. One person would make her caps; another would give her a pair of gloves; a third lent her a gold medal when she was going to go dancing: and this servant treated them like pals, friends, said "tu"* to them, which made them blush and feel ashamed.

From the day that the rain started, there had been breakdowns on the lines, the fall and winter curse of the telegraph office. Procida had immediately sent a service telegram, saying that they could no longer see the islands of Ponza and Ventotene for the rain; immediately afterward, Massalubrense telegraphed that it could no longer see Capri; the traffic signals were therefore interrupted. After three days, the line of islands that starts with Pozzuoli, touches Ischia, Forio d'Ischia, Casamicciola, and Procida, and is partly under the sea, partly in the air, then underwater again, began to suffer: the current came in spurts; they corresponded with great difficulty. In the evening, there was a complete breakdown; no one answered at all. Lost in thought, the assistant director went to the door of the men's section, called the shift head and told him:

"We've lost all communication with the islands."

"Are many telegrams at a standstill?"

"Seven."

"That's not bad; we'll send them by regular mail."

Under that continuous rain, with that humidity that saturated the air, the roads, people, clothing, their very souls, telegraphic service was a work of patience. When they came to work, the assistants looked at the sky, made faces implying little faith, and called their correspondents. Sometimes, at the beginning, service went

---

*"Tu," the intimate form of address, is used only among social equals; for a servant to use it familiarly with these middle-class girls was insulting.

well, for an hour or two, but at a certain point, the signals disappeared and the assistant thought: "Here we go, God help me." But more often the breakdown announced itself in the morning; the problem manifested itself immediately in the correspondent's good morning that Naples couldn't hear, and in Naples's good morning that the correspondent couldn't hear. The seven hours of service passed by, spent in vain attempts to make themselves heard, tapping the keys hard, making long, clear, very slow signals.

"Please, Director," murmured the assistant, "our battery is too weak. Add something more."

"You already have a reinforcement of thirty units. What more can I do?" answered the director regretfully.

"It's useless, useless," replied the assistant. "Otranto will never hear me."

The outgoing or incoming current suffered from a strange, capricious disease that affected it intermittently, that would leave it alone for two hours and then knock it out for a day. It would fluctuate, growing suddenly stronger, then plunging into mortal weakness. The powerful fluid generated by a bit of copper, a bit of sulfuric acid, and a bit of zinc—this very strong fluid that no one has yet explained, this great natural phenomenon, as inexplicable and as great as heat, light, electricity, strength, will, thought—was sick, attacked in its strength and in its potency. Strange convulsions wracked it with pain, so that it seemed that the machines would split apart under its strength: it would beat hard, dry blows repeatedly on the metal, as though it were knocking or crying out for help. In the prostration that followed these blows, the machine's needle quivered indistinctly, a movement so slight that it seemed a breath.

"Director, Director," said Annina Pescara mournfully, "certainly Bologna is saying something to me, but the signals aren't coming through."

"Tune the machine."

The machine was taken apart; the timing mechanism was adjusted more finely; the hairspring was shortened so that it would take the current better; the needle was moved closer to the paper. Tuned in this way, the machine resembled one of those refined human temperaments in which shivering takes place immediately, in which the nerves tingle at the slightest sensation: the mechanism was tuned. Then, feebly, a few signals appeared, broken words, fragments of sentences: it seemed the weak, indistinct delirium of a dying person. And a breakdown was declared, so as to avoid responsibility:

"There's a loss of current over Bologna."

And yet the telegraph operator remained on the line, trying again, still trying, still hoping to be able to correspond. The illness that afflicted the current was so bizarre! From one moment to the next it could improve, for an hour, or a day. And with this uncertainty the telegraph operator spent the hours in useless attempts, constantly trying and trying again, with the fatalism of the young. From time to time, deep sighs were heard:

"What's the matter?" asked Caracciolo, who found the breakdowns fun, because they didn't have to work.

"This Catanzaro line will be the death of me," answered Grazia Casale.

And from time to time:

"There's no longer contact with Benevento."

"What sort of breakdown is there?"

"There's continuous current."

But the worst problem was the contacts. Because of the rain, the poor roads, the poorly maintained wires, a bird alighting on the wires, or any sort of accident, very frequent in the winter, two wires going in the same direction crossed and a "contact" took place. All of a sudden, while they were talking with Reggio, Torre Annunziata appeared on the line, and the transmissions crossed, got mixed up, the correspondents argued, the currents meshed. And Clemenza Achard's sad voice said very softly:

"We've lost Reggio; there's contact with Torre Annunziata."

That day, November 12, it had stopped raining in the morning, but the sky had remained gray and overcast, almost black on the line of the horizon, behind the hill of San Martino. And in the clouds there was a muffled, continuous rumble of thunder; there was a blue flash of lightning on the horizon. At four, the shift head, whose face was tired and bored, appeared at the door of the women's section, called the assistant director, and told her:

"I've lost contact with Sicily."

And they looked at each other with the preoccupied air of people facing an unsolvable problem. The director went back and communicated the news to the assistants.

"We've lost contact with Sicily."

The girls looked at each other, shaking their heads: little by little, it seemed that the Naples office was being cut off from all the other towns that it was connected with. For four days there had been no news of Venice, which sent its telegrams to Rome; Campobasso sent its telegrams by mail; there was no news of Ancona, no communication with Benevento. Now this isolation from Sicily, which was the most significant, seemed like total abandonment, absolute isolation. That day, all the other lines were going badly, not because of the damp, but because of the lightning flashes in the air that were striking the lines and breaking up the transmission signals.

"Ladies, don't touch the metal part of the keys with your fingers; you can get a shock," the director advised.

But some of them found the game of getting a shock amusing. All they had to do was touch one of the rheophores, or the upper part of a key, or a pad on the outside of the machine to feel a little vibration pass from their fingers to their wrist, from their wrist to their neck.

"Borrelli, Borrelli, don't fool around with electric shocks: you could be hit by lightning."

"Those are old wives' tales, ma'am."

Maria Immacolata Concetta Santaniello made the sign of the cross every time the thunder got louder, and you could see her lips moving, as though in prayer. Peppina de Notaris would move back with a slight gesture of fear every time the lightning struck. Peppina Sanna would make a face, as though all that electricity was getting on her nerves. Sofia Magliano, as she tried unsuccessfully to get an answer from Cosenza, talked with Maria Morra about that beautiful Adelina Markò, who had resigned in July and had gotten happily married to a young man from Salerno, a shopkeeper, in August: she had said good-bye to sentimental fancies, which had made her develop a crush on the widower of forty, and she was now happy, as she had written to the director. Now the beauty of the section was Agnese Costa, who was tall and slender, with a beautiful white neck, a large head, and two big gray eyes. Emma Torelli was also engaged, to a telegraph worker, and the wedding was to take place in five or six months. They discussed these things, rather nervously, excited by the useless efforts to get a reply from their correspondents, by the lightning flashes, and by what they were saying. They had never been able to find out the truth in the case of Juliano: she had suddenly disappeared, but she had been called into the director's office three or four times; they had seen her go up from the other room, with her big misshapen man's body. And the director had also been in the Signor Director's office three or four times, to confer with him at length; and she had come away with her face contorted and her lips that were the color of dead roses even paler. The Juliano scandal affected the whole section: it was a scandal that was unclear, but that made them feel vaguely uneasy. And to think that she was so ugly! But a whole jumble of signals appeared on the lines to Cosenza and Catanzaro where Maria Morra and Sofia Magliano were working, and shortly afterward the assistant director announced:

"A pole has been struck by lightning near Salerno: there is contact over Cosenza, Catanzaro, Reggio, Potenza, and Lagonegro."

Six lines were down at the same time, but they weren't dead: in those machines there was a muddle of currents, of transmissions, of strong pulses interrupted by the electricity in the air. The thunder rumbled louder: at all the points of contact, where metal touched metal in the machines, there was a small spark.

The insulators, with metal tips, like the teeth in a comb, also gave off sparks over and over. In the meantime the director came in, dressed in black, with a black crepe veil over her hat and black gloves: her eyes were red and swollen. She began to talk to the assistant director in a low voice: the assistants looked at her, growing suddenly pale at the sight of that mourning, no longer caring about the electricity: surely she had come back from *up there*, where she had gone with the other assistants. They didn't dare call her and ask her what had happened *up there*. A bolt of lightning flashed in the dark blue sky and there was a crash of thunder; lightning had struck in the city. All the machines creaked; in all the rheophores and keypads there was a slight flashing. The shift head appeared at the door of the men's section and shouted:

"Storm: there's danger! Cut the communications!"

The assistant director hesitated for a moment, faced with such a serious measure, one that is taken so very rarely; but another bolt of lightning fell closer by.

"Cut the communications!" commanded the shift head.

Immediately afterward, quiet spread through the office. Naples was isolated: the keyboards, the machines, the insulators seemed to be struck by sudden death: the current was dead. And around the director, who had come from the cemetery, the circle of assistants mourned the dead Maria Vitale.

The Novice

I

Humming a popular tune, Eva Muscettola walked around the brown oblong table covered with workbaskets, small and large; she searched with restless fingers in these baskets, removing pieces of cloth or muslin that had already been sewn or that were not ready to be sewn, narrowing her very bright but nearsighted eyes to see if there was anything missing—spools of thread, a needle case, scissors—making a number of pretty faces, according to whether the contents of the basket struck her as orderly or disorderly. A rosebud was stuck in the belt of her black silk dress, a very red rosebud, already almost open, similar to Eva's beauty, still incomplete, but already apparent. She was singing, putting needles from a card into the needle case of Giulia Capece, who never had any sewing materials, when Tecla Brancaccio came in, the first to arrive, with her firm, masculine footstep, wearing that day, as usual, her man's jacket with the white shirt collar, high and closed, a man's tie, and a horseshoe pin.

"Oh, my dear, dear fiancée," cried Eva from a distance, seeing Tecla arrive, "you're as punctual as a young man for a date! Have you been riding again this morning? How's Gypsy?"

"Fine, she just lost a shoe day before yesterday," answered Tecla in her rather hard voice, taking off her long kid gloves, rolling them up, and throwing them after her felt cap.

"And how's Carlo?" asked Eva in a low, affectionate tone.

And Tecla buckled a strange iron bracelet.

"But why are you so stubborn, Tecla? Carlo is fond of you, but *she* is stronger than you are, my love."

"Maybe!"

"Don't you see that she always wins? She's beautiful, she's blond, she knows how to cry, she's full of wiles, she loves Carlo madly . . ."

"I love Carlo, too."

"Yes, but married women are stronger than us girls," added Eva, expressing an unconscious philosophy.

"That may be true, but I'm not giving up."

"And what can you do?"

"Wait."

And in her low, pale forehead, her gray, shiny, cold, metallic eyes, her thin, dull rose lips, her squarish chin could be seen the strength and patience, the unconquerable will that come from waiting. Immediately, without saying anything more, Tecla sat down at her place, pulled up her workbasket that was larger than the others, took out a coarse striped material, the slip for a small mattress, a very rough cloth that her iron fingers pierced rapidly; the seamstress didn't even raise her head when Giulia Capece and Chiarina Althan came in; her work and thoughts absorbed her completely.

"And so did the box come from Vienna, Giulia?" asked Eva, taking the fur coat from Chiarina Althan's arm and smiling at her.

"Yes, I wish it hadn't ever arrived!" exclaimed the beautiful girl, slender as a reed. "After so much curiosity, so much waiting! Didn't I have you read the letter from my aunt in Vienna? You would have thought that the box contained the seven miracles! Really! Are Viennese dressmakers making fun of us? Don't we have eyes, taste, and intelligence that they should send us blue dresses loaded with roses?"

"Oh, Jesus!" exclaimed Eva, scandalized.

"And a hat trimmed with a stuffed green parrot," added Chiarina, with her rather enigmatic smile. "It seems that it's Giulia's aunt's parrot, a sacrifice to the relatives, in anticipation of her coming into her inheritance. When you wear that hat, Giulia, it sends a message to your friends and appeals to their affection to take pity on your misfortune."

"I'll never wear it, never!" exclaimed Giulia, nearly in tears. "I'll give it to Concetta, the maid."

"And your aunt will disinherit you," retorted Chiarina, laughing.

Giulia shrugged her shoulders. In any case, she was poor, very noble, from a family laden with debts, trusting only in her own beauty to make a great marriage, and all the old family friends, foreign aunts, and confessors were busy finding millions for this splendid creature, who meanwhile was spending her fortune in advance. Giulia reluctantly began to sew a baby's shirt, making very long stitches, breaking the thread every minute, looking at herself from time to time in the mirror across from her, her graceful body bent over like a flower, her long chestnut eyelashes delicately shading her cheeks, her red mouth looking like a shiny, juicy pomegranate. Chiarina Althan, next to her, was cutting out a baby's apron from a piece of pink and white cotton; and her very fine features, which though not beautiful, exuded intelligence, with calm but deep eyes and a thoughtful mouth, bent over the material full of attention and interest, as though she were reading a book or admiring a painting. Meanwhile, Eva had also taken her place and was hemming some baby clothes with long stitches, singing, while Tecla Brancaccio was cutting out with squeaky scissors a piece for the little mattress that she was stitching, which she threw on the floor. The two Sannicandro sisters came in, arm in arm: they were two little statues of pink-tinted white porcelain, two sweet little round dolls, with upturned noses, curly hair, and a childlike air, although they were fifteen. And they immediately began to recite their lesson, like well-trained dolls:

"Good morning, Eva. Papa sends his best."

"Good morning, dear, and thanks."

"Good morning, Eva. Mama sends her best."

"Good morning, dear, and thanks."

They took off their identical coats, put down their identical hats, revealing identical black silk dresses. Then, after remaining speechless for a moment, they went on with the lesson.

"Is your mother well, Eva?"

"Yes, dear, she was at the Union last night; now she's sleeping."

"And your papa's well, Eva?"

"Yes, dear, he's at Gifoni, hunting."

"Is your brother Riccardo well, Eva?"

"He's fine, but he's in Scotland, for the races."

And she immediately brought the two girls, who were looking at one another, satisfied with their recitation, a pile of baby clothes to hem. In that great work for the Abandoned Children's Home, the Sannicandro sisters' specialty was hems: they hemmed every day, always, unceasingly; entire kilometers of hems came out of those patient little mechanical statues' hands. They were always glad to hem, raising their heads from time to time to ask:

"Do you have the white spool, Eva?"

"Do you have the little scissors, Eva?"

Maria Gullì-Pausania entered slowly, with her gait of an Olympian goddess: she deigned to smile at Eva, who ran to meet her, and offered her her brown, cold, upper-class Sicilian cheek, exchanged greetings with Tecla, Giulia Capece, and Chiarina Althan, and took her place, with measured, harmonious movements, rubbing her right hand where a little red spot had appeared, pushing back her white cloth cuffs, pulling up her workbasket, where she numbered in red all the pieces of linen that her friends gave her after they finished with them. And she did her work with a certain solemn slowness, with an air of refinement, being resigned to a menial task, with the affected nonchalance of a superior mind humbling itself through goodness of heart, marking the linen with such dignity of movement that it seemed that she was always thinking of the immense happiness of those children who in their childhood would already have the luck to wear a little white skirt marked by her, Maria Gullì-Pausania—whose house was second only to the king's in Palermo, whose family possessed two principalities, three marquisates, four sulfur mines, and an entire province of orange and lemon trees. She raised her eyebrows when she saw Elfrida Kapnist come in, almost running, the Hungarian with the big, dark, dull, wild eyes, the brown, curly hair that no comb could tame, a palely colored face as long as a goat's, a coat in a strange yellowish color, and a dress that was too short in front that showed her slender feet. Elfrida was welcomed with a range of more or less friendly smiles; Eva herself was slightly embarrassed to receive her, for the rumors that circulated about Elfrida went from the very good to the very bad. She was a gypsy who had escaped from a tribe—no sir, she was a counsel's daughter, noble but poor—she was a ragamuffin—she had had a lot of land confiscated in Hungary—she was the daughter of a horsewoman—her mother was a Radziwill—she received gifts of clothing from young men—the duchess of Mercede gave her dresses. Meanwhile, despite these contradictions, with Elfrida's devilish spirit, her bottomless gaiety, her liveliness of a rather free foreigner, her strange sort of attractiveness, she went everywhere, partly invited, partly tolerated, partly unwillingly entertained, but always present, always merry, showing her little white gypsy's teeth, dancing all night, eating at all hours, heedless of her old clothes, her washed gloves, and her unruly hair that defied hairpins. She kissed Eva on both cheeks in a lively manner and announced, as she began to sew:

"Olga Bariatine is marrying Massimo."

They all raised their heads, including the two Sannicandro girls.

"Is it certain?" asked Tecla Brancaccio.

"Absolutely certain. They're getting married in May; Olga wants to go to Russia on their honeymoon."

"Olga must be very happy, isn't she?" said Eva, in the tender tone of a person who desires other people's happiness.

"More than happy: last night Massimo stayed at her house until twelve, which he had never done."

"Poor Olga!" sighed Giulia Capece. "With all that money, to marry such a pauper."

"A gambler—my brother meets him every year in Monte Carlo," murmured Eva, thoughtful for a moment.

"Bored, and boring," added Chiarina Althan.

"Why did he decide to get married? The Dauns are very noble; who knows anything about the Bariatines?" asked Maria Gulli-Pausania, looking at a pile of new dish towels to be marked for the orphanage's kitchens, undecided about whether to make another sacrifice to charity.

"Naturally, the very noble Signor Massimo Daun probably hasn't found either a friend who will lend him five hundred francs or a loan shark who will trust him, and so he's finally returning the ardent love of Olga Bariatine, who after all is beautiful, rich, and good."

"But reluctantly, very reluctantly," continued Elfrida Kapnist, who was hemming caps. "Last night at a dinner with men friends, he swore like a Turk, at marriage, at Little Russia, and at the whole Slavic race."

"How horrible!" exclaimed Eva. "I wouldn't want to get married at that price, even to a man I adored."

"That's because you don't adore anyone," observed Tecla Brancaccio calmly.

Angiolina Cantelmo, who had just come in then, smiled faintly. She was a tall, delicate person, with big liquid blue eyes, with cheeks tinted with fine, rosy blood, a Japanese rose of transparent porcelain. She belonged to the most noble and ancient Neapolitan family, the old house of Cantelmo, in which kindness, beauty, bravery, and generosity were traditional; yet for two hundred years a tradition of misfortune had plagued the house. A great moral and material fatality descended through the branches; legend spoke of a crime to be expiated, and neither the honesty and courage of the men nor the beauty, virtue, and piety of the women were enough to free them from it: a Cantelmo, male or female, was always dying a violent death. A terrible tragedy had taken Angiolina's mother, and a beautiful brother and sister, blond and rosy cheeked, had already been stricken by tuberculosis. As for Angiolina, two years before she had become engaged to Giorgio Serracapriola, a handsome, rich, elegant, skeptical, and indolent young man; and she, in a pious manner, like a good, respectable girl, had begun to love her fiancé. The marriage had been broken off, for reasons of interest between Giorgio's and Angiolina's fathers, and Giorgio had left for a trip on a yacht, a bit indifferent after all. She had said nothing, she hadn't complained, she hadn't said a word to anyone; if anyone spoke to her about him she answered with a faint smile, and she grew thinner and rosier, like a candle. She was always cold, though, and she spoke in a low voice. She told Eva Muscettola that they could plan to dedicate the orphanage by the first of December, but that in the meantime, eight or ten of the girls who would live there had to be confirmed. They would have to find godmothers, tell the archbishop, choose a private church—the talk became general, each of the seamstresses offered to be a godmother; even the two Sannicandros both offered at the same time, as though reciting a lesson; even Elfrida Kapnist, whom many accused of being a Protestant, heretic, Turkish, or worse, while, in fact, she couldn't accept being the godmother of an ordinary ragamuffin.

"Couldn't we have the service in the Cantelmo Chapel?" Eva asked Angiolina.

"Yes, if you like. But the children will be frightened. Our chapel is so sad, and then it's so, so cold!"

"Don't you hear Mass there every Sunday?"

"Yes, because I have to," answered Angiolina, "but I would prefer any little church with some sun. Papa always has rheumatism when he leaves it, and Maria has a cough."

"You never cough, do you, Angiola?" asked Eva, looking up from some towels on which she was tying a fringe.

"Me? No, never. I'm fine." And she smiled faintly, gathering a skirt.

"Here's the fiancée, here's the bride," called Anna Doria as she came in, pulling Olga Bariatine, the plump little blond, with a mouth like a rose and soft gray eyes. The bride bowed her head, blushing, embarrassed, embracing her friends who had surrounded her, with great tears in their eyes; especially Eva, the good one, who had her arm around her neck and repeated in a low voice, as though she were praying for her:

"May God help you, may God help you, dearest, dearest . . ."

"Do you know why Olga is getting married so soon and so happily, ladies?" yelled Anna Doria, as they all went back to their places and their work.

"Probably because she deserves it . . . ," suggested Chiarina Althan.

"Not at all, not at all!" screamed Anna Doria, still standing in the middle of the room.

"Because she's so pretty and so nice," suggested Eva Muscettola.

"Not at all, not at all," raged Anna Doria. "All of us more or less deserve to get married, all of us are more or less nice, and pretty . . . and yet, how many of us are turning into old maids! I'm not speaking for myself, who am already in mothballs. Do you know why? Olga is getting married early and to the man she wants because she doesn't have a mother: our mothers interfere with our marriages."

"Oh! Oh! Oh! Anna, Anna!" most of them said, scandalized.

"Are you mad, Anna?" asked Chiarina Althan.

"What do you mean, mad? Yes, mothers are affectionate and caressing, who would deny it? I'm not a beast, in spite of my extravagant claims. But our mothers are the natural enemies of our getting married. They're too young? Then they're the ones who deserve to shine, so they keep us closed up in the house, they leave us in short dresses until we're sixteen, because we're competition for them! Too old? Then they hate people, they don't want to see anyone, youth annoys them, memories bother them, they don't care about other people's happiness, they're egotistical, old! Too elegant? Fiancés are wary of elegant mothers-in-law. Too strict? They chase away the ones who like to take it easy in life. The pretentious one craves titles of nobility; another is inflexible on the question of religious piety; a third claims that they should live together; a fourth demands that they go to the provinces; one has a whim, another a fixation; one doesn't like blond men, another detests thin people: good-bye marriage! I assure you, dear friends, those who manage to get married while they still have mothers accomplish a marvelous feat."

The ugly girl, already thirty, thin and awkward, with thin cheeks clumsily colored with a rouge that she made herself—one of her extravagances—remained still in the middle of the room with a triumphant air. Her friends lowered their heads without answering, struck by a deep sense of pain, offended in their good feelings, in their respect for motherhood. And they thought of the daily tragicomedy in the Doria household: a mother who had loved luxury and pleasure too much and who had confined Anna in a sort of dark adolescence until the age of twenty, a mother who had suddenly turned to the austere life, with all the defects of maturity, miserliness, bigotry, pigheadedness, intolerance—facing every day the rebellion of Anna, Anna the crazy one, who fought violently with her mother over everything, who felt ugly and took her revenge, treating everyone spitefully, but most of all her mother, the old fool, as her daughter called her. Yes, they all suffered for Anna Doria's brutal words; but the two Sannicandros, who kissed their father's hand every night before they went to bed and had their mother bless them so that they could sleep well, looked at each other, very pale, with the puffy little mouths of children who want to cry. No one spoke and Eva, who had a more open character than all the others, tried to put in a placating word:

"Here's Anna, who wants to make people think she's naughtier than she is: you pretend to be bad, my dear, but no one believes you. Our mothers love us, in their way: it's not up to us to judge them."

"And you do very well, for your part, Eva," answered Anna Doria nastily, upsetting her workbasket to find the scissors.

Eva went pale and quiet, hurt. A deep uneasiness reigned among the seamstresses; it seemed that no one wanted to interrupt that silence. Tecla had bravely prepared a second mattress slip, when Giulia Capece asked Olga:

"Where do you get your clothes, Olga? Not from Vienna, I hope, if you don't want to be killed!"

"Don't get them from Vienna, Olga," interjected Chiarina Althan immediately, taking the bull by the horns to change the direction of the conversation. "Imagine, they sent Giulia a hat with a big rooster on it: this was supposed to give her an idea of how to be a good housewife."

"Oh, but a rooster, Chiarina!" protested Giulia, deeply afflicted by the nightmare of that Viennese hat.

Olga told her friends who were listening to her that she got everything, everything, from Paris: in a convent of nuns they were already embroidering the linens for her trousseau, with her motto "Forever," along with her initials: she had not yet thought about clothes, but for ball gowns there was only Worth, for sportswear there was only Reuss, for day dresses Carolina; and her friends had stopped working and were listening intently, with a vision of materials, hats, veils, and lace before their eyes.

"Have you thought of having silk blouses made?" asked Elfrida Kapnist.

"No," answered Olga, "I didn't know that they were in style again."

"They're very much in style, in a soft, very light silk, blue, pink, cream, with real Valencia lace. All the society women . . . and others, have them."

Olga didn't answer; Maria Gullì-Pausania wrinkled her eyebrows and moved her chair, so as not to touch Elfrida's chair. So she always knew what the young men were saying at their dinners and what overly fashionable women were wearing? Olga had gone back to saying that Massimo would like to make her a gift, probably jewels, the famous ones of the house of Daun, but that she absolutely did not want them; she was making a marriage of love, she didn't care at all about jewels. The girls who were sewing smiled approvingly without raising their heads, each thinking to herself how good and ingenuous Olga Bariatine was; Massimo had first pawned and then sold the famous jewels of the house of Daun; he was a poor devil in debt who couldn't have given his fiancée a little silver ring. Then there was a quarter hour of silence; they were all working, seized with great zeal, thinking of the eighty abandoned children, girls and boys, who were depending on their labors for their clothing. Eva, the good one, the most vibrantly affectionate, had told them that charity is not merely the giving of money, but that one has to add one's own time and work: that, finally, two or three of the morning hours, until lunchtime, could be sacrificed, working for the poor creatures without bread, shelter, or clothing. And that daily activity, that having to occupy herself continuously with others, that coming and going, satisfied Eva's need for movement and her feeling of altruism, filled her rather empty and lonely days—her mother appearing and disappearing between one ball and another, sleeping half the day, dining in her own apartments, too young for her daughter, who was already too big—her father who adored every kind of sport, who was always in the stables, or hunting, or shooting pigeons, or at the races—her brother who was always traveling to Monte Carlo, or Baden, or Paris. Eva loved all of them: mother, father, and brother, but as they would have it, in the free intervals that their dominant passions left them, and this was not enough, not enough to satisfy her burning need for love, her exuberant vitality. Therefore, to give vent to her feelings, she had used her fire, her flame of affection, to found this girls' charity for abandoned children, and she threw herself into this work with the limitless voluptuousness of good souls who cannot rest from loving and doing good works. It had taken a great deal to convince her friends, to get them together, especially the incompatible ones, that Maria Gullì-Pausania, whom no one could stand because of her airs, that Elfrida Kapnist, whose looks were so strange and dubious! And the ones who were just entering, arm in arm, Giovanella Sersale and Felicetta Filomarino, whom she could never get to come early, who dropped in during the last half hour, distracted, always talking in a low voice between themselves: everyone knew Giovanella Sersale's secret, that she was supposed to marry Francesco Montemiletto, but that he, after courting her for two years, had finally married her older sister Candida; and Giovanella had never gotten over this betrayal: she wore this proudly, like mourning; she would not hear of other fiancés; she would never get married. All of a sudden, nobody knew how, there had sprung up a great friendship between her and Felicetta Filomarino; they were always together; they often had red eyes, a similar melancholy afflicted them. Then what was Felicetta's secret? Quieter and more reserved, she confided only in Giovanella; and certainly, during their solitary conversations, they mourned together their faded youth. Their presence gave a more serious tone to that girls' meeting: each of them, bending her head over her sewing, thought of the cross she had to bear: Tecla Brancaccio of her uneven struggle with a rival who was constantly preferred, Giulia Capece of her beauty that found so many admirers, but not a husband with an income of two hundred thousand lire, Chiarina Althan of the silly, frivolous surroundings where her intelligence was being wasted, Elfrida Kapnist of her poverty that sometimes made her undergo terrible humiliations, Angiolina Cantelmo of the curse that hung over her house, Anna Doria of her atrocious existence, beyond compare, Eva Muscettola of her unsated desire to be greatly loved, to be able to love greatly; only the two Sannicandros were cheerful; they were completely happy, because that day they were going for a drive to the beach with Papa and Mama; and Olga Bariatine was deeply happy, she who had loved Massimo Daun with such ardor and was now reaping the rewards for her love; and Maria Gullì-Pausania felt very happy, because a descendant of Sicilian kings cannot feel otherwise.

"Good heavens!" cried Eugenia of Aragon, entering and throwing her hat in the air. "Are you contemplating the Apocalypse? Are you doing penitence for your sins, girls? Should we all cry together? Oh, Eva, Eva, what have you done?"

"Nothing, dear, nothing. We're working."

"But you'll die, working so hard. Do you want to ruin your chests, and your eyes, and your fingers? All this sewing will make you sad and depressed! Maybe the children will have clothes, but someone here will kill herself, I'm sure."

She threw herself on a chair, crossed her legs, and grabbed the sewing out of Angiolina Cantelmo's hands.

"You, too, you prude? But why don't you send these children some money, lots of money, instead of torturing yourselves sewing? I'll give you a thousand lire for your children, Eva dear, if you stop sewing that big piece of material of yours; today I'll tell Papa to send you a thousand lire. Stop, little Eva, stop! Perhaps noble girls sew? I don't know how."

"That seems strange to me," observed Anna Doria, nastily.

In fact, Eugenia of Aragon, who had a dowry of sixty million, who joined in her person the nobility of three families, Aragon, Ognatte, and Mexico, who had lands in Europe and in America, who owned twelve different estates, and was related to the Bourbons of Spain and the Orleans of France, was a little girl that the duke of Aragon had had with a dressmaker. The beautiful and good duchess of Aragon, stricken with sterility, because she adored her husband and saw that their immense fortune was going to be lost in the hands of worthless nephews, had wanted her husband to legitimize and adopt the dressmaker's poor daughter—and this creature of the streets had almost ascended a throne, being adored by her father and, strangely, by her adoptive mother. She had retained a somewhat rough simplicity that no English governess had been able to change, a noisy goodness, and she had acquired the nonchalant extravagance of a person who doesn't have to count pennies. Nor was she ashamed of her origins: Anna Doria's nasty comment made her laugh.

"Girls, why don't we all go home to lunch? Enough of these shirtless children; come away, we'll tell Mama to send you a hundred shirts for these little ones. Come, there are some clothes at home that I have to show you, and a little monkey that I bought; let's go; come on, Eva, you tell them, who look so astonished. I have a carriage outside that will take five of us easily, and yours, Eva, another five; Maria, you probably have yours, too, you never go without a carriage; you're first-class Spanish nobility. We'll all fit in; we'll look like a school."

And to convince them all, she threw herself on Chiarina Althan's neck, waltzed around with Eva, kissed Olga Bariatine, upset all the workbaskets; and her lower-class liveliness was so contagious, her gaiety so fresh and youthful, that a ray of sun penetrated all those hearts, and everyone smiled radiantly once again.

II

A golden rocket left the shadows of the port, rose and fell brilliantly in the starry spring sky, and fell back, spent, into the sea: immediately after the signal rocket, a line of flares lit up on board the flagship battleship *Roma;* other flares were lit on the *Castelfidardo,* on the royal sloop the *Cariddi,* on the transport ship the *Vedetta,* on the Russian battleship the *Svetlana*—all the merchant ships, brigantines, tubs, fishing vessels, all the *Immaculate Madonnas, Divine Providences, Annamaria Cacaces* that fill the port of Castellammare, lit up with colored lights, so that the whole sea was fantastically illuminated, and the giant red ship of wood and iron, the *Italia,* without masts, squat and heavy, which had been launched that morning, looked like a big fat marine idol, silent, pompous, and motionless, to whom everyone was burning candles and incense.

On the flagship, after the brief fireworks display, there was dancing everywhere. Admiral Gaston, big and tall, almost colossal, with a chest as wide and solid as the stern of a battleship, his nice little wife, and his two oldest daughters—fifteen years old, dressed in blue, with wide sailor collars that showed off the delicate white of their necks, and big straw hats thrown back on their blond hair, real sailors, kind and exuberant—had invited the whole aristocracy of Naples and Castellammare, all the naval officers, and all the foreigners who were already vacationing in Sorrento at the end of May. At the foot of the two wooden stairways, to the right and left, there was a continuous arrival of little boats carrying fireworks in both bow and stern, and a timid but continuous ascent of ladies and girls, who climbed with a certain fear, not without pleasure, without looking at the black abyss of the sea beneath, who sighed with satisfaction as soon as they had arrived on the bridge. Up there they were struck by the novelty, the strangeness of the spectacle, and how unusual it was; a great curiosity seized them; here and there were heard little shouts of surprise and pleasure. A band of Bersaglieri* was placed in the center of the ship, around the mainmast, and it struck up the dance tunes with a certain military flare, with the fury of attacking soldiers, or of pirates sacking a ship. Here, on either side of the mainmast there were some seats, but no one wanted to sit there: the girls and married women were dancing like devils, and in between they were visiting the ship; the foreign women, showing foresight, had brought folding chairs, *pliants;* as for the young men, they preferred to furnish some local color, to curl up in three or four on a pile of ropes; and the women, in order to look interesting, all pretended to walk unsteadily, to

---

*A corps of the Italian army created in 1836; literally, "sharpshooters."

have a sailor's gait, and every so often they would ask some naval official who was very busy with the dancing:

"What if the anchor should move?"

"It's very strong," answered the latter, laughing. On the vast stern deck, all decorated with flowers and banners, people were dancing madly, as though that were the last day that all those women and young men could possibly dance. Eugenia of Aragon, simply dressed in white wool, with a hat covered with white feathers, and a pair of earrings with stones as big as hazelnuts—a luxury permitted only to a spoiled girl—danced, and danced, and danced, without ever stopping, spinning like a top, going from one partner to another without stopping to breathe for a moment, with shining eyes and flushed cheeks, amusing herself like a child: in vain did her fiancé, Giulio Vargas—almost as rich as she and very much in love—beg her, now and then, to rest. She would make a delightful face, then tell him in a gentle tone:

"Oh, Giulio, Giulio, I love you so much, if you'll just let me dance."

This was said with that great sentimental languor, that irresistible languor that characterizes the voice and eyes of a Neapolitan in love; and if Giulio hesitated, she took his arm and carried him away; at the first measure they were spinning around, too. Giulio felt the attraction of that noisy youth. Every time that Eugenia passed Eva Muscettola, she told her, raising her voice a bit:

"So dance, Eva dear, dance: look at me!"

Eva, on the arm of her escort, Innico Althan, a lieutenant in the navy, the brother of her friend Chiarina, was dancing quite a bit, but she preferred to chat and laugh with Innico, a tall, thin, dark young man, who wore his uniform with great elegance and who combined with the gaiety natural to southerners the touch of melancholy of those who have traveled far and who are destined to leave again. So, slowly, in the past few months, a deep affection had sprung up between the two young people, made up of intentions more than words, consisting more in certain small emotional particulars than in great events of the heart. He certainly felt the affectionate solidity of Eva's soul, despite the disorder and abandonment of a family that lacked a domestic center; he felt that flow of tenderness going out from the girl's heart to her friends, to children, to the poor—and she, for her part, admired that young man who had managed to remove himself from the atmosphere of vice and frivolity of his friends and companions, pursuing a long, hard career, often far from his loved ones.

"How beautiful your battleships are," she said to Innico, looking at him with eyes filled with gentleness.

"But they're not always decked with flowers and banners; we don't dance the polka on board, as we're doing this evening."

"What does it matter? I like them so much," she murmured, bowing her head beneath her blue hat, a breath of air trimmed with daisies.

"You should see it in a storm, this good ship! How solid it is, how it resists and doesn't yield!"

"Don't talk to me about storms, Innico," she said, perturbed.

"And why not?"

"I can't think about it . . . I can't think about it; when the weather was bad, I'd never sleep . . ."

"Then you'd have to embark with someone you love . . ."

"Why couldn't I?"

"The law doesn't allow it."

"The law?"

"So dance, Eva, dance, now that Innico is here," yelled Eugenia, laughing and shaking her big jeweled earrings.

It was a waltz, and many married women, tired out, had sat down on the blue velvet sofas, but the girls resolutely kept on. Elfrida Kapnist—audaciously dressed in red brocade, with satin slippers gleaming with pearls, in a dress so daring that it scandalized many women, with that air of an unkempt gypsy, with those big eyes that were both wild and gentle at the same time—clung to the arm of Willy Galeota, the most stylish young man in Neapolitan society. Willy Galeota had been courting her for a month, persistently, as one might court a married woman, following her everywhere, dancing all night with her, talking to her in a low voice, not letting anyone get close to her; and she accepted his court tranquilly, as though it were nothing, with the serenity of foreign girls, without prejudice. And, as usual, people said the most horrible and the nicest things about her: Willy was her lover; Willy couldn't obtain a single word of love from her; she and Willy had met at night in a closed carriage in Posillipo; she wouldn't let Willy visit her in the two poorly furnished little rooms where she lived; Willy treated her like a dancer; Willy was going to marry her. She feigned not to know about, not to hear, this ripple of gossip in which she was attacked and defended, in an equally exaggerated manner; and she danced the waltz languidly, looking her escort in the eyes, mutely and confidently seductive. For a moment Giulia had been angry with Elfrida, since Willy Galeota was the most marriageable man on Giulia's list; but when Giulia found herself surrounded by the prince of Sirmio, the very rich Roman patrician; the magnate of Hungary; Giorgio de Neri, the very rich Florentine; the count of Detmold; the first secretary of the German embassy; and other young men, she felt better—her court was complete; all the women envied her; she danced, chatted, laughed, licked ice cream, beautiful in her Worth dress, with seven ropes of pearls around her neck, while her mother watched her from a distance, smiling at her with eyes damp with joy, to see her so beautiful and so popular. Maria Gullì-Pausania, the classic beauty with the pure Siracusan profile, knowing full well that dancing is more suited to irregular types of beauty, was not dancing but was strolling among the couples, making her very simple black silk dress flutter harmoniously, looking a little like Minerva under her black silk hat, on which she had put fresh May roses: Peppino Sannicandro gave her his arm, an expression of bliss on his imbecilic features, the silly satisfaction of one who couldn't put down his whalebone walking stick—a whalebone walking stick was suitable for a shipboard dance—he had found this inanity very witty and repeated it to everyone happily, earning smiles of approval from Maria. Later he had invented this silly line to ask his friends, who were about to go to the races:

"How many fillies do you take to the races?"

Maria laughed quietly, flattering the vanity of this cretin, and they didn't talk much; he said almost nothing to her, in his idiotic bliss, but he was very happy to escort one of the most beautiful girls in Naples: she remained silent, with her composure of a wise, thoughtful goddess. Suddenly, the music stopped; the couples began to walk about; trays of ice cream were handed around; the sound of women's voices rose from the bow to the sky.

Below, in the admiral's quarters, there was a coming and going of ladies and officers around the buffet table, the clinking of glasses, the clicking of teeth, couples bumping into one another. The two Gaston girls, with their big sailor hats pushed back on their blond heads, rosy and laughing, brought their friends to the buffet; then they finally stayed there with the two Sannicandros, both dressed in pink, who ate with the gluttony of adolescents, first salmon with mayonnaise, then vanilla ice cream, then a slice of hunter's pie, then sweet jelly; beside them Anna Doria, since she couldn't find anyone who would ask her to dance, drowned her troubles in food, with the enormous appetite of nervous old maids; and Eugenia of Aragon, who was dying of hunger, she said, had come along to join them; she would gladly have eaten a plateful of vermicelli with tomato sauce. And all the women, married women and girls, who came through those big, shiny, wood rooms, with the big, soft, deep sofas made of jute, with brass handles that looked like gold, felt a deep sense of well-being, and they almost sighed, seized by a love of foreign countries, envying the officers who escorted them their wonderful travels, while the officers, laughing, smiling, dark, and likable, lent themselves to these sentimental seagoing fantasies of the ladies, concealing from them the troubles, vulgarities, and long periods of boredom of naval life. Chiarina Althan, who didn't like dancing much and who was a keen observer, had sat down on a sofa near the buffet and was watching with interest those who were eating, admiring the bottomless appetites of the Sannicandro sisters, rosy and happy, who were eating candied chestnuts and drinking consommé; the ravenous appetite of Anna Doria, whose mother made her fast three times a week; and the large proletarian appetite of Eugenia, whom Giulio Vargas was feeding as though she were a child, laughing and joking. Then, when she saw Tecla Brancaccio enter the buffet room all alone, dressed in blue, her sleeves and neck embroidered in gold, with curly hair and a hat on her head like a young officer, she said to her:

"Shall we have some ice cream together, Tecla? Come see how our friends can eat."

"I'm looking for Carlo," she said, narrowing her cold, metallic eyes.

"He's not here," answered Chiarina.

"Then I'll go somewhere else."

"No, dear, don't go look for him," said the other, detaining her.

"He's with *her*, isn't he? Where? I'll go find him right away."

"Oh, Tecla, stop it. Why chase someone who can't marry you?"

"Because," she said, shrugging her shoulders. "I'm going to look for them, Chiarina."

"Then I'll come with you." And she got up, seeing that there was no way to dissuade her.

Arm in arm, while Chiarina tried to lecture her, they walked the whole length of the battleship, from bow to stern, but they kept to the edge, because people were dancing between the mainmast and the forebridge. Lovers leaned against the railing, looking at the sea and the stars, talking in low voices.

Some solitary individuals were leaning there, too, looking off into the distance. Because they were looking for Carlo Mottola and Lady Maria di Miradois, the two girls didn't see Olga Bariatine, who was facing the railing, looking toward Castellammare. The little blond Russian had been waiting for two hours for Massimo Daun, her fiancé, who had promised to come early to dance with her; and with his usual strange air, he had left the beach, with Luigi Muscettola, Eva's brother, and Lodovico Torremuzza, the Sicilian fencer, and two or three others. And he hadn't come back; she didn't feel like laughing or dancing; she was worried and nervous; she couldn't tear herself away from the railing, studying every boat that came near the *Roma,* suspecting only one thing, unfaithfulness, never imagining what those young men could be doing for two hours, in a hotel room around a table, gambling, pale from their passion.

Tecla and Chiarina couldn't find Carlo Mottola and Lady Maria di Miradois anywhere; they went up to the bow. There there was no dancing; the awnings that covered it were beginning to move in the evening breeze. Leaning against the railing as though it were a balcony, with their backs turned to the others, Felicetta Filomarino and Giovanella Sersale bent their heads in the shadows, looking at the phosphorescent sea. And from the slight nervous movement of Giovanella's shoulders, from some tremors, from the curve of her neck, one could tell that she was sobbing, while Felicetta Filomarino stood motionless beside her, not daring to confide her secret, not even to the stars in the sky or the waves in the sea. Tecla and Chiarina stopped near Angiolina Cantelmo;

she was standing upright, near the bent mast on the bow where the flag is attached, wrapped in the white folds of a crepe shawl, and holding on to the mast with her hand, she studied the darkness with her big blue eyes, as though she wanted to travel with the battleship through the seas of the Orient, searching for the little yacht in which he was fleeing. And in spite of her white dress, she looked thinner and taller and more transparent than ever, as though a torch had been lit in a porcelain vase.

"Aren't you dancing, Angiola?" Chiarina asked her.

"No, Maria is dancing, down on the stern," she said, stretching out her long, thin hands.

"Have you see Carlo Mottola and Lady Maria di Miradois?" asked Tecla, who always went straight to the point, without hesitating or being ashamed.

"They were here a little while ago: they've gone away."

"Good night, Angiola."

"Good night, Tecla."

And the slender creature turned back again to watch the sea, dreaming, perhaps wondering what attractions of an Oriental island were holding her fugitive. Chiarina and Tecla went back down the stairs. There was a great bustle on board: the admiral had allowed the guests to visit the dining room and the officers' rooms, the hold, and the machine room, for those who were able to stand the hot temperatures, beneath those low ceilings; so that a throng of people crowded the stairways, men and women progressively disappeared, as though swallowed up by the hold; heads appeared on the other side; there was a shout of astonishment, women cried out in fear, half-real, half-simulated. Eva Muscettola had reappeared on the arm of Innico Althan, who had showed her his little room, with the porthole where a rose was blooming, and the rose was now on the breast of Eva, who was reflecting; Eugenia of Aragon, seized by a crazy whim, was begging Giulio Vargas to give her a battleship; she insisted that she wanted to go to sea; she no longer wanted to live in stone houses; Giulio promised her a yacht, when they got married. And finally, Tecla Brancaccio and Chiarina Althan found Carlo Mottola and Lady Maria di Miradois in the cannon room on the bow: there the admiral, with his big face, clean-shaven around his mouth and chin, with graying side whiskers, one hand leaning on the enormous black breech of the cannon, was explaining the firing mechanism to four or five ladies, who listened in deep surprise. The two lovers—Lady Maria di Miradois, a blond Spaniard, fiery, languid, and passionate, dressed in white silk, covered with jewels from her little hat to her shoes, and Carlo Mottola, a slender, dark young man, handsome in a classically Italian way mixed with a hint of the Orient in his color and features—were holding hands, listening to the cannon explanation. And unperturbed, Tecla Brancaccio went up to them, smiled at Lady Maria, and shook hands with Carlo Mottola, saying:

"Oh, Carlo, I was looking for you. Weren't we supposed to dance the waltz together?"

"Of course: we can dance a quadrille together."

"Let's finish hearing this explanation, shall we?"

And all four, Carlo, Maria, Chiarina, and Tecla remained in a group, listening, not embarrassed in the least, used to having to smile in the midst of drama; the admiral had picked up a howitzer and was holding it up; he showed it to the ladies, told them to try to lift it. They tried, laughing, and failing: Lady Maria di Miradois gave up, making an adorable face, but Tecla, extending her arms slightly, pressing her lips together, with a wrinkle that cut into her forehead like a scar, raised the howitzer.

"You're very strong, Tecla," murmured Lady Maria.

"Very strong," answered the latter quietly, adjusting her cuffs.

And this was the only sign of the great passionate struggle that raged at the bottom of these three souls.

But as they left the cannon room, a bright light struck the group. From the shore of Castellammare, from the terrace of Stabia's Hall, an electric spotlight projected its great white ray on the battleship *Roma,* and it struck the big ship on the side, illuminating fantastically first one side then another, according to the passing fantasy of the person who was directing the light. First the white light had fallen on the foredeck, where the tall, slim, almost ghostlike figure of Angiolina Cantelmo had appeared, ideally transfigured in that brightness; then it had jumped from the bridge, where they were dancing a great quadrille, and there appeared in its beam, in the processional circle of the women's *moulinez,* the two Sannicandro sisters, very lovely, their eyes dazzled by the light, the two Gaston sisters, whose blond hair looked like a golden stream, Maria Gullì-Pausania, with the wise, pure profile of Minerva, with the solemn, regal pace, Giulia Capace, whom the very white light surrounded with a snowy halo, and behind them, in a continuous circle, the line of beautiful women's faces, surprised and flattered by that light. From the beginning the pale, bright ray had fallen on the foredeck, inundating the two bent heads of Giovanella Sersale and Felicetta Filomarino in light; and Giovanella, with her pale, emaciated face, looked almost ghostlike, Felicetta looked almost dazzled, bathed in whiteness, both stricken with the same illness. As the light moved, there was a confused, happy shout of surprise, timid people hid in dark corners, girls and young men gathered together, as though they were posing for a photograph; from the foredeck, the light had reached the poop deck: at the door of the buffet Elfrida Kapnist stood straight and insolent, holding out a crystal glass to Willy Galeota, who was pouring Bordeaux and champagne for her at the same time, and she laughed and laughed, unperturbed, with her black curls covering her forehead and her pale, dark face of a troublesome gypsy.

Leaning against the railing, still motionless, still alone, watching the shore of Castellammare, Olga Bariatine waited for Massimo Daun, but her face no longer reflected the anxiety and agitation of the person who waits, hoping and fearing: instead one could read there a resigned fatigue, a mute, painful patience, the relaxation of every feature, the dejection of the one who waits without hoping or fearing; and the lively, passionate, and voluptuous figure of Elfrida Kapnist, in the rather wan splendor of the electric light, took on an almost diabolical appeal, while the sweet face of the Slavic girl was softly illuminated, in a melancholy brightness, in which her blond hair, scattered with blue flowers, and her large eyes, sad with wait-ing, made her resemble a pale Ophelia looking at the frozen Baltic, sighing for a mad Prince Hamlet beneath the moon. Again, the light was projected on the dancers: Tecla Brancaccio had asked Carlo Mottola to dance the quadrille; they were dancing without speaking, but close to one another, the girl almost dominating the young man, while Lady Maria di Miradois, patient and calm, like one who is biding her time, was not dancing but was watching them, with a strange smile on her lips. Tecla was smiling, too: in the light you could see her small, very white teeth shining, like those of a ferocious cat, while the beautiful mouth of Donna Maria smiled deeply and intimately, like a woman who is all-powerful in love. Finally, the electric light fell for a while on the poop deck: there Eugenia of Aragon, dragging behind her two or three instru-mentalists, had formed a small orchestra and was going around organizing a tarantella, a real Neapolitan tarantella, and her pas-sion had communicated itself to four or five couples; the popular dance, now soft and loving, now fast and passionate, had begun, amid the applause and enthusiasm of the spectators. Eugenia of Aragon gave herself up to this mad joy, spinning like a top, dancing to perfection with Giulio Vargas: she felt right at home, said Anna

Doria, the nasty old maid. And dancing with a certain lively, simple sweetness, Eva Muscettola swayed in the brightness of the electric light, dancing with Mario Capece, but her eyes and mind were elsewhere, precisely over there with Innico Althan, who didn't know how to dance the tarantella, who was talking very seriously with Natalia Muscettola, Eva's young mother. And in that white light, in that soft night, on that perfumed sea, in Eva's heart a new, infinite, irremediable tenderness was born, and overflowed.

III

In the vulgar first-class salon, in white stucco, furnished with uncomfortable ugly sofas in red velvet, illuminated by gas flames that flickered in the autumn evening wind blowing down the corridor where there was coffee and newspapers for sale; in this big, sad, stupid waiting room, the first to arrive had been Eva Muscettola and Chiarina Althan: they were accompanied by Signorina Anderly, Eva's governess. The two girls were inseparable, since Innico Althan's marriage with Eva had been fixed: Chiarina's fine, sharp sensibility got along well with Eva's kind, sensitive soul. They began to walk up and down, buttoned up in their dark overcoats, their veils pulled over their eyes, like two patient travelers.

"What a silly thing a honeymoon is!" Chiarina was saying, watching a traveler who put down his suitcase on the big, dark table and went out again, prey to the nervousness of those who are going away, that nothing can calm.

"No, no, dear Chiarina, it's very romantic . . ."

"Bah! Too many hotels, too many indiscreet waiters, too many strange faces, useless, boring wandering."

"You wouldn't go on a honeymoon?"

"No, but it's not up to me."

"Ah! I forgot that you don't want to get married; I'll have a sister-in-law who's a nun. Why don't you want to get married, tell me?"

"Because."

"I'll find you a husband, you'll see."

"Do you love your neighbor as yourself?"

"Oh," said the other, blushing.

And they went to meet Anna Doria, who was entering alone, her cheeks painted with the rouge that she made up herself, with a little white veil that was intended to tone down that creaminess; that evening she had decided to paint her eyes by underlining them with a piece of burnt cork, and she looked so strange, so ugly, that even good Eva couldn't help smiling.

"Mama had a monsignor and two abbots to dinner," she explained. "I left halfway through. Mama was furious, as usual: I left her in a state. Here I am for the funeral march."

"You're nicer than usual," murmured Chiarina, laughing.

"You bet! Wouldn't she be better off dead, Olga, rather than accepting this rascal Massimo?"

"Girls would always rather get married than die; you, too, Anna."

"Me, too, naturally, but I haven't yet fallen in love with a buffoon."

"Why do you dislike Massimo so much?" Eva asked Anna.

"He's not worth talking about: he's a confirmed cold, depraved person. Imagine, he spent all last night in a gambling den, and this morning he was an hour late for the religious marriage. Olga cried all through the Mass."

"Who knows if it's true about the gambling den?" said Eva.

"Good heavens! Your brother was there, too!"

"I don't think so . . . ," said Eva, growing pale.

"What, you don't believe it? He lost seven or eight thousand lire, too."

"He'd promised not to gamble anymore," murmured Eva.

"Then ask Tecla, who I came with; she stopped outside to buy a book."

Tecla had also come in, in a black wool jacket lined with astrakhan, all frog fastenings and braid, with an astrakhan beret; she had bought a novel by Balzac, *Albert Savarus*.

"Yes, they gambled all night. Carlo lost twenty thousand lire," she said, smiling.

"And this doesn't bother you?" asked Chiarina, while Eva bowed her head, worried.

"Not at all."

"And why?"

"When Carlo is deep in debt, he'll have to marry me, as a way out. Donna Maria can't give him money; I can."

"And you're satisfied to be married as a way out?"

"He'll love me later; he has to end up loving me," answered Tecla, with the profound stubbornness of someone who wants only one thing.

The room was filling up with the more hurried travelers, who arrive an hour before their departure; the group of girls stood aside, and the two Sannicandros entered, together with their father and Maria Gullì-Pausania, their future sister-in-law, arm in arm, walking slowly, so pretty in Alsatian bonnets of red satin.

"We brought Olga some roses," said the first.

"White roses, because she likes them," added the second.

And they looked at each other, happy to have so much wit; then the first began again:

"We met your mother in the carriage, Eva."

"She was with your brother Innico, Chiarina," the second went on.

A doubtful smile appeared on the lips of Anna Doria, and Chiarina and Tecla looked at each other for a fraction of a second, as though questioning one another, but Eva smiled, completely happy, watching the door, to see whether her mother and fiancé had appeared. Maria Gullì-Pausania was chatting in a low voice with the prince of Sannicandro, a robust old man with a red face and a white mustache, a father-in-law who was already letting himself be captivated by the great classical airs of his future daughter-in-law, hearing with what reverence she spoke of the arms of the Sannicandros and of the Sannicandros' ancestors, who had fought under Roger the Norman. Giulia Capece and Eugenia of Aragon had come in, too: Giulia still accompanied by her flock of young men, diplomats, Russian barons, continuing her tiring role of noble, beautiful, poor spinster looking for a rich husband, Eugenia of Aragon with her putative mother, the beautiful, fresh, blond, sterile princess, and Giulio Vargas; they were to marry in a year. Now in the heart of this fiery girl of the lower classes who had become a princess, a fervent love had sprung up, a passion for Giulio Vargas; the two fiancés paraded their love everywhere, holding each other's arm or hand, looking fixedly into each other's eyes, talking in a low voice, smiling meaningfully. Giulio was wearing a tie the color of Eugenia's dress, Eugenia a man's pin on her collar.

"Now you'll see, we're all going to feel like fifth wheels," said Anna Doria.

In fact, after hugging and kissing all her friends, one after the other, with that noisy effusion that proper people criticized her for, holding tightly to her chest a big bunch of hyacinths, roses, violets, a rarity in the fall, that she had brought for Olga, Eugenia went to sit blissfully in a corner with Giulio, exchanging a word with him from time to time, shaking her head sweetly, while Maria Gullì-Pausania thought that she was more like a dressmaker than ever: it was scandalous to show one's love so publicly. Now the girls, ladies, and young men who came to say good-bye to Olga Bariatine, who was leaving on her honeymoon, were divided into two or three groups, chatting, laughing, whispering, indifferent to the bustle of arriving travelers—in a low voice, so that Giulia Capece wouldn't hear, Anna Doria was saying that Madame Charlotte, the dressmaker in the Passage Verdeau in Paris, had gone bankrupt through the fault of Giulia; in two years she had supplied her with a hundred thousand lire worth of dresses and had never been paid a cent; she had gone on giving her dresses, counting on Giulia's eventual marriage, but in vain, there was no marriage, and Charlotte, the poor thing, had suspended payment.

"But wasn't Rocco Caracciolo going to marry Giulia?" Tecla asked Anna.

"No, no. Caracciolo was *otherwise* committed."

"What *otherwise*? Who *otherwise*?" asked four or five girls, overcome with curiosity.

"A ballerina, Flame: he couldn't break it off; it was really a serious commitment."

And the girls, some lowering their eyes, some blushing, had moved closer together, concentrating, stirred by curiosity for that other world that they didn't know, that they were not to know, but of which they occasionally found an echo in their homes and in their conversations.

"What? What do you mean, Flame?" said Elfrida Kapnist, leaning her brunette head into the group of her friends. "You don't know anything. Annina Doria is behind on her news: Caracciolo got away from Flame, by giving her thirty thousand lire, all at once, for her and the child . . ."

"What child?" asked Eva ingenuously.

But silence reigned; everyone had lowered their eyes and were looking around, as though distracted; decidedly Elfrida Kapnist was too free in her speech, she was intolerable. And the bad impression increased: Elfrida was wearing a shabby black-and-white-checked dress that cost forty thousand lire, and she had two shining diamonds in her ears, worth three thousand francs.

"What is Willy Galeota doing?" Annina Doria had the courage to ask.

"He loves me, as usual," Elfrida answered immediately.

"And when are you getting married?" insisted the other, trying to trip her up.

"Soon, soon," said Elfrida, turning her back and going to join Giulia Capece.

Eva kept turning around toward the door, a bit impatient, waiting to see her mother come in with Innico Althan, but her mother and fiancé did not appear; Giovanella Sersale had arrived with her sister Candida Montemiletto and her brother-in-law Francesco Montemiletto. Strange to say, Giovanella's face no longer showed that profound sadness, that incurable spiritual illness that manifests itself in one's every fiber, in one's color and features—instead, her face was calm and concentrated, as though closed within a dream, a thought; it almost seemed that, with a superhuman effort, she had reached spiritual liberation, a state of serene contemplation. She was no longer going around with Felicetta Filomarino, the sad girl who jealously hid her secret, whose pain ate at her: instead, she always went out with her sister and brother-in-law, with her sister who had taken a husband, a fiancé, away from her, and a mysterious smile flickered on her lips. Angiolina Cantelmo had come in with her sister Maria and her father: she was no longer Angiolina, no longer a woman, but a slender stalk, thin, white as a fine rose, without the shadow of any blood beneath her skin, a waist so small that it seemed that it would break in two every time she moved, hands so thin that the smallest gloves fell into a thousand folds on them. And one could see in her the desire to look as though she were still healthy and beautiful: she wore a coat with rich folds in order to hide the thinness of her body, with a thick white lace scarf wound around her skinny white neck; a white veil dotted with black fell over her cheeks in order to give them a fictive vivacity. Her eyes were shining, she was smiling: when her father, the duke, who had been tried repeatedly by domestic tragedy, had seen his good, beautiful daughter wasting away for love of him who was traveling far away, he had gone to his father, the prince of Serracapriola, to beg him to consent to this marriage for the sake of his daughter who was dying of love. And the prince had consented, even for his absent son, provided the dowry was increased by two hundred thousand lire; his son could hope for and ask much more, but Cantelmo was a friend and relative; father and son would be satisfied with half a million, since the girl was dying of love. The handsome traveler had come home, indolent, cold, and skeptical in order to pay court to his fiancée, and the delicate creature had sprung back to life, the way fragile white roses open up on warm winter days. Her face was transformed by happiness: she talked but little, in a faint voice, but one which always trembled with emotion. When she entered, she immediately saw that her fiancé was in the group with Giulia Capece; the smile that she sent him was like words, light, affection, feeling, a whole soul taking flight. And immediately those who loved her and understood her—Eva Muscettola, Tecla Brancaccio, Eugenia of Aragon, Chiarina Althan—surrounded her, looking at her with great tenderness, not daring to ask her how she felt, talking to her in a low voice, pushing her toward the far side of the room, so that she wouldn't catch cold in the draft. A group of young men had come in—Willy Galeota, Peppino Sannicandro, Carlo Mottola; Mario Capece had also arrived, carrying a bunch of heliotrope and lilies of the valley for the departing bride; the private conversations became general; everyone was astonished that Massimo and Olga hadn't arrived; it was only twenty minutes before the departure for Rome. Eugenia had Giulio swear to her that they would never leave Naples when they got married; they would shut themselves up in the immense, flowering villa of Aragon; she loved Naples and hated every other place in the world.

There was a great stir: Massimo and Olga had come in, arm in arm; everyone surrounded them; their greetings sounded almost like a cheer. She was prettier than ever, in her dress of dark blue wool over a red cashmere skirt, held in place by a little swallow hidden among the tunic's folds; a swallow seemed to take flight from her dark blue felt hat; she was very pale; Massimo had his usual air of a man who was annoyed and annoying. When Olga saw everyone who was waiting to say good-bye to her and the friendly hands that were reaching out to her and the beautiful flowers being offered her, amid so much affection, attraction, and so many memories, she was seized with a nervous tremor; she couldn't cry, but her eyes stung and her throat was choked with sobs. And slowly, she took leave of all those who had been her friends, exchanging with each of them a tender word, a promise, a regret, or a hope; Massimo talked wearily with his friends, his hands in his pockets, his hat pulled down over his eyes, the picture of complete boredom.

"We brought you roses, Olga," said the first Sannicandro sister, looking at the bride with big eyes full of tears.

"They're a souvenir of Naples. Don't forget, Olga," added the other one.

She bent over the roses, smelled them at length, kissed them, then without another word, kissed the two girls on both cheeks, and the two girls, after exchanging a look, stuck out their lower lips at the same time, as they always did, and began to cry.

"Oh, my dears, don't cry, don't cry," she said, trembling, and signaled to Maria Gullì-Pausania to come comfort them. Their future sister-in-law came forward regally, kissed Olga coldly on the forehead, and said to her calmly:

"We'll come to Paris in six months, Olga. I'll be there with Peppino. Will you be there?"

"I don't know, I don't know," murmured Olga Daun confusedly, looking furtively at her annoyed husband, who was already heading toward the door.

And Maria Gullì-Pausania took her little sisters-in-law, who were still sobbing, into a corner, began to talk to them quietly, like an old grandmother preaching wisdom, and they listened to her, raising their eyes to her face, like children trusting their grandmother's promises.

"Here are some hyacinths, my dear," said Eugenia of Aragon. "Come back, Olga."

"I'll come back, Eugenia."

"Come back soon: it's cold there, here it's hot, Olgarella."

And she leaned, completely trustingly and lovingly, on Giulio Vargas's arm.

"Remember the evenings that we've spent together, Olga," said Tecla Brancaccio in a low voice. "Here you are now, getting what you wanted. Be happy, my dear."

"May you get what you want, Tecla!"

"I must get it or die," answered the other firmly.

"Will you do me an errand in St. Petersburg?" Giulia Capece asked the bride. "Is it possible you could get me a Russian fox coat? I'm dying to have one."

"I'll remember," murmured the bride, looking around with the dreamy eyes of one who no longer understands what's happening.

"My Olga, I wish you a life that is always serene, a heart that is always in love," Chiarina said to her softly.

"How is that possible, Chiarina?" the bride answered in the same tone, in a pained voice.

"Be good, be good; don't think about it," replied her friend, touching her forehead, as though to bless her.

But at the door Massimo Daun was growing impatient, reaching the height of his bad temper: the employee was announcing the departure for Rome in a loud voice, everyone was hurrying; the bride started out, too, followed by a procession of her friends. A great wind blew under the awning, the gas flames flickered; Massimo Daun stood before a reserved compartment throwing shawls and flowers on the seats, in a bad mood. A feeling of sorrow now dominated all the people who had come to see Olga off: that little blond, good and affectionate, a beautiful flower who had matured in the Neapolitan sun, who was going off in the world, embarking on the ocean of life where there was such danger of shipwreck, moved everybody. Even Anna Doria, the angry old maid, was touched at the sight of that little being, defenseless and without protection, throwing herself into the fray where the probability of getting crushed was so great.

"Write to me, Olga, write to me, don't forget."

"Yes, yes, I'll write," said the other, speaking as though in a dream, with trembling lips and eyes that were incapable of tears.

"Courage, my Olga, courage and strength," Elfrida Kapnist said into her ear, "then nothing can frighten you."

"Good luck, Elfrida," answered the bride, leaning out the window, nearly fainting.

Angiolina Cantelmo came up to her, and the two girls stared at each other for a moment, with a look so intense and profound that their lips found nothing to say. Angiolina held Olga's little hands tightly in her thin hands, almost as though she wanted to communicate to her magnetically the sweet things that she would have liked to say. Her voice failed her.

"The Holy Virgin . . . ," she managed to say, very faintly.

"Oh, Angiolina," babbled the bride, almost interrupting her.

And finally, the tears poured from her eyes; she cried in silence. Eva Muscettola hugged Olga in her arms, feeling her cry on her shoulder, saying:

"Remember that we love you, always, always: I love you so much, my Olga . . ."

The bell rang.

"Olga, Olga," said Massimo in a dry, whistling voice.

"I'm coming," she answered, obeying.

In groups of three or four, they said good-bye at the station door, and all got into carriages to go down to Naples. And Eva had gone back to the thought that preoccupied her; in vain did Chiarina talk to her of happy things:

"Where can Innico be?" Eva burst out.

"Well . . . I can't imagine," answered the other, disconcerted.

"Oh, Chiarina, do you believe that he loves me? What will I do if he doesn't love me?"

She threw herself into her friend's arms, sobbing, while the carriage took them home, and her friend comforted her with tender words, caressing her as though she were a sick child. In truth, though, Chiarina Althan was sad and thoughtful.

IV

The elegant carriages entered the spacious cloister of Santa Chiara, filled with winter sun, from the main open entrance on the Via del Gesù Nuovo; they let off the guests at the church door, in front of the raised quilted curtain, where a glimmer of candles could be seen; then they went to find a place to wait, over there, in a corner of the great deserted piazza, near the other bolted entrance on the Via della Rotonda. The curious flocked to the open entrance, trying to see something, but one had to have an invitation to enter. Some guests arrived on foot dressed in black, with white ties showing under their overcoats, opera hats, and light gloves, as though for a wedding; they showed their invitations, entered the cloister, disappeared into the black mouth of the church, which seemed to be illuminated at the end by an aureole of candles. Ladies arrived on foot dressed in black, glittering with pearls, clutching prayer books in their hands. The curious thought that it was a big wedding, and they waited patiently for the bride, in the Piazza del Gesù Nuovo, on the stairs and under the porch of the Normal School.

In the church, all plaster and gold, decorated like a salon, attractive and bright, they had lowered the red curtains over the panes of the large windows in order to block out the light; and from the right of the chapel, where the good saint Maria Cristina of Savoy sleeps, up to the door, the men were gathered; from the left of the chapel, where Giotto's Madonna looks at the crowd with her pale, milky blue eyes, over to the popular chapel where the Eternal Father is worshipped, the miraculous Eternal Father of Santa Chiara, the ladies were gathered. The two galleries were surrounded by red velvet poles: at the entrance, ten servants of the house of Muscettola stood straight and motionless: the duke of Mileto, brother of the duke of Muscettola, and the prince of Montescaglioso, brother of the duchess of Muscettola, were doing the honors; on the high altar, kneeling on a red velvet cushion, leaning against a prie-dieu, the duchess of Muscettola, dressed in black, held her face in her hands and was praying, crying, or thinking. And in the Church of Santa Chiara, to the right and left, all the Neapolitan aristocracy crowded in, the white and the black, the Spanish and Sicilian, the Calabrese and the Salernitan, the one that lives in Naples, Sorrento, and Castellammare and the one that lives in Scotland, England, and Paris, dropping by Naples now and then to introduce French and English fashions.

Oh, it isn't easy for the Neapolitan aristocracy to meet with such solemnity in a church, in a dance hall, or at a public feast! Many of the men and women who were in the Church of Santa

Chiara for the house of Muscettola had not gone six months earlier
to the Church of Santa Maria degli Angioli in Pizzofalcone for the
marriage of Elfrida Kapnist and Willy Galeota, that marriage that
had angered the old maids of the aristocracy, scandalized many
brides, and astonished everyone: the intransigent still considered
Elfrida an adventurer, the indifferent were going to wait and see;
that marriage had disturbed all of society, introducing an element
of rather bohemian liveliness, a bit of rich gypsy life.

They hadn't all gone to the funeral of Angiolina Cantelmo, who
had died quietly on an evening in May by a window in the sad old
Cantelmo palace, with one hand on her sister Maria's head, while
she smiled at Giorgio Serracapriola: the funeral had been held
without guests, in the cold Cantelmo Chapel, among close relatives, with the duke present, crying, aged ten years, spilling his few
old man's tears on the poetry of his vanished dear soul. Giorgio
Serracapriola had left again on a steamship for Japan, leaving
behind the memory of his gentle fiancée, who had loved him so
uniquely.

Nor had they gone to the funeral of Luigi Muscettola, Eva's
brother, who had shot himself in the heart one night as he left a
gambling den. People had intervened: suicides could not even be
buried in holy ground; they had had to write to Rome, to the pope,
for permission, but there was no service; everything had been done
at night, in secret.

Only the Sicilian nobility had attended the wedding of Maria
Gullì-Pausania with Peppino Sannicandro; it had been held in
Palermo, with tremendous pomp, with valets dressed in medieval
costumes and a gun salute on their return to their villa-castle outside the city.

A similar reunion of the nobility took place again after a month,
after the magnificent funeral of Eugenia of Aragon: the noisy,
lively, likable creature had died in childbirth, after providing an

heir to the Vargases and the Aragons; nothing could have saved her; because she was young, overflowing with vitality, very rich, happy, in love with her husband, death to her was a horrendous thing; in her delirium she cried out that she didn't want to die, that her loved ones should save her, for the love of God; she threw her arms around Giulio's neck, hugging him so hard that she nearly suffocated him; she died in despair.

Now, the same people, more numerous, perhaps, due to the novelty of the occasion, had come to the Church of Santa Chiara. Punctually at eleven o'clock, the novice entered the church and walked the whole length of it up to the high altar. She was dressed in a long gown of white brocade; on her chestnut curls she wore an enormous white veil, in which she was completely enfolded; large jeweled earrings sparkled at her delicate ears; she wore an elaborate brooch at her neck, a buckle at her waist; her white-gloved hands carried a bouquet of orange blossoms and a prayer book bound in white velvet. She was all in white, from her head to her toes, and her beautiful young face was white. She kept her eyes lowered, almost closed, but without serenity: that face reflected a supreme peace.

Peace, not serenity. She wasn't smiling, so she wasn't serene. Her lips seemed to have given up smiling forever: they formed a dignified line that nothing could cause to curve any longer in the merry laughter of youth. Thus, the bottom part of her face, which had always looked rather mobile, imparted a sudden aging to the whole face. She seemed to be someone else, with the death of her smile. Eva Muscettola, the novice, was transformed.

A murmuring began as she passed by; some women's voices said softly, sorrowfully: Eva, Eva, Eva, but she didn't even turn; she continued on her way, as though nothing could interest her any longer. Behind her came the two godmothers: the princess of Tricarico, the mystical, pious great lady, with her regal bearing and a face that was pale from prayer and tribulation; and the duchess of Mercede, a Spaniard, tall, thin, with fine lips, with eyes like coals, straight and proud . . .

When she arrived at the high altar Eva knelt, made the sign of the cross, went up to her mother but did not embrace her; she kissed her hand: the duchess had put out her face, but she jumped back, as though she were sorry. The novice knelt between her two godmothers: Cardinal Riario Sforza began the Mass, slowly, barely moving his body, on which age and asceticism had taken their toll. The men, standing straight, had the stupefied look of those who feel the solemnity of an occasion without daring to abandon themselves to that emotion: only a few old men, the duke of Aragon, the duke of Cantelmo, and the duke of Isernia, who had recently been struck by tragedy, dared to bow their heads, they who had regained their faith through misfortune.

Instead, on the other side, the women were praying, kneeling, abandoning themselves in that mystical hour to their feelings, eagerly seizing that hour of contemplation. Tecla Brancaccio, of the strong iron will and courageous soul, was watching Eva Muscettola, bowing her head and praying: she, stubborn and iron-willed in the struggle with Maria di Miradois, had won; the Spanish woman had left for Barcelona, Carlo Mottola had made up his mind to marry Tecla, against his will, still burning with his old passion. Tecla had won, painfully, despairingly: but Eva, on the high altar, dressed in white like a bride, holding in one hand a lighted candle, in the other a silver cross, having put down the flowers and prayer book, Eva, the beautiful and good, had lost, had been beaten; and Tecla, not knowing Eva's great secret but understanding the spasm that it had created, prayed and prayed, for the losers as well as the winners, for Lady Maria di Miradois as well as herself, for poor Eva as well as those unknown persons who had irremediably saddened her.

Anna Doria, supporting herself with her elbows on a chair, with her head in her hands, stricken by a nervous fit of melancholy, prayed as she held her rosary to her lips; Eva's renunciation of life, that separation from all things human, persons and feelings, that voluntary death of the Christian heart that abhors suicide, abhors the world, and turns only to God, seemed to her the end of her own life; it seemed to her that she herself, Anna Doria, at the age of thirty-five, without affection, without a future, had no other choice but to go shut herself up in a convent.

Giovanella Sersale, her head bowed in painful contemplation, did not have the courage to pray; her soul was immersed in sin; she loved sin; she didn't have the courage to save herself from it; she was unworthy of prayer, unworthy of kneeling before God; never could divine mercy pardon her: oh, Eva, up there, who had placed the silver cross on her chest, had escaped from the storm, she was in safety, she had renounced, but she, Giovanella, could not; no, she had to lose herself, had to die in sin.

Next to Maria Gullì-Sannicandro, who was praying decorously for her who was fleeing vain pomp and, rather than make a spectacle of her sorrow, was shutting herself up forever in a cloister, Giulia Capece was praying, thanking the Lord for having mercy on her; in two months she was leaving for England; she was marrying an old prince; Naples was getting too sad now; girls were dying or becoming nuns; brides were dying or going away, like Maria di Miradois; adventurers were marrying princes; Giulia prayed quietly, without distressing herself, feeling only pity because of Eva's beauty, which was going to waste away in a convent.

The two little Sannicandros, so very pretty under little black hats, had knelt down next to one another, very close, and were saying the rosary together; the elder began, in a low voice, the second responded, continuing, and they prayed fervently; there came to both of them a great desire to save their souls, to become nuns;

they would have liked to become two saintly creatures, the two saints of the house of Sannicandro; and Felicetta Filomarino, the girl without hope or joy, whose heart was a mystery to all, rather than perish in spiritual sin like Giovanella Sersale, was imploring the Lord to have Eva's vocation.

All the women were praying, moved by the occasion and by the rite, giving vent to their sorrows in the contemplation of the innocent twenty-year-old who was going away to die in a convent: even Elfrida Galeota, the gypsy who had become a countess, prayed; she prayed, remembering the childhood prayers that her wandering life and her hardships had made her forget; she prayed with a heart that was humbled in victory, for her who had always been good to her, for Eva, who was voluntarily disappearing from the scene. And the one who was immersing herself most deeply in prayer was Chiarina Althan, that good and intelligent creature: she alone knew the horrendous secret that had destroyed the life of Eva Muscettola; she alone knew the extent of that sacrifice; she pitied the girl but prayed for those who had killed her, for those who had never had peace.

The Pontifical Mass was ending. The seated cardinal blessed the Franciscan nun's habit that Eva was to put on, spread out on a silver tray; then, bowing deeply to the altar without swaying, without raising her eyes, without seeing anyone, Eva, followed by her two godmothers, crossed the church again, went out the cloister door toward the entrance to the convent, where the other nuns were waiting for her: behind came the priests singing psalms. Again, some friendly hands reached out, almost touching Eva's wedding dress; voices called to her, but like the first time, she didn't hear. Her mother had remained on the high altar; everyone was watching her, to see whether she was crying; to lose one child after the other eight months apart, to see the end of one's house: a young man dead from a revolver shot, a girl who was becoming a nun, must be an unbearable blow for a mother's heart. But the duchess did not raise her head; she remained alone on the altar; the duke was traveling abroad; he had refused to be present at his daughter's taking the veil: the family was destroyed from top to bottom; the Muscettolas would die out, the heredity would pass to the Miletos. Eva had given her dowry to the home for poor abandoned children.

There was an interval of silence; the sun had reached the small portico; it almost came in the door; three windows were heating up intensely, casting a reddish light over the white marble, plaster, and gold of the lovely church. Suddenly, next to the high altar, a small door opened, the one that led to the convent: in front of it was Eva. They had taken away her white dress, the veil, the flowers, the jewels, the satin slippers, all the worldly trappings. The brown tunic of Franciscan nuns fell from her neck to her feet in large folds, cinched at the waist by a white cord: her feet weren't visible; her hands had the yellowish whiteness of wax; her beautiful chestnut-blond hair fell loose over her shoulders. Seeing her in that coarse habit, Giulia Capece felt a great pang in her heart and began to cry silently. The officiating cardinal, who had entered the monastery with Eva, left the abbess's side, went toward the future nun, blessed the white scapular, and Eva put it around her neck, automatically, without looking anyone in the eye. She still had the same peaceful look that no other expression, either of sorrow or joy, disturbed: this immobility of the face that everyone had always seen so lively hurt one's imagination more than any expression of sorrow. Finally, Eva knelt beside the small door and bent her neck; a nun left the others and went over to her, gathering all her hair together and squeezing it in her fist; the abbess, a stooped little old lady with a large jeweled cross hanging from her scapular, leaning on a cane, advanced slowly toward Eva. In the church everyone craned his neck, stood on tiptoe to see what was happening in front of the small door. The novice was praying as she knelt; one could see the movement of her lips; the old abbess held a pair of long scissors with a very shiny blade and passed them under the clump of hair, which the nun held up in a tight grip. Feeling the cold of the steel on her neck, the novice gave a long shiver, perhaps of terror; the women who were watching stopped praying, anxious, trembling; they all felt the same shiver. The scissors, unsteady in the trembling hands of the old abbess, made a squeaking noise without cutting; they didn't bite into the hair; they turned over; it seemed that the operation would never end; those five minutes seemed an excruciating eternity: the clump of cut hair remained in the nun's hand, soft as a dead thing. Some of the women in the church recoiled, their faces very pale, as though lifeless. Elfrida Kapnist, Countess Galeota, lowering her head with the brown, curly, and rebellious hair, her head of a free, audacious bohemian, cried over Eva's cut tresses. They had thrown a black veil over the novice's bare head, which suddenly appeared diminished, as though it had become very small, like those of some dead people.

The service was not yet over: the novice Muscettola, by the highest favor of the Holy See, had obtained permission to be spared the year as a novice; her vocation was so deep, so irresistible that she wanted to take her vow on the same day she took the veil. In vain, even her confessor had advised her to give up this idea, to do the year as a novice; perhaps she might regret her decision and she would always have time to change her mind, but she had turned out to be so decisive, so unmovable, that they had naturally had to have recourse to Rome. And Rome had consented; now women were no longer becoming nuns; such an ardent vocation would serve as an example. Then the novice got up, in the middle of the choir, in front of the small door: four nuns with lighted candles came to surround her. They gave her a long parchment written in Latin: she read it slowly, slowly, but without a tremor in her voice, without emotion, a voice that already had the monotony of nuns' voices. It was the long form of the vow of enclosure that she recited by the light of the four torches: the grave Latin words frightened the souls of all of those praying women; even the men could not shake off that emotion; a profound silence reigned in the large church. At the end Eva stopped, and in Italian said the four vows: chastity, poverty, obedience, and perpetual enclosure. She put out her hand and swore in a tranquil voice: she took the pen that they gave her, signed the scroll; after her the abbess and the cardinal signed. Anna Doria cried uncontrollably, with little, dry, hoarse sobs.

Then the service became even more lugubrious. In the middle of the choir, a rug was spread on the floor; the nuns led Eva to it, made her lie down flat, like a dead person; they crossed her hands on her chest; they covered her with a black velvet blanket trimmed with silver, on which there was a skull and crossbones, the symbols of death. Around her, at the four corners, four large candles blazed, and immediately the bells of Santa Chiara began to toll the death knell. The nuns chanted the *De profondis*. Frightened, the two Sannicandros were crying, clinging to one another, because they thought that Eva was really dead. Maria Gullì-Sannicandro felt her eyes fill with tears, at this funeral of a live person. Eva, hidden under the blanket, stiff as a cadaver, was censed, blessed with holy water; the nuns circled around her in a procession, carrying the cross. Oh, how Giovanella Sersale, who could find no more tears, so burning was her passion, would have liked to be dead, dead, dead, in a deep sleep where torment never again comes to wake us; dead, dead, in that great rest where there is no more thought, no more love, no more suffering! How Felicetta Filomarino would have liked to be the nun, the mystical soul who had ascended from the love of humanity to adoration for the Creator, who felt her spirit being liberated more and more from the bonds of earth! The prayers for the dead went on, deeply sorrowful, while the sun heated up all the windows veiled in red; the death knell went on tolling, and the curious who were crowding the street wondered if this were a wedding or a funeral.

The cardinal walked toward Eva and told her in Latin: "*Surge qui dormis, et exurge a mortuis, et illuminabit te Christus!*" The evocation was repeated three times; the nuns removed the mortuary blanket; Eva got up, kneeling on the rug, then rose to her feet. The cardinal blessed her and left the choir: the nuns kissed her, one by one. The small door was closed, while the nun prayed with the others: "*Ego sum resurrectio et vita . . .*"

All the women bowed their heads and cried for the nun.